All-American

Boy

"*A quintessential American masterpiece*" – Ron Wiggins, Palm
Beach Post

"*A literary triumph – a tremendously important work*" – Steve
Keller, Springfield Times-Register

"*Timeless – he's captured an era, and in doing so has captured
our hearts*" - Alison Thomas, South Florida Book Club

Grey Knight Press
mail@greyknightpress.com

To
The Old Gang

Many of whom are in these pages

"There's a fine line between mischief and criminality" – Principal Woody "Wood Pecker" Dunwood

Books by George Poncy
Published by Grey Knight Press

Strait of Hormuz
This Eternal Darkness
All-American Boy
Something Has Happened
In the Motorcade

- As George Williams -
Snow on the Palms
Blackjack to Win:
A Layman's Guide to Beating the Game
The Man on the Grassy Knoll
The Quest for God:
Shadows at the Back of the Cave
How to Create a Black Hole
in Your Washing Machine

Acknowledgements

Susan Allen, Chatham Historical Society

Cover photos courtesy Chatham (NJ) Historical Society

All-American Boy

A novel by
George Poncy

Chapter 1

Gather 'round cats
And I'll tell you a story
About how to become
An All American Boy
- *The All American Boy, Bill Parsons, 1958-*

WHEN I think back on things – not my strong suit, really – I can trace it all to Mrs. Schongarth's moronic suggestion that I skip the eighth grade. It sure as hell wasn't my idea.

"He's a brilliant boy," she'd told my mom, who of course lapped it up like a thirsty kitten. What a crock. I guess the whole town found out how brilliant I really was at graduation, when I caused the gigantic uproar, disrupting the whole stupid ceremony and just about blinding Principal Dunwood. I didn't even know I'd poked him in the eye at the time. Of course, he didn't have to jump on me and try to grab the microphone, either. I heard later that half of Windham said they'd been there to witness the madness, but I guess that's just human nature, like about every old person in New Jersey swearing they were at the Hindenblimp disaster.

I think I can't be too brilliant anyway, because despite any alleged intelligence I haven't been able to figure out some of the things that happened to us during my senior year at

Windham High. I mean, most were probably typical high school experiences, fun stuff and all, and as I think back on last year we seemed to kind of float through most of it. I imagine that's probably normal, with sports and dating and some hell-raising. Even studying now and then. I guess when I say hell-raising, I'm including my first and only (not counting the FBI "interview") police interrogation, courtesy of Chief Duff Carlin, and the explosion that caused so much damage. In fairness to us, though, we had no idea of the concussive power we were dealing with. I mean, chemistry can be pretty tricky, and maybe Mr. Wisner should have warned us more emphatically (?) But some of the events have really bothered me, and I can't figure them out at all. Not that I haven't tried. Sometimes I think I am figuring out something meaningful but then everything starts itching me, or some guy will come in the room to visit, or it's time for freshman soccer practice, or I fall asleep.

You see, Windham is a nice town with lots of well-off people, a great place to grow up, but maybe that's not completely true because if that's the case how come so many people are dead in just a couple of months? And not just deceased, like some kind of peaceful passing in the night, but violently dead, yanked from life with no warning at all. And why is it that sometimes there's no air to breathe thinking about our fathers' jobs on Wall Street and gray flannel suits and the goddamn Erie Lackawanna, like a steel coffin rumbling straight to Hell, and that stupid day my brain had a blowout with everybody staring at me? I shudder thinking about those sinister 3 x 5 index cards on the Sweet Shoppe bulletin board. In Windham, for Chrissake, a "desirable upscale suburb" according to the New York Times. Is it so desirable because all the maids and gardeners and chauffeurs and handymen have to be gone by sundown? Is every place like that?

Is there another Kathy Obermeister, ruined by Wolfie's one-eye, sobbing her heart out on her pillow while the monarch butterflies dance in her garden and little Wolfies dance in her womb? And feeling like somebody is standing on your chest whenever you think about it? Does every All-American town have a Mrs. Moffitt, all sweet and baking cookies for us and then checking into an ivy-covered, historic inn and committing an unimaginable horror?

And worst of all. . . worst of all, did we help destroy our classmate? Jones, Brownie, Herbie Schultz and me: were we responsible for what happened to Jerry Garragues and his family?

Maybe it depends on whether I think about it on a sunny day at soccer practice, or late at night, laying on my back gazing out my dorm window. I don't know.

Sometimes on a really clear, cold night I think I see Sputnik floating by, but only if I look out of the corner of my eye. Maybe it's like that.

Does Evil exist by itself, or is it in some of us, or is some of it in all of us?

I wonder.

I wonder – is it like a spider web, visible only against the night's dew, linking seemingly unrelated events in some fierce design toward something unspeakable at the center, where Mrs. Broadhead's eyes stare wildly out, unblinking and tinged with madness? Was that the first strand to be woven, spinning from my smashed bicycle like some crazy spinning wheel as it turned and whirred *clickety-clack* in the street, everything else frozen in that horrific moment except what was flowing out of Johnny Broadhead? Who even knew all that stuff was in him?

I guess that's a dumb question, because of course it was, and that means it's all crammed into me and Dan Jones and everyone I know, even the lovely Mary Anne Moffitt. How sick is that.

I thought it might help to write down last year's events, sort of in order, but they came out kind of random and I don't really know how to fix it. We just started a Creative Writing course, but I haven't learned anything too practical yet, except that Assistant Professor Murphy keeps saying stuff like "adjectives are the tool of a weak mind." I think that's his favorite expression. I hadn't known adjectives were the tool of a weak mind. I suppose mine must be pretty anemic. In high school I wrote stories with quite a few adjectives and got A's, so maybe the whole school is out of touch, I don't know. Next we'll probably learn adverbs came from behind the Iron Curtain.

Anyway, regarding writing my story, you're supposed to know enough to maybe write an outline first, which I didn't really do, except possibly in my head. Also, I guess I need to figure out who the protagonist is. Maybe it's me, because I'm writing the narrative, but really I'm not sure whose story it is, exactly - maybe all of ours, the Class of 1959, or even Windham in general. Can a whole town be a protagonist? I guess that doesn't make much sense. I mean, Nick told the story of Gatsby, which we analyzed my senior year at Windham High, including whether or not Nick had gotten laid off Jordan Baker - to the consternation of Mr. Glendenning, our fill-in English teacher - , and maybe it's kind of the same thing. I could be just the vehicle. Anyway, if I turn this in, I might be killing two birds with one stone, but I am hoping I can figure things out first so there is some definitive conclusion. I haven't found one yet, though, and it bothers me to think that maybe I never will.

I'd really like to ask Father Corr, or somebody, but after all he's a priest so I don't see how I could. I sure as hell don't know, because I only grew up in one place so I have no frame of reference, plus I'm still a teenager, despite my IQ score. Which wasn't *that* great, anyway, unless you listen to my mom. Hardly even my dad does that.

Chapter 2

Up in the mornin' and out to school,
The teacher is teachin' the golden rule...
-    *School Day, Chuck Berry, 1957*

They made me take this I.Q. test when I was maybe twelve, which would have been around 1955, and it did me no good at all. The whole stupid deal was some new program they were trying out because President Eisenhower was scared of the Russkies, or maybe Red China. I guess in Cathay they never hung around in groups of two or three, or shot the breeze at their local Sweet Shoppe, if they had one, because the Movietone News and EC Comics always referred to them as 'Mongol hordes' or the 'Yellow Peril', all running and screaming down Pork Chop Hill shooting at our G.I.'s across the 38th Parallel.

Anyway, it didn't make much sense to me, since over here they just operated the laundries or made egg rolls and seemed quite polite. Orientals were brought over to work out west on the railroad, as we learned in Mr. Kritzinger's American History class, and they labored really hard for little wages and obeyed the law, mostly. Maybe it's something in the air over there.

For my mom, the concept of her son skipping the eighth grade was like the Second Coming. She got all flaming and excited, especially with me being her firstborn and all, having ruined her celebrity career, and she said the school had confirmed her suspicions that I was some kind of junior Einstein or something. Really, I don't think she had ever given the subject any thought until Mrs. Schongarth, the Windham Junior High Social Studies teacher and part-time guidance counselor, made her stupid suggestion. Either that or my mother refused to believe an ordinary kid could derail her career as a concert pianist - she had to have given birth to somebody like Jesus or da Vinci to justify the whole thing. Or maybe Judas, come to think of it.

All I could do is shake my head and hope it would all blow over. Evidently I was smart enough to skip a grade, but not smart enough to have an opinion about getting shoved ahead of my classmates and having to compete in sports with a year's less physical growth – not to mention the girls. What was the goddamn rush? I would have rather been left back a year if I had to get yanked out of my natural place in the world. I'd be the best ballplayer in the class and have an extra year of maturity which would have really helped with dating and everything. Although I think maturity was never my long suit.

Naturally, mom was all atwitter and got some kind of bug up her ass to find out just how smart I was, so they dragged me off to an institute. The tester was a woman who gave me all sorts of crap to do, including math problems and verbal junk where you read paragraphs and answered questions. There were puzzles you had to mentally fold up, and sets of objects where you had to tell which item didn't belong with the rest. The testing lady, Mrs. Leibbrandt, was quite pleasant, and mother like, with a sensible dress and a nice smile. I kind of felt sorry for her, especially when we spent some time on a section about ink blots. I told her stuff about the blots, which was actually kind of fun, or would have been, if I wasn't afraid they might commit me if I said some of the stuff I was really thinking when I looked at those cards. They told me it was part of the I.Q. test, but maybe it was some kind of sanity test because everybody knows about those ink blots. They all looked like vaginas, anyway, or at least what I thought vaginas probably looked like at age twelve. After awhile I said they did, even though the testing lady was a woman, and motherly, which was kind of embarrassing, because I figured whatever the hell else I made up might be even worse.

I don't know if they make any kind of allowances for the testing person being a woman and the testee a kid, who might be reluctant to say all those blots look like vaginas, but if they don't they should. At least that's my opinion. They also gave me something called a Thematic Apperception Test, I think, but I might have the name wrong because I stole a glance at the booklet and tried to read it upside down. Mrs. Leibbrandt showed me these old-timey drawings that probably Freud drew, for Chrissake, and the guy wasn't much of an artist. Dan Jones, my best buddy in high school, could have done it much better and the pictures would have been funnier, to boot. You were supposed to make up a story about each picture, and several of them involved family situations, so it didn't take a genius to figure out they were really trying to find out what you thought of your family life, and if you wanted to have sex with your sister, and crap like that, so the trick was to say everything was nice, unless you wanted revenge on your parents.

But after awhile I figured they would think I was not telling my true feelings if everything was sweet and airy, so I kind of went the other way, and pretty soon the guy in a picture had a butcher knife he was just about to whip out and plunge into the bosom of the unsuspecting young maiden looking at him in a trusting manner. I guess I waffled a bit on that test, but maybe they take that kind of thing into account.

I wondered afterward why they gave me that mental stuff, besides the I.Q. test, and I hope it was because they just added it in like a bonus, kind of like when my dad bought a new Buick Roadmaster and got them to throw in the radio for free. I hoped that was the case, and not because somebody suspected I was maybe one click off somewhere. I started to think that maybe they were using the I.Q. thing as a cover to see if I was really sane. I mean, I know I went kind of off the deep end when I saw Johnny Broadhead lying in the street, a couple of months before, but who wouldn't?

Johnny hadn't been my good friend or anything, but I had known him since second grade and probably anyone my age seeing that mess in the street would have gone off a little bit. Thank God I wasn't too close, but I still could see everything wet and glistening, streaked to the curb, and him laying there all broken and not even like a person, but some kind of smashed marionette, with blood all over my busted bike, and his mother's eyes boring into me like I could do something about it, or had something to do with it, all horrified and screaming, and I don't want to discuss it any more.

Anyway, Mrs. Leibbrandt asked my mother not to tell me the results, since it's supposed to be bad for a kid to find out how smart or dumb he is, or if he's nuts, but she must have told me my IQ a zillion times. I think mom tells everybody she meets, including people in the Shop-Rite when she's getting the groceries. She probably goes around ambushing other ladies' carts at the cereal display and telling them my IQ score while the Cheerios are tumbling off the shelf. I wish she'd go back to concert touring, sometimes, which might calm her down, but then who'd iron the clothes and overcook the meals?

It's not like I went off the charts, for Chrissake, but I did score above the dullard level so from that time on I was doomed to hear the score like it was etched in stone, especially when I screwed up. That's probably not a good analogy because if I died before she did my mother would chisel my IQ number right on my tombstone, I'll bet. I got good grades in high school, and graduated with pretty much an A average, but there are a lot of smart freshmen here and I guess I'm maybe average, if that lucky, so I've had to work my ass off first semester. I hadn't been used to that.

By the way, they did make me skip that grade. If I'd really been smart, I'd have thrown the dumb test.

Chapter 3

Ours is not an easy age
We're like tigers in a cage
What a town without pity can do
-Town Without Pity, Gene Pitney, 1962

Windham, New Jersey is a postcard community; the township is especially photogenic. Rolling hills, leafy countryside and meandering rural roads belie its proximity to New York City. White rail fences, horses and farm animals are common roadside sights. Our town is along the Erie Lackawanna rail line, west of New York by about 25 miles and ten light years, culturally.

I quoted all that, except the last phrase, from the hilarious Chamber of Commerce brochure they put in Mr. Wertz's real estate office. Dickie Wertz brought it into school one day and we all cracked up. Even Mr. Kritzinger got a chuckle. Can you imagine? It belies, all right. The only farm animal I ever saw in Windham was the big plastic cow on top of the milk store out on Shunpike. It sure would be funny as hell to see some porky fat pig try to cross Route 24 around 5:30 pm. There'd be bacon all over the road.

The population is just under ten thousand. When the New York Times ran a series of articles about the best places to live within commuting distance of the city, we were third on the list. Big dumb deal. Among our classmates, the joke was that we'd sure hate to live in the fourth. Anyway, the Windham Courier ran the story to death, blasting it all over the front page for about two weeks. Most of the commuters lived in the township, wore expensive suits, and read the Wall Street Journal or New York Times, instead of the Daily News or Daily Mirror, which they probably really wanted to read. The few riders who wore sport jackets or short-sleeved shirts lived in the borough and had crummy jobs in places like Newark or Hoboken. At least that's my conclusion.

To the west lay The Great Swamp, which was kind of a pretentious name, because it wasn't all that big and did not contain many creatures that could harm a man. It was wet, though, and maybe you went into that soggy acreage once to explore it, but after you got bitten by six zillion mosquitoes and picked up a leech or two that was enough. The marsh just stayed there, soaking, attracting no interest from anyone, except when one of Windham's finest stumbled on an abandoned still while hunting ringworms or something.

The township stood atop a terminal moraine, which, according to Mr. Kritzinger's geography lesson, meant the pile of rubble left at the end of the last glacial advance about ten thousand years ago. The borough was down below, which township residents figured was fitting, at least socially. Borough houses were older and smaller and sometimes fronted along busy Main Street, which was not too desirable. Township houses were generally clean and new and located in subdivisions with fancy names that were supposed to remind you of England, although hardly anyone had probably ever been there. These houses had several levels and all the latest appliances, including our unique hanging refrigerator that trapped our parakeet once for two hours.

In 1959 the town was mostly German, I think, with a few Scandinavians thrown in, because just about everybody was blonde and blue-eyed. The place looked like a regular Third Reich West; the girls were the best looking bunch, probably, in any high school in the United States. You should see my yearbook. Actually, I would like to see my yearbook because it got lost over the summer. I couldn't find it when I packed up for college.

We were about the second class to occupy the new Windham Senior High School, which looked like an automobile showroom stuck onto a factory. The L shaped building fronted along Main Street, down in the borough, at the end of a long, oak-lined driveway ending in a circle in front of the main entrance. The Sweet Shoppe, our after school hangout, was across the street next to the Shop Rite supermarket.

There were about 450 kids in the whole place. The school I mean, not the Sweet Shoppe. Almost everybody who graduated WHS went on to college, because it was that kind of upscale town, and the few who didn't became police or firemen. So the cops were Aryan, and the residents were blonde, and the town was clean and nice and lots of people had two cars and new split-level houses with dishwashers and attached garages. This was no crummy Levittown. The police station was conveniently located next to the train station, down in the borough. The cops could keep an eye on whoever got off at the Windham station. In the mornings, the men in the gray flannel suits took the express trains and headed east for the city and important jobs on Wall Street or wherever. The westbound locals carried the day maids and handymen. At night the process was reversed. That meant that if the cops saw a colored person getting off a train after 10 a.m., the offender was immediately intercepted and, without a valid reason for being in Windham, escorted across the tracks to the other side and put on the first dusty local back to the city - sort of a 20th century Underground Railroad in reverse. This also applied to any Negro in town after about 4 p.m. Most people thought it a convenient policy and kept the town relatively crime-free.

I guess I thought so too, or at least took the whole concept for granted, until my bicycle chain broke in Madison, the next town over. They fixed it for free at Po's garage. Afterward, it always bothered me that maybe Po couldn't have fixed my bike in Windham, had he worked there, if the sun was shading towards dinnertime. He'd have had to get on the train or motor off on Route 24 to wherever he lived, maybe in Jockey Hollow. Old Po had a nice smile, really peaceful and gentle. His face was a well-oiled, worn baseball glove, stained dark from saddle soap and thousands of dusty ground balls. Pure white teeth gleamed against supple black leather. Even his old overalls were the texture of soft cloth.

But there was no one to tell my thoughts to. And later, when Po lay cordoned off and still at the edge of the road, snagged by another strand of the web – but that was toward the end of my senior year, just before our disastrous class trip.

Chapter 4

So be my guest you've got nothin' to lose
Won't you let me take you on a sea cruise?
- Sea Cruise, Frankie Ford, 1959

Chief Duff Carlin leaned across the scarred, oak cop desk and looked me straight in the eye. He folded his beefy arms and leaned them on the blotter right behind the wooden sign reading CHIEF DUFF CARLIN. I got the impression he'd done this many times before to young criminals like me. Maybe he practiced it. It was an uncomfortable feeling.

"Mr. Garragues could have died, you know," he said. "It was damn lucky they found your classmate before he drowned."

"Yessir," I said. "It was terrible. I couldn't sleep that night." Was this appeal for sympathy too obvious? Maybe not; I heard my mother's intake of breath. Chief Carlin nodded, slowly.

"Now look, son, we know it wasn't you. You're a good kid, but you've been in bad company." In the other chair, my mother nodded vigorously. "We know the whole thing was Dan Jones' idea. We know he was the guy who injected the booze into the grapefruits and oranges, right? Just tell us who bought the vodka."

What did they do, get fingerprints off the rinds? Could they do that? I didn't think so, since citrus seemed to have pebbly surfaces, but then again I wasn't up on latent print detection except for what I read in the True Crime pulp magazines. The covers always showed some half-naked sexy broad tied to a chair, with a hoodlum or two in a cheap double-breasted suit and dago fedora leering over her. Not exactly book report material, but we liked it.

Did Chief Carlin really expect me to squeal on my classmates, especially Dan Jones, my best friend? I had held the fruits down so they wouldn't roll around while Jones inoculated each citrus. That made me an accessory, I figured. No doubt the Mayor's office was exerting pressure on Duff Carlin and his men in blue. That is, if our town had a mayor. Did we? I couldn't remember. I wasn't even sure who our class president was. Maybe it was Dick Orr.

I tried to affect a look of innocence. I knew my mom was waiting expectantly for my answer. I didn't disappoint her.

"Chief Carlin, I'd really like to help you. Really I would. But I don't know anything about it. Honest. I don't think Dan Jones does either."

Chief Carlin studied me for a moment, then leaned squeakily back in his battered swivel chair. Sunlight streaming through the dirty blinds behind his chair made a convict pattern on my chest. I might have heard water dripping somewhere, but it could have been my imagination. Maybe it was the Interrogation Room. Could I take it? I wondered. I hadn't done so hot at the FBI "interview" earlier in the year. My mother broke the silence.

"Chief, I know when my boy is telling the truth. Believe me, he's an honest boy. He gets good grades. He's never been in trouble before." Good old mom, backing me up like that, conveniently ignoring a few minor incidents like when the cop brought me home in seventh grade. It had been a thousand to one shot, a snowball from forty yards. Would the Duffer buy her act?

Chief Carlin swiveled in his chair, facing my mother. The Chief was doughnut fat. Why do all fat cops wear shirts two sizes too small?

"Well, Mrs. Williams, I think that's all for now. I might have some more to say about this later. George, I hope you've learned something from all this."

Boy, had I. For one thing, we used way too much vodka. It probably didn't help that the hypodermic needle Herbie Schultz had lifted from his father's medical bag had bent a couple of times, and might have been leaking excess potato juice. We had tried to be careful and not leave puncture marks.

Our senior class trip to the Jersey shore had become a disaster, just like the year before. Things started downhill when most of the citrus was eaten before lunchtime, on empty stomachs, and Jerry Garragues decided to swim to England. He'd sat up amidst a nest of high octane orange peels, lurched to his feet and teetered toward the surf and the United Kingdom. Sand and water squished out of his Bass Weejuns at the water's edge, where he swayed for a few moments, still fully dressed. Everyone was curious to see how far he could get before he drowned. It turned out he didn't get very far at all, because he fell into the trough just beyond the breaking surf and disappeared, arms akimbo, without a trace.

Michele Hoyt screamed and hollered for Miss Van Aldewehe, our luscious art teacher, who was chaperoning the trip along with Coach Weber. A couple of lifeguards ran and dove into the surf.

"I'll look over here!" Coach yelled, and splashed in as well. I really hoped Miss Van Aldewehe would follow and get her bathing suit wet, but instead she hopped around from side to side on the sand, hands to her cheeks, saying "Ooh, oh."

The lifeguards flailed around and dove under repeatedly, while for some reason Coach Weber stood in one place peering down. It took a minute or two to find Jerry, which seems about two years when someone's drowning. He only weighed about 140 pounds, rail-skinny, so when Coach shouted, reached down and grabbed his arm Jerry's whole limp body came flying out of the water, like linguini with clothes. A curious crowd gathered around our unconscious, soggy classmate. One of the lifeguards bent over him and began artificial respiration. I couldn't believe how much stuff came up out of Garragues: quarts of seawater mixed with pickled grapefruit, orange pulp and stomach matter.

Later, as he was being loaded into the ambulance, Jerry made, for him, a pair of astute observations.

"Where's my shoes?" was the first. He sat up, looked under the gurney and around the ambulance. Of course, the Bass Weejuns were but another victim to the eternal sea.

"No wonder I threw up," he said, in his second moment of truth. "My stomach was full of puke."

There was other stuff that went wrong on the trip, and a lot of throwing up and disgusting behavior, including Sherry Stahl's bra winding up on Tommy Enright's head and a slimy condom on the gearshift knob of the bus, but Jerry's brief trip off the continent was a definite highlight. Not as luminous as Miss Van Aldewehe's bathing suit, though. Somehow they'd found out about the vodka and the spherical citrus screwdrivers and that's why I was sitting in Duff Carlin's office, Chief of Police of the Borough of Windham, New Jersey.

Later, I found out from Jones that Chief Carlin gave the exact same performance when he and Mrs. Jones were called in to the chief's office an hour after we left.

"Now look, son, we know it wasn't you. You're a good kid, but you've been in bad company. The whole thing was Williams' idea, wasn't it? Just tell us who bought the vodka."

Actually, that was Jones' best reconstruction of the Duffer's conversation, since he could hear only about two of every three words. His ears were still ringing from the blast a couple of weeks earlier, but there was no way he could seek medical attention without going to jail, and the rest of us with him, most likely. He was really concerned for awhile, but his hearing did clear up over the summer.

But hey, at least they saved Garragues, dragging him out of the gray water and pumping all that sand and sludge out of his lungs. He went home the next day and seemed little the worse for wear.

Then.

Chapter 5

Chapter one says to love her,
You love her with all your heart
-   *The Book of Love, The Monotones, 1958*

Jones, my partner in crime, lived in the borough, and his house was really nifty because it was built in the 1700's and George Washington had slept there. I know lots of people say George Washington slept in their houses, but in this case it was documented. The guy seemed to sleep around as much as Shirley the Machine, our band groupie. He tied his horse to a tree in nearby Madison, and the dumb town left the tree in the middle of the road and paved around it. Big stupid deal. It was probably some lieutenant's horse, in any event.

Anyway, the rooms in Jones' house were undersized and not very level and sometimes you had to duck to go through a doorway, because the colonists were quite small. Jones didn't have to duck, since he was maybe 5'10", and built like a weightlifter, but I bashed my noggin a couple of times. I'm sure you remember all the suits of armor from the Middle Ages, in museums and castles, which were also miniaturized because human beings didn't grow to modern size until they had better nutrition. At least that's what Mr. Kritzinger said. The poor bastards - no plumbing or sandwiches or Clark bars.

You couldn't smoke in parts of Jones' house because of the age, and fire was a risk. Most of us smoked except the girls, and even some of them puffed an occasional Newport in the Sweet Shoppe after school. Brownie said high school girls who smoked were sexy.

"You mean because their mouths are open and they're like breathless and stuff?" I had inquired. Maybe he was alluding to some kind of chemical reaction with menthol tobacco. Jones, Brownie and I were sitting in a back booth sipping vanilla cokes sometime in the early fall, right before soccer practice started.

Brownie looked at me like I was nuts.

"What's the matter with you?"

I got asked that a lot. It wasn't really a question.

He explained that smoking meant the girls were of lesser moral character, and maybe would go all the way, or at least let you get farther, so they were sending us boys messages.

"Plus, it's a sucking exercise," he concluded. Jones nodded agreement.

"Jesus, George, you play in a band. You're supposed to know about broads."

Well, in a limited sense he was right, in a rock and roll sort of way. I hadn't made the smoking connection, though it seemed logical.

Mr. Schmid, owner of the Sweet Shoppe, was rumored to have been a guard at a place called Bergen-Belsen during the war. Evidently it wasn't much of a resort, at least according to the New York Daily News, although Mr. Kritzinger kind of dismissed it as hyperbolae. That's probably why Mr. Schmid kept a low profile and tolerated us ordering small cherry cokes or egg creams and sitting in his booths for an hour or so after school, when we weren't playing a sport. Egg creams were great, but you had to tell the soda jerk to spoon off all the foam or else you didn't get much soda. You'd think the guy would learn after being told ten thousand times but maybe that's why they called him the soda jerk.

I am digressing, and I need to make more of an effort to keep this on track. Assistant Professor Murphy says everything has to advance the story, and not to dawdle around on crap that doesn't have much to do with what happens. "When in doubt, throw it out." That's his other literary expression. He's probably right, and knows a lot more about literature and creative writing than I do, but maybe I like to meander around and smell the flowers while he runs pell mell for the Second Act. I can't help wondering if he knows so much how come he's not writing for a living? I mean, I don't see his name up there with James Michener and William Shirer and Rachel Carson. Or even Evan Hunter, the guy who wrote *Blackboard Jungle*, the book that started all that stuff jangling around inside my twelve year old body, and which I kind of wish I hadn't read at that age. Maybe nothing too meaningful ever happened to Assistant Professor Murphy, or he doesn't have much of an imagination, or he didn't grow up in a place like Windham.

Come to think of it, maybe he's the lucky one.

Chapter 6

Young love, our love
We share, with deep emotion ...
- Young Love, Sonny James, 1957

Some time before we got kicked out of Burn Brae Country Club, in early fall of my senior year, Wolfie met Kathy Obermeister at one of the club's dreary family functions. The Wolf was two years younger than me, which was eleven years older than our parents' big surprise, little Raymond. Wolfie's real name was Wolfgang, named after Mozart, of course, which was my mother's nutty idea. Can you imagine? Thank God they hadn't done that with me; I'd probably be Johann or Ludwig or Igor. All of those old masters had whacko first names. As it was, at least my brother called himself The Wolf. It could have been worse.

Kathy and Wolfie liked each other right off, and both sets of parents thought this was very cute. After a few dates, though, Wolfie deflowered her. Her parents wouldn't have thought that was too cute. They were pretty young to be having sex, I thought, but that's what he told me. It sounded like he might have been telling the truth. As a result, Wolfie liked the club temporarily and, for a few weeks, stopped hitting into the foursomes ahead of us, except when they were really slow. All he did that I know of was break into the clubhouse office and change all the players' handicaps while he copied down a new batch of member charge account numbers. The Wolf had been mildly concerned he might have been overusing the numbers he already had, but to our knowledge no member had complained about his bill. The new handicaps screwed everybody up royally for about six months, and we ate again for free.

The whole business of Wolfie having sexual intercourse with Kathy Obermeister, if indeed he did, was one that bothered me for quite a while. Not that I've exactly been a priest myself, but the thing was she was a virgin and just a nice, sweet teenager. Lest you think I'm hypocritical, I should say the girls who hung around our band were a different species, like Shirley the Machine, and it didn't much matter what you did with them. I know that sounds cold, but it's really not, because the girls themselves didn't much care. If you treated them nicely, it made not the slightest difference, except you went out of your way for nothing. No good would have come of it.

Of course, after Wolfie had his way with Kathy he dropped her, because that was that, he said.

"Hey, when you're done eating, somebody clears the dishes, you know?"

I was disappointed. I had ascribed a higher standard for my brother. I suppose that was silly. I didn't even really know Kathy Obermeister, except that her father was a partner in a big Wall Street firm, but that didn't mean she deserved it. They lived in this neat old house a few miles away with gardens and French doors. I was there a couple of times. There were always butterflies in her garden, it seemed. Beautiful black and gold monarchs. I don't know what the hell they were doing there, but I sort of always linked the thought of those butterflies living in that beautiful garden with something sad. It was as though

Wolfie had pulled their wings off. If one flew high enough, perhaps it could look in Kathy Obermeister's window above the roses and honeysuckle, following the muffled sounds and see her, uncomprehending, lying in her bed, sobbing away with Wolfie's quick little sperm darting around inside her newly-functional womb.

Kind of nutty, I know.

Chapter 7

Blown by wind, kissed by snow
All that's left is the dark,
You're gone from me
Oh, oh, tragedy
- Tragedy, Thomas Wayne and the DeLons, 1959

Graduation was screwed up somewhat because about three days before the ceremony Bird Mueller put a shotgun in his mouth and blew the back of his head clear into the next room. There had been no warning that we knew of, no sign at all. Mueller had a ready smile, and was pretty well-liked. The Bird had become our friend senior year, in an easy comfortable way, even though we hadn't really known him that well beforehand. He had transferred in from Green Village at the beginning of sophomore year.

He played tennis, which was not too common, and was supposed to be pretty good, besides being a hell of a varsity basketball player. He seemed to be one of those guys always at ease with his surroundings, but I guess that proved things weren't always as they seemed.

The news left us stunned. The administration called a special assembly the next morning, first thing, to tell us, but most everybody had heard about it already. Jones was late to school and when we lined up to go into the auditorium he said, not very softly, "Where the hell's the Bird? He out sick?" and a horrified Mrs. Stuckart had to rush over and talk to him. Mueller was aces, a really class guy, and I guess still water ran deep. He spoke mostly with his hands, and his grace, shooting the eyes out of a basketball and making All-State for WHS. The Bird had been slated for a free ride at Seton Hall in September on a full basketball scholarship, which would now go unclaimed.

He was quiet and so no one knew what demons haunted his mind enough to do a horrific thing like blow the back of his head into the next room with a twelve gauge. You have to watch the quiet ones, I guess, if only because you don't have a clue what their minds are doing.

I kept thinking about Mrs. Mueller finding her son, if indeed it was Mrs. Mueller who discovered the body, and all the mess. The thought made me shudder, thinking back those years to Mrs. Broadhead when she saw what was left of her boy in the middle of Passaic Avenue, and my bent and broken bicycle. And then, worse, the memory of her eyes when she locked onto me, sealing our mutual terror, fusing me indelibly into her nightmare, forever linked by the first filament of the web. I see those eyes sometimes, right when I don't want to, if I don't sleep through the entire night.

And afterward, when Mrs. Broadhead had been carried away, they had cleaned up Johnny, mostly, and then with the big Windham pumper hosed the rest of Mrs. Broadhead's firstborn into the storm drain and limed the street. They limed the goddamn street, a white smear, like some kind of one-dimensional tombstone. Mrs. Broadhead wasn't there to see that, the part of her son that never made it to the coffin but drained into the Windham sewer system.

Who cleaned up the Bird? I wondered. The coroner? Did they do that, or just take pictures? His mother? Certainly not his mom. Some maid, probably, who came in on the Erie Lackawanna for this grisly errand, and then disappeared back into the night, wordlessly, carrying this memory and maybe infinitesimal particles of Bird under her nails back to some grim city tenement, maybe with a smug satisfaction, or worse: the knowledge that she had done what she was supposed to do. And the wallpaper. Was that a speck of the Bird or just an imperfection in the fleur-de-lis?

How could Mrs. Mueller ever forget that, if you saw your boy's head blasted out like that? How could you forget finding your son in two different rooms? I never forgot it, and I wasn't even there and I wasn't his mother.

It would be July before we knew why Mueller had shot his last basket and the back of his head off; I hoped to God his mother never found out. It wouldn't be from us. Our strange trio - Brownie, me and Coach Weber - would keep his ghastly secret forever, and another strand from the web settled, almost invisibly, on Windham.

*   *   *

Somehow, I got started telling you about stuff that happened toward the end of our senior year, which is all out of order. You have to go back to the beginning, while everybody was still alive, and everything seemed normal and things hadn't yet spiraled out of control. The thing is, I can't really fix a time when stuff started to go wrong, and maybe that's got a lot to do with what's bothering me. Life was swell, and the Yankees were about to knock off the Milwaukee Braves in seven games to win the World Series, before the goddamn New York Giants ruined our youth in overtime against old Johnny U. Everybody loved Johnny Unitas, especially that bullshit story about him coming off the sandlots right into the NFL and setting all kinds of records, but after beating our beloved Giants in overtime he was on my list for awhile.

Chapter 8

Up in the morning and out to school
The teacher is teachin' the golden rule
-     *School Day, Chuck Berry, 1957*

We got a new gym teacher senior year, Coach Weber. He replaced our ancient rheumatic coach, Coach Buhler, who had finally retired, or maybe died.   I mean, the guy was about fifty years old, anyway.   Weber wasn't very old, and this probably was his first teaching job. For the whole year, we never saw him in anything but his black sweat suits with red striping. At least, I hoped he had more than one suit, since he wore the same outfit just about every day. They weren't even our school colors, for Chrissake, which were a corny blue and gold, like a zillion other high schools.

Mr. Weber had gotten off on the wrong foot from the start. I mean the first five minutes. He tried to take attendance, which no other gym teacher had ever done, because he didn't know any better. He kept mispronouncing everybody's name.

"Ku-NATH?"

"That's KU-nith. Here."

"Van-A-der?"

"It's VAN-a-der. Present."

"Well, at least here's one I can't get wrong. Jones?"

"That's Jon-ESS, Coach." The whole class burst out laughing.

The other mistake he made from the get-go was an attempt to get chummy with the hoodlums in our gym class. This was short-lived.

"When I call your name, tell me what your friends call you. Let me know if you have a nickname," he had said. In a little while, he got to Jack Frankfurter.

"Well, I can guess what they call you, Mr. Frankfurter. Heh-heh. What's your nickname?"

Now of course we all called him the Wiener, as in Oscar Mayer wiener. Once I believe that terrific Oscar Mayer Wienermobile had come to Windham, the big hot dog on wheels, but it was a dim kid memory. Everybody loved that truck, didn't they? The Wiener, who kind of looked like an uncooked Sabrett anyway, played it to the hilt. He gave Coach Weber a blank stare.

"What do you mean?"

"Well, I mean . . . maybe you have a nickname," was the lame response.

"Well, Coach, I'm not sure I know what you mean," the Wiener said.

"Aah, well, skip it. Griffin, Dale?" Coach was trying to move on.

"Sometimes my mother calls me late for supper," the Wiener said.

"That's all right," Coach said.

"My dad calls me a goddamn idiot," the Wiener persisted. Another round of laughter from the class. Coach Weber looked surprised.

"HEY," he said. "Don't use that kind of language in class." More gales of laughter.

"Sometimes my father - " The Wiener was relentless.

"HEY!" Coach Weber yelled. "I said STOP IT. Now let's move on."

It was too late. Boisterous laughter was again disturbing Miss Van Aldewehe's Art class next door.

That was the beginning of the tension between Coach Weber and Jack the Wiener Frankfurter. For whatever reason, chemistry I guess, the Wiener decided he didn't like Coach Weber. I asked him about it one day in the cafeteria, while I was trying to open my half pint of chocolate milk.

"What've you got against Coach?" I asked, fumbling with the stupid carton. The guy seemed nice enough to me, if kind of naïve about the Class of 1959, treating us like students instead of inmates.

The milk carton was aggravating me. The goddamn things were harder to crack than a safe. They were supposed to peel open and make a spout, but all they ever did was shred. When you tilted one up to drink, half the milk poured out sideways and down your neck. Nice. For three cents, you'd think you could get a decent drink.

"Ha," Jones said. "The milk's all running down your neck."

"There's something about that guy," the Wiener said. "Something real wrong. You'll see."

"It's all over your shirt," Jones said.

"What do you mean?" I asked, dabbing at my neck with a disintegrating napkin. "How can you say that?"

"Now there's shredded napkin all over your neck," Jones said.

"You'll see," is all the Wiener said.

It wasn't long before the next confrontation. Coach Weber had the really odd idea that one day a week we should have a class, which he called History of Sports, instead of playing something. Who cared about History of Sports? We just wanted to play softball or dodge ball or whatever was normally scheduled that period. On this day, Coach Weber talked about jousting and other English stuff where the whole idea was to poke a hole in the opponent. Actually, we were pretty interested and wondered if somehow we could work this game into gym class.

Coach was drawing this nifty mace and chain thing when half an egg salad sandwich hit the blackboard, square on the chalk picture. Of course his back had been to the class, so Coach Weber couldn't tell it was Jack the Wiener Frankfurter who threw it. Who wanted to eat egg salad anyway? Actually, he could tell who threw it because as the Wiener let it go some of the egg salad flew off and got all over his shirtsleeve. Also the other half of the sandwich was still on his desk, before it wound up in Bruce Himmler's fagbag. The half sandwich had hit and stuck with a splat noise, and slowly sank to the chalk tray leaving a trail of yellow mayonnaise and yolk. It kind of reminded me of a large yellow slug track.

"Mr. Frankfurter," coach said, eyeing the Wiener's sleeve, "get down to Mr. Dunwood's office *now*."

"Hey, I didn't do anything," was the reflex answer.

I could tell Mr. Weber was struggling to stay calm instead of wringing the Wiener's neck, something that would be repeated at times during the year.

"*Now*, mister."

The Wiener took his time getting his stuff together before sauntering out of the room. I wondered if he would slam the door, but he closed it with a soft click which somehow seemed more insolent than if he'd banged it. Jones and Brownie thought their clashes were funny, but they made me uncomfortable, to tell the truth. There's nothing wrong with showing a little respect, plus I don't think the Wiener knew how close he probably came to becoming a quadriplegic.

Chapter 9

Hide it in a hiding place where no one ever goes
Put it in your pantry with your cupcakes
- *Mrs. Robinson, Simon and Garfunkel, 1968*

It's not so hard writing about the fun times, and even the other times, but when the topic is yourself it can be a different story. Sometimes it can be painful. I probably should have written this chapter earlier, to keep things in order, but I've been putting it off. Of course I don't tell my parents much of anything, and, being the oldest, I don't exactly have heart to hearts with Wolfie and Raymond, but Brownie and Dan Jones are privy to most everything. I mean, they're real buddies and will be for life, I hope. But I haven't told anyone about this next part. It's a strand of the web that touched me personally, ensnaring me as I fought to break free, fearing the spider scrabbling towards me from the center. It's not funny, and it's not a great memory. If I do turn this whole thing in to Assistant Professor Murphy you can bet your ass this chapter won't be in it. Here goes.

The grade I skipped was the eighth. When I began the ninth grade, I didn't know everyone in that class too well. Because I was younger, I became sort of an unofficial mascot for the first few months. It was a good-natured thing and kind of died a natural death by maybe Thanksgiving, but when classes started in September that's how it was. This reputation that I was some sort of brainiac preceded me, which was unfortunate, but as soon as people got to know me they realized it was a myth. Everything settled down, especially when they found out I was a rock and roller with my own band, Froggy and the Gremlins, and an unsuccessful recording artist.

It started in Mrs. Carnahan's Geometry class. Now Mrs. Carnahan was no knockout, believe me, and she was – I hate to admit it – *old*. My guess would be forty if she was a day. When she walked into a pool of light by the window on a sunny day, drawing a trapezoid in the air with her chalk, you could see the wrinkles, sort of. She had these freckles on her skin – not the kind of freckles little redhead kids have, little happy polka dots, but the ones old people get when their skin starts getting kind of like parchment. The weird thing, though, is that I thought she was pretty sexy. She was still shapely, and she was fond of these see-through white blouses and tight skirts with high heels. Although you could pretty much see through the blouse, her slip was of course opaque but for some reason the whole deal seemed pretty exciting to me, especially since she had these round, heavy breasts that were more sultry than perky. If you know what I mean.

None of the ninth grade girls wore anything like Mrs. Carnahan's outfits, nor did they have sultry breasts. I wasn't too up on what sort of undergarments went where in older, mature women and it was actually kind of intimidating but sexy too, kind of like a puzzle that unlocks some great treasure. I couldn't admit this to anybody, of course, because Brownie would call me a necrophiliac and Jones would bray with laughter while branding me a pervert. Besides, like I said, she wasn't too good-looking.

So now there I was, a ninth grader who was really chronologically an eighth grader, and who should've been thinking of nothing but the Mick's batting average and why he was better than Willie Mays, except that that damn Blackboard Jungle had screwed up my mind as well as my glandular system, and I found myself fixated on Mrs. Carnahan. I mean, I was fixated on Mickey Mantle too, but that's just normal for any Yankee fan. Anyway, when I hit the rack at night I was no longer thinking about the Yankees or the Rangers or Bo Diddley or even the lousy Knicks, like I had before ninth grade. I was thinking about Mrs. Carnahan, and it didn't make too much sense, even to me. Somehow her being not good-looking made her more exciting, because after all she probably had to take what she could get, and therefore was likely more accessible. At least, that's what I thought, probably. I hadn't done so hot on those ink blots the year before anyway, so what the hell did I know?

I started imagining all sorts of really perversion-type stuff, starting with her clothing and ending without it, right there in the geometry classroom, amidst the protractors and triangles, raising clouds of chalk dust. The thing is, once you start that kind of stuff it's just about impossible to stop. So now my body felt like somebody tightened all the tendons and things, zeroing in on my crotch, like a rubber band winding a model airplane propeller. You get the idea. Pretty soon the model airplane has to take off or the rubber band busts. And this was about every stupid night. So what else was I supposed to do?

This went on for a couple of months as my obsession became more feverish. After all, Mrs. Carnahan was married, which meant she did it every other day and probably had developed a craving, like cigarettes maybe. That really was an exciting thought. The thing was, it wasn't just sex. I realized I wanted to protect her. From what, though, I didn't know.

I imagined all sorts of juvenile stupid things, like Mrs. Carnahan giving me detention. In my reverie I could hear the sounds of ball playing outside, maybe Brownie or Orr smacking a line drive while I sat in the second row. In this particular stupid scenario, I hear Mrs. Carnahan sigh, seated at her desk.

"Is everything all right, Mrs. Carnahan?"

She looks up at me, trying unsuccessfully to hide her watery eyes, but a tear runs down her cheek.

"Everything's just – never mind. Thanks for asking." She smiles sweetly.

"It's all right. It'll be okay, I'm sure." I'm wearing a sappy smile. I'm certain she's having a problem at home. In reality, although I never even saw Mr. Carnahan, I hate his guts. I hear a sniffle.

"It's Mister Carnahan, isn't it?"

Suddenly she begins sobbing. I jump up, run up to her desk and put my arms –

Oh, what the hell. I told you it was stupid.

Only here's the thing. It wasn't. In my heightened state of awareness in that classroom, I noticed small things that seemed to back up my deluded night visions. At times, Mrs. Carnahan didn't seem all together, distracted, as though maybe some things from her personal life were intruding on her classroom demeanor. I mean, we all think of teachers as sort of not real people, maybe going into suspended animation after school, without any personal life or human activity, until the next morning. But, as I said, I had no trouble imagining Mrs. Carnahan doing non-teacher stuff like maybe shopping or watching Milton Berle or making supper for Mr. Carnahan, who

I still hated, even though I had no good reason. And, over a month or so, I think she began to notice me. I mean, I think she began to realize that I had thoughts about her.

At first, she looked at me oddly. Not so anyone would notice, maybe just a glance here or there, but I sure picked up on it. So far my Mrs. Carnahan fantasy was manageable, if only just, but it all got out of control in a hurry.

I got detention:

"George, what's so funny?"

It was another of Dan Jones' caricatures. I couldn't help it; they always made me laugh out loud. This one showed Mr. Kritzinger on a leash, being led around on all fours by Mrs. Kritzinger, lifting his leg against a fire hydrant. Mrs. Kritzinger had a teacup handle.

"Aaahh –"

"Maybe you can explain it to me after school."

I felt like I'd put my finger in a light socket. The rest of the morning was a blur. Jones, of course, had no idea. He just cracked up that I was getting punished for his drawing. Someone was always getting punished for his drawings, it seemed; they were a kind of artistic lethal weapon. As the day careened by, I found it hard to breathe when I thought of my 3:10 rendezvous. At 3:05, I had that familiar feeling as though I was going onstage or in goal for the state championship soccer game – all my molecules were whirring and spinning too fast.

The day's memory was crystal clear compared to my recollection of that study hall, though. I do remember Mrs. Carnahan telling me to sit in the first row, and looking up at me from behind her desk every couple of minutes and smiling as she read my expression, which I don't believe was too composed. I recall her coming around from her desk after awhile and standing very close to where I was sitting. All of a sudden my face was about the temperature that would melt lead. She put one nylon-encased leg up on the desk across from me, looking at me intently as she did so, and I know she was saying something but I have no idea what. The next thing I knew she'd taken my hand and held it in both of hers. And then she said the words that sent me into hyperspace:

"Do you like me, George?"

Yeah, I know it sounds nifty, and really good, and I had lucked out, and probably that's what I thought at the time, although I can't remember a damn thing about what I thought, if anything, except now my brain was the temperature of the sun. I barely noticed that something small had bit me on the hand; my palm began to hurt.

But later I thought about it a lot. And, as I say, it wasn't funny. Not then, not later.

That's all I'm going to write about it now.

". . . Do you like me, George?"

Chapter 10

In Chapter 4 you break up
Won't you gimme just one more chance?
- The Book of Love, The Monotones, 1958

I was sitting in the Sweet Shoppe with Brownie, Jones and Robbie van Arsdale on a beautiful Indian summer day, as we usually did from about 3:10 to 4:00. Robbie was a junior, a really good dresser, one of those guys who always looked like he just stepped out of the shower, brandy-clean and unwrinkled. On the other hand, my clothes looked like nobody ever ironed them within five minutes of getting dressed, which drove my mom crazy. Shirttails would climb out of my pants like they had a mind of their own. I missed the occasional belt loop. It's not like I didn't try, though.

Robbie was some kind of weird religion, Mormon or something, where they didn't like doctors, or maybe it was lawyers. Nobody liked lawyers, anyway. He couldn't go to the dances or smile or have any fun. He was allowed to have sex, though, I think. His parents were nuts. Who would live like that?

Outside, the sun was dazzling, the sky the deepest blue. You know the kind of day I mean: everything is sort of extra alive, sharp and colorful. The air had the tang of fall crispness, with just a hint of burning leaves.

Inside the Sweet Shoppe, though, the burning smell wasn't just a hint. The air was so polluted you didn't need to light up to have a smoke. It was in the beginning of my senior year, a week before soccer practice would begin, so Brownie and I had free time for the next five days. Brownie, our All-American midfielder, had a first name, but even the teachers called him Brownie. Between him and Jones, it was always a sunny day, and something better was just about to happen. Some people just enjoy life, you know? These guys didn't have an introspective bone in their bodies.

Michele Hoyt and a couple of her friends had seen us come into the Sweet Shoppe. She stopped by our corner booth as they were leaving.

"Hey, Brownie," she said, smiling sweetly.

"Hey, Michele," he answered. "Get laid this summer?"

She ignored this. "Are you pregnant? Looks like you're gonna have a baby elephant."

We started to laugh. Brownie had put on maybe ten pounds over the summer, courtesy of Ballantine Beer, and needed to take it off for soccer.

"Yeah, Michele, look." He stood up and unzipped his fly. "The trunk's already out."

Michele screamed and scooted out the door. We howled.

"HAH!" Brownie exclaimed. "Pretty good, eh?" I told you he was quick. His philosophy was simple: life's a bowl of cherries, but some guys get the pits. Brownie just spit them out. I was glad it was Brownie who was with me when we made our ghastly find after graduation: the epitaph on that giant concrete tombstone, shimmering quietly in the awful heat, waiting for us.

I spotted Dick Orr through the tobacco haze, over by the bulletin board, which hung on the back wall by the juke box. He was another good athlete, and about the same height as me and Brownie. There seemed to be a lot of guys around 6'2" or 6'3" in our class; maybe it was because they were fluoridating the water from the reservoir. Orr was leaning against the wall, reading the messages on the index cards. Anyone could post a message on the board, or, if you had something to buy or sell, put it up on a three by five index card with thumbtacks from the boxes on top of the juke box. I waved Dick over.

"Hey, George," he said, and sat down in our booth. He ordered a vanilla coke.

"What're you looking for?" asked Jones.

"A car," Orr replied. Cars were a very popular subject on the bulletin board. "I get my license next week. I'm looking for a Bel Air, maybe, if it's cheap enough."

"I'm thinking about painting mine," Brownie said. He owned a 1953 Nash Rambler. The thing was ugly as sin, and looked like a small Lincoln taking a dump. The seat tilted all the way back, though, so it was a very desirable car for dating.

"Why?" asked Robbie van Arsdale. "The paint looks okay."

"Well, suppose I need to make a getaway," Brownie said, with what would prove an uncanny prescience.

"From what?" I inquired.

"I don't know, but you gotta be prepared. Here's what I was thinking. Suppose I painted one side of the car one color, and other side a different color. Then the cops would have two different descriptions."

That was the craziest idea I ever heard, but maybe it had some merit. My eyes were watering in the smoky haze, a permanent fixture. If the place ever caught fire, nobody would know to get out. Two booths over, Mary Anne Moffitt was barely visible through the pollution. Too bad.

"I thought about painting it camouflage, so nobody at all would see it, and there wouldn't be any description. But then I figured people would plow into me if they didn't see the car at all." I hadn't thought about that before. Maybe that was why the Army painted their trucks all green instead of camouflage.

"Anything funny on the bulletin board?" asked Jones. There was usually some wag advertising rubbers for sale, used only once, and stuff like that.

"Nah," Orr replied. "Hey, what's the 2640 Club?"

None of us had ever heard of the 2640 Club. I needed to stretch my legs anyway, so I got up and wandered back to the board. There were the usual notices about rides wanted, and junk for sale, and the notice Dick mentioned, on a three by five:

% Notice %
Tuesday night's meeting of the 2640 Club
is cancelled. It will be rescheduled for
later in the week.

The card was unsigned. That was curious. There was something kind of familiar about the number, but I couldn't place what it was. An address? Phone number? . . . maybe it would come to me.

Something light and silky touched my face; I brushed it aside.

*   *   *   *

A week later Brownie taped his car right down the middle, with masking tape, and painted one side yellow and the other side green. The end result, of course, was probably the most noticeable car in North America. When he called us out of the Sweet Shoppe to show off his artwork, we cracked up. The thing was hilarious, like a half ripe avocado. If you looked closely at the finish, you could hardly tell he used a brush except down by the rocker panels. I didn't know you could paint a car like that.

It didn't matter to Brownie in the slightest that we laughed at his creation. You couldn't hurt that guy's feelings with a hammer. He just shrugged it off and was pleased when Regina Lundgren told him his car was cool and rode with him out to the reservoir on Friday night. Brownie said they spent an hour on the green side of the car, which was pretty funny. Maybe she saw his baby elephant trunk.

Chapter 11

Yes, everybody's somebody's fool
Everybody's somebody's plaything . . .
- *Everybody's Somebody's Fool, Connie Francis, 1960*

Nobody loves everybody. I'll bet even Jesus got pretty vexed with the asshole that stuck a sword in his side. Somebody always rubs somebody else the wrong way, and in my case it was That Bastard Heileman.

Actually, Heileman rubbed everybody the wrong way.

Every class in every high school has a That Bastard Heileman: a real sonofabitch. Lots of guys are funny, and wise off, but there's a difference. Heileman would make fun of classmates and hurt their feelings. If there was a weakness, he would jump on it. Nothing was out of bounds for That Bastard.

We had a classmate, Johnny Wingo, who had been crippled with polio when he was a kid. As a result, he gimped around with one bent leg and one useless arm. You could hear the Gimp coming down the hall, if nobody else was around: step, shuffle. Step, shuffle. It was kind of a cripple version of the Stroll. Brownie told him he ought to be on American Bandstand; he might start a trend and maybe get laid. That might sound cruel, but the idea actually cheered the Gimp and gave him a goal of sorts.

Most people with disabilities develop some compensating ability in other areas, or at least people tell them that to make them feel better, although the truth is God didn't make a level playing field. In the Gimp's case, though, he had no special talents we or he could discover. On top of all that, he was gullible, so the guy practically had three strikes against him from the start. Of course, we called him the Gimp but that was good-natured. I mean, did he think we didn't notice? But with That Bastard Heileman it was different. He was *mean*. He would ride the Gimp all the time and tell him he was never going to get laid, unless it was to another gimp. That might have been true, but there was no need to say it. What made it worse is that we didn't have a female gimp he could use for companionship.

The subject of That Bastard Heileman came up on a Friday, our last free day before soccer practice would begin. As always, Brownie, Jones, Robbie van Arsdale and I were sitting in the Sweet Shoppe after school nursing vanilla cokes and smoking Marlboros.

"You know what That Bastard Heileman said to the Gimp at lunch?" I asked.

"What?" asked Jones.

"He told the Gimp he read in some journal they just found a cure for gimpitis, but it costs ten grand."

"Gimpitis?"

"He said that?"

"Yeah," I said. "I heard him. He told the Gimp he'd bet his old man didn't have enough dough to fix him. I swear I'm going to cream That Bastard."

I think I'm a pretty even-tempered guy, but That Bastard Heileman was like a flashpoint.

"If it's yesterday it won't be soon enough," Brownie said.

"You'll bust your hand and you won't be able to play the guitar," Jones said. "Better let Brownie do it."

"If I'd have heard him, I think I would have popped him right there in the cafeteria," Brownie said.

"I can feel it coming," I said. "We're going to get into it."

It only took a week. I was walking behind Sherry Stahl in the hallway after Social Studies when That Bastard Heileman passed by. He leaned toward Sherry and said "Oink." I didn't even think. I shoved him hard in the chest. We scuffled for a few seconds.

"Behind the track after school, Williams," he said.

"You got it, asswipe," I said.

Naturally, news of the impending fight flashed through the school before one could squeal another oink. Sherry Stahl just about wet her pants telling all the girls I was defending her honor, when really she'd had nothing to do with the whole encounter. At 3:10, half the student body was circled around Heileman and I as we squared off in a hollow behind the track, where we couldn't be seen from the school building. Heileman was about my height and weight, but I felt confident I could kick his ass. After all, That Bastard didn't play any sports that I knew of.

Boy was I wrong. Heileman didn't play a sport, but the guy worked in his old man's rose greenhouse after school, shoveling and hauling cubic yards of dirt like some human steam shovel. His muscles were hard as rocks, and he was strong as a farm animal. For another thing, he wore a big ring on his left hand, something I hadn't noticed until we started sparring and he cut the inside of my mouth a couple of times with left hooks. After a minute or two, I was spitting blood and definitely not winning. We hit the ground wrestling, and I took another shot or two in the face. Just as Jones had predicted, I about busted my hand on his cheekbone.

As we rolled around, I glimpsed flashes of black and red, and they weren't all from getting belted. After another minute, an arm reached in and pulled me away, just as I had gotten on top of That Bastard and was wailing away on his face.

It was Coach Weber. I was panting and bleeding, and my mouth hurt like hell, and part of me was glad the fight was over. But another part wondered why coach let me get softened up and just watched until I managed to wind up on top.

My mom was horrified to see the damage, which I couldn't really hide, but I think dad secretly felt pretty good when I told him I wound up on top despite my battered face and That Bastard Heileman didn't look much better. Mom was going to call the principal, for what I didn't know, but dad nixed it. She didn't usually listen to much of what the old man said but he was pretty firm about it.

Of course, Wolfie laughed his ass off and said I looked like a hamburger before it went on the grill. Even Raymond giggled and pointed at my nose when it started to bleed at dinner.

Infinitely worse, Sherry Stahl adopted me as her hero and I couldn't avoid the embarrassment all year. Jones and Brownie wouldn't let me forget it, in any event. Sherry even hinted something about the prom, but I feigned ignorance.

Oink.

Chapter 12

Many a tear has to fall
But it's all in the game
-    *All in the Game, Tommy Edwards, 1958*

Despite the Wiener's airborne egg salad sandwich, Coach Weber seemed undeterred from his mission to educate us on the History of Sports. A few weeks later, he decided to show us a wrestling film that he brought in a large metal film can. He had Bruce Himmler, the head A. V. guy, set up the projector. Bruce was the only student with a briefcase, the soft-sided kind like he was some important government scientist working on the A-bomb, for Chrissake.

Actually, since all that nasty business about his uncle during the War, nobody was going to give Bruce clearance to use a government rest room, much less read about A-bombs anyway. Bruce had tried to deny he was related to the Nazi war criminal, but we knew better. How many guys do you know named Himmler? Come to think of it, he was probably related to half the families in Windham anyway. I bet he'd have gotten his cherry cokes for free from Mr. Schmid, if we'd have let Bruce patronize the Sweet Shoppe. Probably all the Nazis in town had the sense to stay away from each other, I bet, until everybody forgot about the storm troopers and all. Actually, since it seemed like PBS would never stop showing *Victory at Sea*, the damned war would probably go on forever.

But anyway this time we were supposed to watch this wrestling film on the school's 16mm projector, and it took Bruce about five minutes to set it up. These two guys were wrestling in black and white, since this was a cheap movie, all scratchy and grainy and jerky, like maybe from colonial times. Coach Weber was explaining the different moves as the film lurched on. He was saying things like "He's got him in a cradle, boys."

The problem came when some kid poked his head into the room and said they needed Coach Weber in the office for a minute, a scenario that would be repeated later in the year with disastrous consequences for the entire population of Windham borough. That's when Jones became the Audio Visual guy for about thirty seconds. As soon as Coach left, Jones shoved Bruce Himmler out of the way and fiddled with the projector. He shook a fist at Bruce when he was through, which told Himmler that if he said anything he would eat a knuckle sandwich after school. A current of anticipation ran throughout the room.

A few minutes later Coach Weber came back and sat down. He nodded to Bruce to resume the movie. The two black and white guys started wrestling again and Coach started commenting again, still saying things like, "He's trying to put him in a cradle, boys," when all of a sudden one of the wrestlers leaped up backwards, seemingly in defiance of gravity, and landed lightly on his feet like some kind of graceful ballet dancer. We all started to guffaw, because we realized what Jones had done. You couldn't tell, really, when the two guys were rolling around on the mat. Coach Weber said,

"What?!??"

which of course made us laugh even louder. The film actually went on for about a minute more, with Coach Weber's mouth hanging open, because he was too slow to realize the projector was running backwards. Every second the class was getting more hysterical. When he finally yelled at Bruce to shut off the machine, most of us were unable to breathe from laughing so hard and tears were rolling down our cheeks. Coach glared at the Wiener, who was laughing as hard as anyone, but he had no evidence. I expected any minute to see Miss Van Aldewehe come in from next door and complain we were disturbing her Art class again.

It would have been worth a detention just to see her come in with that soft, pouty look. I loved Art.

*   *   *   *   *   *

Actually, the incident with Coach Weber pretty much tells you about the guy, which is why I've included it. I mean, it's an anecdote, sure, but now it doesn't seem as funny as it did then, especially in light of future events. Coach really wanted to teach us stuff, but didn't seem to realize we didn't particularly want to learn anything, at least in the classroom. Maybe it's because he was so young, or grew up in the Midwest or something. In a way, it's kind of sad, like when a really old aunt or somebody gives you a bicycle for Christmas and you're about ready to get your driver's license. It's sad to realize she spent quite a bit of dough for the wrong thing. I hate that stuff.

Who could have thought, back in the fall, Coach Weber would be involved in such disturbing things, so close to the center of the web? And that I would have to figure out that life wasn't so pat, not black and white at all, but a murky gray, sometimes, and it wasn't always possible to tell the heroes from the villains, unlike on TV or in the movies?

Certainly not me, or Dan Jones, or even Brownie. And that's about all who could know, except maybe for Chief Duff Carlin, and we weren't about to ask him.

But all that was later, in the spring, when the spider was spinning furiously and events seemed to happen so fast and got very confusing. Back in September I wasn't thinking about any of those things; probably my deepest thought was the next soccer game or band job.

Chapter 13

Back in the classroom
Open your books
- *School Day, Chuck Berry, 1957*

While Home Ec was required for girls, boys had to either take Shop or Art. Shop guys invariably came from the borough, and wore rolled up T-shirts with their unfiltered cigarettes stuck in the sleeves. Township boys smoked Marlboros, and the girls puffed on Newports, but the borough youth smoked Luckies or Camels, with the sexy woman hidden in the camel's leg on the package. They usually did things like set the timing on motors and hack up metal in vises in preparation for their future dead-end jobs, ripping off executives from the township when their cars went south or they needed some shop-type stuff done to their houses.

Lots of guys, including me, opted for Art because of Miss van Aldewehe. She was the pinnacle of Windham voluptuousness, and you can't get higher than that. She reminded me of a ripe tomato, all juicy and smooth. She was nice, too. She didn't catch on that all the guys went into an erotic haze when they stared at her, so she must have thought we were all really stupid because we gave answers like "Uuhh . . ." when she asked a question. She did really dumb things like tell the class stuff such as "Please," instead of just ordering us, as in:

"Please don't mix the water colors with the oil paints."

So of course all the paints got mixed together and the school board had to authorize purchase of all new Art supplies, including brushes, because they got ruined, too.

Jones was Miss van Aldewehe's favorite student for two reasons. One, he charmed her with his sappy smile, All-American blonde crew cut and big blue eyes, and two, he was a really talented artist. One day he had the Wiener call her over and ask a question about the painting he was working on, because he sat in the next row opposite Jones' seat. While she was bent over looking at the Wiener's picture Jones painted part of her shoe with red oil paint. Actually, when Miss van Aldewehe was bent over the Wiener's painting I was looking at her ass, eyes glazed in reverie, and it took me several seconds to realize what Jones was doing with his detail brush.

Once a year the school held a combined Achievement Fair, where all the Art and Shop stuff was exhibited for parents and siblings. My senior year was the best Achievement show ever, because the night before a bunch of kids broke into the school and added their own contribution to the Fair. Shop class had built a frame house, made of small sticks which might have been toothpicks and Popsicle sticks, and it was quite elaborate. It had taken a couple of months to put together, and had cutaway sections to view the construction details. There were labels saying stuff like JOIST and FIRESTOP, or at least there were the night before the exhibit. Of course, the midnight raiders doused the house with lighter fluid and torched it, so that in the morning when the Fair opened most of the house had burned away, and the roof collapsed, but the neat part was that it looked just like a real fire would in a real house, if you overlooked the people. The people were plastic and just melted down into shapeless lumps, except that the ones farthest from the fire sort of slumped.

The whole thing was pretty funny, almost hysterical when you actually saw what was left of the house, but in another way it wasn't too funny at all. Those shop guys were probably proud of their miniature home. They were never going to make too much dough operating lathes and crap, wearing dirty overalls and eating hard-boiled eggs and cold sandwiches out of lunch boxes on their half hour lunch break for the next forty years. They would always be Rocky or Ace or Dutch and not Robert van Arsdale III, for example, although Robbie had nothing to do with the junior class' vandalism. They weren't going to ride the Erie Lackawanna and get sloshed in the club car and make tons of dough sitting around New York offices wearing stupid ties like the township kids. But some of the vandals who torched their exhibit were from the township, probably, maybe all of them. It was kind of disquieting, in a way, as I thought about it.

Actually, for all I know, the kids who burned it down might have been the same ones who built the damn thing.

Chapter 14

He walks in the classroom cool and slow
Who calls the English teacher daddy-o?
- Charlie Brown, The Coasters, 1959

When we returned from Thanksgiving break, we had a new English teacher. This was very unusual. No explanation was given, but Mr. Freisler was gone. Vanished. There was no official announcement. The new teacher was Mr. Glendenning. The guy was pretty old, maybe 40, and he didn't make the same mistake as Coach Weber. He started right in where Mr. Freisler had left off, so evidently he had Mr. Freisler's lesson plan. Very curious.

"My name is Mr. Glendenning," he said, spelling it out for us on the blackboard. "I will be your English teacher for the remainder of the fall term, and the spring term as well for those of you continuing on. I'm glad to be here. Now, I understand that between now and the Christmas vacation we will be turning in book reports. You may use any of the books on the fall reading list. It's already on the lesson plan, so I trust this is not a surprise."

The Wiener raised his hand.

"Mr. Glendenning, I have a question."

This guy had just given us a hefty book report assignment, within five minutes of his first appearance, so we weren't too pleased. He seemed surprised and annoyed at the Wiener's interruption.

"Yes, what is it, Mr. - ah -" He consulted his chart. "Mr. Frankfurter?"

"What happened to Mr. Freisler?"

The new teacher was taken aback. Clearly, he was not used to interruptions.

"You'll have to ask the administration," he said, brusquely. "That's got nothing to do with me."

This was pretty interesting. This new guy was already washing his hands of Mr. Freisler, although he probably never met him.

"Is he dead? In jail?" the Wiener asked. There was a silence.

"He's not dead as far as I know. I have nothing further. I told you, Mr. Frankfurter, this is a matter for the administration. The subject is closed."

Wow. Maybe Freisler got picked up in the elementary school playground over on Hillside, playing Hide the Worm with the five year olds. We couldn't wait to find out.

The book reports were due in about ten days. Of course, no one had started reading except maybe a few girls. There was no way any of us was going to read some weighty classic and write a book report in that limited amount of time. As a result, just about everybody except the Wiener picked the same book, which was the shortest one: *The Old Man and the Sea*. It was actually pretty good, for a required book. I mean, it was kind of bullshitty, too, attributing a sort of pelagic nobility to a goddamn fish, but what the hell. You gotta write about something, I guess. This old foreign guy couldn't just stroll into his local Havana Shop-Rite for a filet of marlin, and even if he could, it wouldn't make much of a story. Instead, he about broke his ass trying to land the whole fish.

It made me feel even more like going to Cuba, which was having some difficulty at the moment with rebels in the hills. We really didn't understand why, because the head dictator guy Batista had casinos and legalized prostitution and no drinking age. Who could want more than that?

"Who wants to read their book report?" asked Mr. Glendenning on the day they were due. A few female hands shot up in the air, plus the Wiener's. Mr. Glendenning seemed surprised.

"Mr. Frankfurter, would you care to read your report?"

"Yeah, maybe in a minute," the Wiener replied. "But I found out what happened to Mr. Freisler. Wanna hear what I found out?"

"No, I don't want to hear about Mr. Freisler," Mr. Glendenning said firmly. "I want to hear about book reports." The rest of us wanted to hear what the Weiner had found out, though.

"Okay," said the Wiener, as though he needed to officially approve Mr. Glendenning's itinerary. "But the reason Mr. Freisler is gone is that Mr. Kritzinger caught him making out with Mrs. Kritzinger in the Teacher's Lounge. It was around five o'clock and Mrs. Kritzinger thought Mr. Kritzinger had gone home with Mr. Wisner."

The whole class was in an uproar. The Wiener had already been in enough trouble for insubordination. The only way he possibly could get away with what he had just said is if it were absolutely true.

"SILENCE!" commanded Mr. Glendenning. He glared at the Wiener for what must have been ten or fifteen years. Then he nodded, slowly.

"All right, Mr. Frankfurter. All right. Mr. Frankfurter, you will repeat what you just told me to Principal Dunwood after class. Won't you?"

"Sure," said the Wiener. "Sure I will. What the hell, Coach Weber told it to Mr. Klopfer."

Our besotted janitor. Another gold star for Coach Weber on his *permanent record*. Home Ec was taking on a whole new meaning, the more I thought about it. I wondered if only girls could take the class. The thing was, though, Mrs. Kritzinger was built like a teacup. Her arms looked like sausages. It wasn't a pretty thought. Mr. Freisler must really have been a horny old bastard.

"That's it. That's enough. Meantime, let's hear what else you have to say, only this time on something to do with English. Let me hear your book report."

The Wiener was just dying to give his book report, we could tell. He brought his paper up to the front of the room. Of all the great authors on the official classics list for book reports, I wondered who the Wiener would have chosen. I didn't have long to wait.

Here is what he read aloud:

"My Book Report
by Jack Frankfurter
English 12A
Mr. Freisler - ah - correction
Mr. Glendenning

'99 44/100 Per Cent Pure Horror'
by (unintelligible)

'This is a classic story of two men who were partners in the soap business. They started a small soap company, which quickly grew to a substantial size. The business was making money hand over fist. The greedy partner, Mr. Duffy, was not content to make half the profits, although both he and Mr. Davis, his partner, had become rich. So during a plant inspection, when no one was looking, Mr. Duffy shoved Mr. Davis over a safety rail into a vat of lye, which as we all know is a caustic substance used for making soap. Being of a nasty disposition, Mr. Duffy ordered all the soap from that particular vat put into special stock, which was to be used only by certain people or for special company events. Of course, a certain percentage of this soap was made up of Mr. Davis, who was killed by the caustic lye."

Our eyes were bugging out. This story was not on the classics list, although so far it was pretty good. Much better, in fact, than most of the crap we had to choose from. Who the hell wrote this, Edgar Allen Poe?

"Mr. Frankfurter!" interrupted Mr. Glendenning. "What are you talking about? What book is this?"

"I told you, Mr. Glendenning. It's 99 44/100% Pure Horror. You know, like Ivory Soap. Get it? 99 44/100% pure. Let me finish, I'm almost done."

Mr. Glendenning was looking at the Wiener in amazement.

"So anyway, one day the surviving partner, Mr. Davis - wait a sec - that's Mr. Duffy, because he killed Mr. Davis -I lost my place there for a second - OK, here I am - Mr. Duffy had taken some of this special soap home. He wasn't a Nazi or anything, although the Nazis made soap out of Jews, as we all now know, which was revealed at the Nuremberg trials."

Across the street in the Sweet Shoppe, I was sure Mr. Schmid winced.

Here the Wiener effortlessly switched tenses.

"So Mr. Duffy decides to take a shower. He gets all soaped up and the first thing that happens is that he gets soap in his eyes, and can't see. It burns his eyes. He tries to turn the water to a colder setting, but because the soap is in his eyes he accidentally turns off the cold and now he is getting scalded. He yells and drops the soap bar. Then he slips on the soap, which is really his partner in some percentage, and falls and breaks his leg. He tries to get up to turn off the scalding hot water but cannot on account of his broken leg."

The Weiner glanced up from his paper and saw mouths hanging open in absolute silence. Encouraged, his delivery increased in volume and dramatic flair.

"Meanwhile the soap has lodged in the drain and clogs it up, so the almost boiling water is starting to climb higher and higher in the shower stall and Mr. Duffy can't get up. He is being scalded like a lobster and finally the water gets over his head and he drowns. So you see how the dead partner got his revenge on Mr. Duffy, first by blinding him, then by scalding him and making him slip and fall and break his leg, and finally by clogging the drain so he drowns. He reached out from *beyond the grave.*"

The Weiner paused in artistic triumph.

'This excellent story was extremely well written and is a classic in anyone's eyes.

Jack Frankfurter
English 12A
428 words."

There was a silence.

"That's way more than the 350 required words," the Wiener concluded.

It was a pretty good story, all right, but the Wiener had gone around the bend. This wasn't Chaucer or Somerset Maugham or even that Beowulf guy. Finally Mr. Glendenning spoke up.

"Mr. Frankfurter, I have a question. I'm curious. Just what classic is that you have described?"

"I told you. 99 44/100% Pure Horror."

"Which classic author on the classic reading list wrote it, Mr. Frankfurter?" asked Mr. Glendenning. He was speaking slowly and carefully now. He had emphasized the word *classic* twice.

The Wiener shifted on his feet a little bit. "Well, it was a collaborative effort, I think."

"What?" asked Mr. Glendenning. "What do you mean, a collaborative effort? By whom?"

"Well, the staff of EC Comics. I mean, I guess, because it didn't give one particular author."

Mr. Glendenning stared in disbelief. A few classmates who couldn't restrain themselves were starting to giggle.

"QUIET!" yelled Mr. Glendenning. He looked, with great care, at the Wiener. He looked like he was studying a dangerous animal. "This is a *COMIC BOOK?*"

Wiener was now looking somewhat uncomfortable. "Well, yeah," he managed. "An EC Classic, though. It says that right on the cover."

That was it. We couldn't help it. Jones and I started to guffaw. Brownie was holding his sides and rocking, hysterical. The whole class broke up. The Wiener looked around, honestly surprised. I swear, the Wiener wasn't even trying to be a wise guy. He was on the level, which made us laugh even harder once we realized it.

Evidently Mr. Glendenning realized it as well. "Mr. Frankfurter, you need to come in and see me at three o'clock this afternoon. This has been quite a day for you. Do you have a problem with that? Is three o'clock convenient?" He was being agonizingly patronizing. The Wiener didn't get it, though.

The Wiener thought over his schedule. "Nah, no problem. That should be OK." He moved toward his seat, then stopped for a moment.

"Hey, Mr. Glendenning. Do I get an A?"

Chapter 15

In Chapter four you break up
But you give her just one more chance
-The Book of Love, The Monotones, 1958

I was still sort of thinking about my brother and the Kathy Obermeister deal a couple of weeks later, although not in a really serious way, but it would just roll around the back of my brain once in a while. I couldn't really determine why this was bothering me, exactly. Maybe it was because in my mind Wolfie wasn't too far removed from playing with his Tonka trucks, rather than Kathy Obermeister. He was just a kid, for Chrissake. I just couldn't picture it, not that I wanted to. I thought back to when I was his age, which wasn't that long ago, actually, but somehow that was different. After all, I had been pushed ahead a whole year.

I wondered if maybe I should have another talk with the Wolf, although I had no idea what I would say, or even exactly why I would say it. But then I figured it was my responsibility, as his older brother. What else was I to do, leave it to mom and dad? They had no idea, of course, and besides, it wasn't a parental issue.

Anyway, I wandered into his room after supper. The Wolf had set up a card table and was building a model airplane. Raymond was sitting on the bed, trying to open a can of furniture polish as he watched Wolfie work. Outside, a light rain was ticking on the window and it was that weird yellow half-light you sometimes got before dark. I snapped on the light.

"Thanks."

"Mom's going to be pissed if you get any glue on the card table. You should've put newspaper down," I said as I removed the furniture polish from Raymond's grasp.

Wolfie held up the glue tube. "Want a sniff?"

Mom had made spaghetti and meatballs, one of our favorites, and chocolate pudding, so I was stuffed. I could have used a wake-up jolt. I leaned over the tube and inhaled. Wow. Cleared my sinuses right up.

"Don't give any to Raymond. An F-86, huh?"

"Yeah," the Wolf replied. "It's not too hard. Wanna help with the decals when I'm done?" Decals were about the best part, so he was being generous.

"Sure," I said. "Don't get any glue on the windshield. It'll get all crapped up. Listen, I want to ask you something. It's about your ex-girlfriend."

"Kathy-o? "

"Yeah. I was thinking, maybe you were a little cold about the whole thing. That aileron's upside down. It doesn't glue, that part snaps in."

He turned it right side up. "Oh, yeah," he said as he snapped it in place. "No need to worry, Georgie boy." Georgie boy? What the hell was that?

"Why not?"

"Well, I was a little hasty. I called her and we're going to the picture show Saturday. Plan 9 From Outer Space and Return of the Fly."

For some reason I felt relieved. "That's good, Wolfie. It shows consideration."

He snapped the other aileron in place. "It shows I got horny again."

Over on the bed, Raymond was licking the varnish off the headboard.

Christ. I shouldn't have wasted my time.

Chapter 16

Roll over Beethoven,
Tell Tchaikovsky the news
- Roll Over, Beethoven, Chuck Berry, 1956

Because I had the audacity to ruin my mother's career as a concert pianist, by being born in the middle of her scheduled tour, the least I could do, she felt, was go to Princeton.

I guess she hadn't looked too swift waddling onstage, like some musical duck, in an evening gown with a bowling ball sized lump in front, flopping down to belt out Beethoven's Fifth. It detracted from the whole ambiance, probably, and besides, she kind of had to sit pretty far back from the piano keys. For awhile, she had a special outfit designed, with extra panels, but that only worked until maybe the seventh month. I was a big baby. So that was that. I guess it was Ludwig van's loss.

Now, she was all excited and living her concert life all over again in a vicarious way because of some kid named Van Cliburn. He was this hotshot young concert pianist from Texas, for Chrissake, and had won or was just winning a big competition in Moscow. Obviously, he hadn't had to go up against Jerry Lee Lewis or Antoine "Fats" Domino. Concert pianists are supposed to come from Vienna, or Madrid, maybe, but Texas? Home of rockabilly legend Buddy Holly? Mom's insurance agent, who specialized in insuring concert pianists and other artsy types, was acquainted with this Van Cliburn fellow so my mother got firsthand reports. I supposed he was pretty good; it must be tough to win in Moscow in front of an away crowd. From what I heard, Van Cliburn's mother was just about my mom's twin. All this translated into the necessity for me to go to Princeton, since I played the electric guitar instead of the concert piano. At least that way my mom could continue living vicariously, which was certainly the least I could do. I could sort of see her logic, although I didn't really agree with it. After all, it was supposed to be my life, wasn't it?

Wasn't it?

"My George is attending *Princeton*," she could say at the country club, or probably to anyone who would listen in the Shop-Rite. The impetus for this came partly from Mrs. Kritzinger, our piecework guidance counselor, since that was about the only college she knew. Windham kids were supposed to go to Princeton, although in a pinch maybe Dartmouth would do. Mrs. Kritzinger loved the blazers.

Sometimes at the country club - whichever one we were in at the time, since we were practically country club Bedouins because of my brother Wolfie's cavalier golf etiquette - you would see old out-of-it guys wearing Princeton blazers. They looked just like regular E.J. Korvette or J.C. Penney blazers, with this big deal seal on the pocket. If you looked real closely, the little sewn words might say "Department of Sanitation" for all it meant to us. I mean, really, who gives a shit? Maybe other Princeton guys, but that's about all. Somehow they think you are going to care also. They must teach them that crap, like Robbie van Arsdale's Mormons.

"We want only the best for you, George," my mother had said, which meant she only wanted what was best for her. Princeton was the only college - excuse me, university - where the interviewer actually came out to your house, kind of like the encyclopedia salesman. I think the reason was to see if you had enough dough to qualify, and if your house was on the right side of the tracks, and if you didn't cover your living room sofa with clear plastic. In our case, we were automatically on the right side of the tracks because we lived in the township.

Actually, I did kind of want to go there, in an odd way, because we had been to Princeton to play the state high school soccer finals. It was a really pretty town, with ivy and stuff, and a tall college-looking tower. It was the sort of tower you might expect to find in England, with some kind of half-assed maiden looking out yearningly toward someplace like Kent. Here, though, all you could probably see in the distance was the New Jersey Turnpike. Most likely just students flunking English climbed to the top and jumped off. It made you almost think about studying, I guess. At least, I could tell that it could have that effect.

There were Princeton students around everywhere, and I looked at them closely from the team bus. They seemed to fall into two groups: geeks and the blazer set. One thing that would be a letdown - the girls. In Windham, I was so used to going to school with movie star looking girls, All-American cheerleader busty blondes with perfectly even white teeth on their wonderful All-American smiles (courtesy of Dr. Hofmann, the orthodontist), that when I saw the broads in a normal type town they were a real letdown. Lots of brunettes and ugly girls with glasses. Some were fat or misshapen. Those Princeton broads sure didn't know how to dress either, that was clear. They weren't too color coordinated, and some didn't even wear stockings or nail polish or have their hair done. I wondered what they did with their time.

Actually, none of us seniors had thought much about the entire college application process. At the Sweet Shoppe one soggy fall afternoon - soccer practice had been cancelled because the field was underwater - Brownie brought the subject up while we smoked Marlboros and drank cokes. There were five or six of us in a corner booth, sitting amid stratus clouds of tobacco smoke. Dieter Becker, a classmate who lived a couple blocks over from me on Linden Lane, was detaching the coupon from a pack of Raleighs. He said they tasted like pig dung, but after four million coupons you got a toaster and coughed up a lung.

"I got a recruiting letter from some college in Missouri," Brownie said.

"Yeah? Soccer?"

"No, miniature golf." That was sarcastic.

"Already?"

"No, I've got ESP. It's coming next month." That was sarcastic as well.

"How much?"

"Hey, it's not specific like that. They want me to come visit. They'll pay my airfare."

"You gonna go?" Jones asked.

"How the hell do I know? Sure, I guess. Free trip, anyway. What about you guys? You guys thought about college?"

"What the hell for?"

I think that came from the Wiener, but I'm not too sure. Anyway, he had a point. Thinking about the future and stuff just sucked the air out of the room, and there wasn't much fresh air in the Sweet Shoppe anyway. Leaving Windham would mean losing all our friends and living in some crummy little dorm room with some stranger and no car or TV, at least until we pledged a fraternity. No more American Bandstand for awhile, I guess.

Brownie looked over at Jones. "Hey, you got the state shot put record. You'll get recruited too, I bet. Dental school's gotta be expensive."

Jones shrugged. "Don't bet. Track's not a big money sport."

"Why don't you go to art school?" I asked. Why do people with terrific talent always look at doing something else?

"I don't need to go to art school," Jones said. He was right, really. He already knew how to draw. He could whip out a caricature, war scene or anything else faster than that guy with one ear.

"What about you, Williams?" Brownie asked. I guess he was the moderator.

"I sure as hell can't draw. I dunno either. I guess I'll see what Mrs. Kritzinger says." We all had appointments to see the guidance counselor, who would give us our Princeton handbooks and set up our interviews.

"Forget Kritzinger. She doesn't know diddley. She'll just give you the Princeton book and have the guy come out to see you." That was true.

"What do you want to do?" asked Robbie van Arsdale, looking at me.

"Do? You mean, like a job thing? Afterwards?" I asked. Why were we still talking about an uncomfortable subject? My ass started itching me. I squirmed on the seat.

"A career, for Chrissake."

Career? I was just a kid. I didn't want a career any more than I wanted malaria. What the hell was a career, anyway, except a job where you had to wear a tie and commute to the goddamn thing? What could be better than having your own band and recording contract, even if it was probably worthless? I guess, if I thought about it, I never really wanted to graduate at all.

Dieter Becker saved me from answering. "My dad wants me to go to Yale. I'm a legacy."

"What's a legacy?" I asked. Was I the only dumb person there?

"What's the matter with you? It means his dad went there," Brownie said. I knew Mister Becker ran some big investment house in New York. There had been an article about the guy in the Courier. I guess Dieter was worth big bucks.

"I don't want to do it," Dieter said. "I don't want to go anywhere."

"You have to go somewhere," Brownie said. But did you?

"Why?" asked Wiener, echoing my thoughts.

"Your dad's a big deal investment house guy, isn't he?" I asked. Actually, I wasn't sure what an investment house really was.

"I don't want to do that either."

There was silence for a time. Maybe Dieter had said something we all were thinking. What the hell, a bunch of old guys getting all dressed up and riding a train for two hours each day to look at numbers rolling across a screen and hustling people on the telephone? In between having lunch and a couple of martinis at some fancy place that cost maybe five bucks, and getting half tanked in the club car on the way home? You had to go to college for that? Shit. Who the hell would want to do that even if you didn't go to college?

Mickey Mantle hadn't attended Princeton, and he didn't look at numbers rolling across a screen. Little Richard hadn't gone to Yale, and he didn't look at numbers rolling across a screen either. Come to think of it, I'd bet Po hadn't even gone to trade school.

Robbie spoke quietly. "You know, I heard they're building a missile silo someplace around Convent Station."

We looked at him. "Where'd you hear that?" Jones asked.

Robbie shrugged. "Some people were talking about it at church."

Anything about Robbie's church lost credibility, I figured, but maybe somebody worked for the military or something.

"One of the elders' nephews is an Air Force officer."

"Isn't that crap secret?" Dieter asked.

"Supposedly," Robbie said.

"A *missile* missile? Like a guided nuclear warhead ICBM missile?" I asked.

Robbie gave me a pained look. If true, that was a big deal.

"A Titan. A whole installation. Maybe about four of them."

"That's pretty cool," Brownie said.

"Yeah?" said Robbie. "I'll tell you how cool that is. Every missile silo is a target for the Russians."

"Yeah? How're they going to find out?" Dieter asked.

"Christ, if we heard it, the Russians sure as hell know about it."

Spies in the Sweet Shoppe?

"We're toast anyway, being so close to New York," Brownie said.

"Yeah? Well now we're burnt toast," said Robbie. He sipped his cherry coke. "So what were we saying about careers?"

Duck and cover. Yeah, right. We didn't even have air raid drills in Windham.

"Screw college, then. Let's all move to Australia," Brownie said. Maybe he had a good idea. Everybody loved those koala bears. Someone held the front door open for a few seconds; smoke eddied towards the rain. A little oxygen drifted in, along with the tang of ozone. It lifted the gloom, thank God.

Chapter 17

I'm out walkin' after midnight
Out in the starlight
-Walking After Midnight, Patsy Cline, 1957

They'd found Po, the nice colored gentleman who fixed my bicycle chain for free, half in the ditch out in the township. It appeared he'd been walking along Green Village Road and been clipped from behind. Chief Duff Carlin's men in blue decided there had been no witnesses. The Windham Courier, which gave the story one whole paragraph, said the cops were checking local garages and dealerships for unexplained repair work. The investigation probably took all of fifteen minutes since there was only one body shop down in the borough and exactly zero dealerships in town.

Some goddamn bake sale got a full column on page three, for Chrissake, but Po's death was at the bottom of page five. The whole freaking paper was only six pages anyway. The disturbing part of the story was that he'd come apart a little. He'd been hit at least twice and had been dead for hours before somebody called the police. Plus there were no skid marks. To me, it seemed like a hit and run felony, but the cops treated it as though somebody had run over a cat.

I didn't know many colored people, at least to talk to. The ones I did were usually fighters training at Ehsan's Training

Camp in the township, guys like Floyd Patterson who was currently getting ready for his title fight with Ingemar Johansson. There were colored sparring partners, too, like Freddy Mack, mostly punch-drunk and incapable of coherent conversation.

Po had been like Patterson, soft-spoken and thoughtful. I'd had five bucks on me when my chain broke, and I offered it to him, but he'd just smiled and refused.

I happened to see the picture in the Madison Eagle, which was weird since I never read that rag before or since, and there was Po's family carrying the coffin in a cemetery I didn't recognize. I thought I'd seen the tall, thin pallbearer before. The caption identified him as Beauregard Jackson, Po's son. You could see he wasn't wearing a suit, but he'd tried to match the jacket and pants. You could tell this even from the black and white newspaper photo. The jacket was too small and his shirt cuffs stuck out. You could tell Beau wanted to look respectful for his father, and as I studied the picture it made me kind of sad, picturing Beau Jackson trying on a couple of different jackets to see if anything matched the pants, so that he could pay proper respects to his dad.

I guess old people read the obituaries to see if some friend or acquaintance passed on, kind of like us kids in high school looking up the ball scores. It's a different story, though, when you might know the guy carrying the coffin and his old man's inside, the nice old guy who fixed your bicycle for free, all stitched together as best the undertaker could, probably. I made a mental note never to read the obituaries, if I can remember when I'm an old geezer.

Chapter 18

We had a quarrel
A teenage quarrel
-   *Rose and a Baby Ruth, George Hamilton IV, 1956*

When Freddy Hirsch called on Saturday and said he wanted a pizza, I had been just about to sneak a pbj sandwich. The whole kitchen stank, because mom was making the old man's favorite dish - pork chops with some other inedible Depression Era crap. Freddy said he'd pick me up around six. He'd graduated a year ahead of us, and had his driver's license for almost three years. I think he might have been left back somewhere along the line, but that's just a guess because of his age.   For whatever reason he seemed to have more friends, or I should say acquaintances, in our grade than his own. I don't think Freddy had any close friends, really.   I guess it was because his brain was misshapen. Not that the class of 1959 was the paragon of normalcy, as you've probably already figured out.

Freddy had driven us several times to Staten Island, where the drinking age was only eighteen, to buy booze and bowl a few games. He was a big kegler and owned his own ball and shoes. The problem was he'd been banned from just about every bowling establishment in northern New Jersey for trying to hit the pin boys as well as the pins.   In his mind, he'd invented a scoring system that included extra points for creaming the poor unfortunates back in the pit. He'd wait until the guy was clearing the pins after his first roll and chuck another ball as hard as he could. As far as I know, he never hit anybody but it wasn't for lack of trying.

The Hirsches didn't have too much dough, so after graduation Freddy went to work for Warner-Lambert up in Morris Plains until he could save enough money for college. Freddy wasn't dumb, just out of balance, so he'd probably get into Rutgers, which sort of had to take unbalanced people since it was a state school. It wasn't too expensive and had terrible teams in just about every sport.

At Warner-Lambert, Freddy somehow got the job of killing used lab animals, and he turned out to be well suited for the task. It sounded like the place was run by Dr. Mengele or somebody. As he explained, the used lab rats had to be homogenized and so he'd invented a game he called Beat the Blade. You get the idea. Freddy had other games too, involving outdated rhesus monkeys and other primates, but we told him we definitely didn't want to hear about them. Actually, Jones and Brownie did want to hear about them, but I wasn't around at the time.

Freddy Hirsch's father was from the old school. His English was broken, and he spoke mostly German to Mrs. Hirsch. He labored behind their old frame house in his greenhouse out in Green Village. He was strong as an ox from shoveling dirt and wheeling it around from place to place, which evidently is a requirement of rose growing, but he was bent over. Older people can be quite strong, hard strong, from years of manual labor. They're usually Europeans, and they're bent over a lot, and they are kind of made out of some hard wood.

Mr. Hirsch looked much older than Mrs. Hirsch, who looked old already. She wore those shapeless European frock things and combat boots. They probably both were about forty, but could have passed for sixty-five. Mrs. Hirsch had brought one big skill to America. She could really whip up a terrific spaghetti dinner, even though it was German instead of Italian, with this delicious ground up sausage in the sauce.

It was a tradition that any fighter training at Ehsan's for a championship bout would sneak out for a night and eat Mrs. Hirsch's spaghetti, sometimes with untoward results. I don't know how it all started, because Mrs. Hirsch didn't seem your typical fight fan, but there it was. I was invited to Freddy's house for those meals, which is how I got to meet Floyd Patterson, Gene Fullmer, Joey Giardello and a bunch of other titleholders.

Mr. Hirsch had old world type thinking, and when he withdrew the savings from Freddy's bank account without telling him because he had had a tough year in the rose business, there was a real family crisis. I guess he had too much European pride to ask his son for the dough; he just took out his own private Marshall Plan.

"Can you believe that?" Freddy asked me, shaking his head as we downed a pepperoni pizza at Nick's. Freddy ate at least two whole pies a week. "Twenty two hundred bucks."

I crunched a crust bubble. "Wow, that's a lot of dough. Is it a loan?"

He just snorted. "Loan, my ass."

"Did you talk to him about it?" I guzzled the rest of my Nehi and signaled Nick for another root beer. It was getting harder to find sarsaparilla.

"Even my mom tried to talk to the old man. Son of a bitch." He shook his head. "He ain't gonna get away with it."

"What do you mean?" As I said, Freddy's gyro was missing a few ball bearings. I was beginning to get worried. They say it starts with creatures, and Freddy was a founding member of the Animal SS up at Warner-Lambert. Not to mention the pin boys he was constantly trying to cripple.

Freddy's eyes narrowed. "I don't know yet, but he ain't gonna get away with it."

"Do me a favor, will you? Let me know what you decide before you do anything."

I knew for a fact Freddy had a Luger and knew how to use it. He'd shot out half street lights in Madison for target practice.

He looked off, nodding slightly, then picked up a piece of crust and broke it in half.

"Don't worry, you'll be the first to know."

Chapter 19

I been searchin'
Oh, Lord, I's searchin'
Oh, child, searchin' every which -a-way
- Searchin', The Coasters, 1957

The Wassermans were one of about three Jewish families in Windham, and I think they were pretty religious. Teddy had to go to his church, or synagogue, on Saturdays, which was a tough break, because most recreational activities were scheduled on Saturdays. The place was a few towns over where there were enough Jews for a congregation. Besides the travel time, Teddy said the service lasted for hours and hours, which must have been agonizing. I don't think even God wants to hear people for hours and hours, wailing and speaking in dead languages that He probably doesn't even much care about anymore. I would think He just wants them to move *on,* for Chrissake, in a civilized way.

At least, that's kind of the impression I got from listening to Teddy describe what he did during the services. The old people wore these striped blankets and skull caps and wailed and rocked a lot. I don't mean wailed and rocked like Little Richard belting out *Good Golly, Miss Molly,* either. Teddy called it "gogging out." Can you imagine a God who'd want to listen to that for hours and hours? Even He would probably wind up drooling or sending a bunch of locusts to end it all.

Teddy said he had more in common with his classmates than he did with the old Jews. Not that some of us Christians were much better, like Robbie van Arsdale's Mormons who married everybody or the Baptists, who believed the way to Heaven was to roll around like alligators in muddy water. At least that's what they showed once on Movietone News, at the picture show, before Flash Gordon's Episode 23 against old Emperor Ming. These Negro Baptists in Mississippi were all dressed in white, with their hands up in the air, like God was going to call on them for answers, or maybe they had to go to the celestial bathroom, and then some white guy dunked them in a sludgy creek. There was some crude music that actually was kind of cool, like John Lee Hooker cool, almost. The Movietone News guy, who I think might have been Ed Herlihy, was describing the scene in some patronizing manner, like we were watching Marlon Perkins' Wild Kingdom.

Anyway, Teddy Wasserman had come over to my house on a weekday evening to study for an upcoming math test. He was pretty good in math.

"How come you live in Windham instead of New York?" I inquired. I knew New York had lots of Jews and Puerto Ricans.

"Well," he said, "I have lots of relatives in New York. They're all jewelers and clothing manufacturers and stuff over on Seventh Avenue."

"Don't you want to live with the other Jews?"

Teddy shook his head.

"New York blows," he said. I certainly agreed with that logic. "Besides, I'm German too, aren't I? I'm a mixed second."

"What? What the hell's that?"

Teddy just shook his head. "Nothing, never mind. Besides, if you want to know the truth, most of my relatives are a pain in the ass. All they want to do is preserve the old ways, which is okay if you're old and your doinker doesn't work anymore, and all you can do is think about the past because you live in crummy New York, so who wants to think about that?'

'But I'm a kid," Teddy continued. "I don't give a shit about the tribes thousands of years ago. Do you give a crap about your ancestors thousands of years ago?"

I had never really thought about it before. "Nah, I guess not. I don't even know who they were or what they did. Maybe I'd like to know about my grandfather the bond smuggler or him marrying his first cousin, but that's about all I know anyway. It's kind of neat having a grandmother who's also your aunt, I guess."

Teddy leaned back in my armchair. We were in my room, math books spread out on my desk, talking in the light of the study lamp. It created an atmosphere for the two of us.

"You want to know something else?" He leaned back and looked at me. "In some ways, you Catholics are like us Jews. I'll tell you one. You're not supposed to go to other churches, are you? Not even to visit."

I hadn't really thought about that too much, either. "It doesn't make any sense, I know."

"Of course it doesn't make any sense. Common sense is missing in most religions, isn't it? God is mysterious, that's the excuse for not using your brain. Who are you to question the ways of God? Except of course it's the ways of man."

Teddy was becoming passionate about the subject.

"Look, Jews will try to drag you into the gog and teach you all kinds of Jewish stuff. But you'll never catch a Jew in your church. We just won't go. Know why?"

"Uuh - " I thought for a second. "The collection?"

Teddy ignored the joke. "Because of the biggest sin of all. Pride. Pride and guilt are our stock in trade, our intellectual commerce. We think we're better than you, which is the pride part, but deep down not really. That's the guilt part. What else can you think when everybody dumps on you? It's very complex, which is another thing we can anguish about. You know we call ourselves the Chosen People, don't you?"

I knew that. It didn't make much sense to me, although Jews were smart, I think, because a lot of them became doctors or accountants. They kind of looked like the Arabs without the pajamas, so maybe they were related. I didn't think the Arabs were too smart, actually, since we'd never heard of them doing anything except maybe trading spices and salt and stuff that we could just get from the Shop-Rite. There was that Ali Baba guy, but he was just a legend.

Teddy brought me back to the conversation. His monologue, actually.

"Don't you think we're just insulting God when we say that? How egotistical that is? Don't you think it was us, the Jews, who said we were special? Do you really think He conspired with Jews to kill other people he created? We dare to rank God's creations in some sort of goddamn numerical order. Am I really better than you, or do I just want to think so? Did God create Mary Anne Moffitt as something lesser than me?"

He definitely had a point there.   "Does my heart beat any differently? Do I think higher thoughts? We all use the Holy books as a weapon, don't we? All of us. You and me. We kill in the name of God."

"I never killed anybody in the name of anything." Not even Johnny Broadhead. No matter what his mother might have thought, in her deranged way.

He paused for a moment, and then grinned.

"Actually, I am a lot better than you, George, but that's just one specific example."

Teddy was really wound up, but the guy was making a lot of sense. The more I thought about it, the more I was realizing that Teddy Wasserman's view of religion and God were more like mine than maybe his own people's. Maybe the Protestants were closer to getting it right.   They just went through the Catholic doctrine like it was a buffet line, picking and choosing what they wanted or felt was right.   Papal infallibility?   Skip that section, head right for the entrees. Limbo for infants? No? Go around that guy, grab some salad. Don't like mortal sin? Leave it off your tray, head for the desserts. Pretty soon you'd have exactly the meal you wanted and could digest it all without heartburn or stomach gas. What the hell.

Maybe if some scholars had similar discussions, everybody would get along better, because they'd reach wiser conclusions. After all, we were just a couple of high school students.

And what the hell was a mixed second?

Chapter 20

I sure would be delighted with your company
Come and do the Jailhouse Rock with me
- Jailhouse Rock, Elvis Presley, 1957

The afternoon was crisp and clear, perfect soccer weather, and we were at home against Morris Plains. The smell of new-mown grass was pure, sweet energy in my lungs, a welcome change from the nicotine fog of the Sweet Shoppe. I was on my way to chalking up my third clean sheet of the campaign. We were ahead 3-nil late in the second half, and I'd only had to stop maybe five shots. Two were just dribblers I scooped up and punted downfield. Even the Gimp, our class cripple, could probably have kept goal so far.

I leaned against the post and watched the faraway action. Our defense was awesome, led by the Greek, who had made All-State for the third straight year. A sweeper fullback, he dominated the section in front of me and made my job mostly a spectator. Between the Greek and Brownie, our All-American midfielder who controlled the flow of the game, we were pretty much unstoppable.

Mr. Greek and Mr. Brown were standing together near the Morris Plains goal. They were fixtures at all our home games. Being foreign, Mr. Greek would bring strange little picnic stuff in a kind of knapsack like Europeans probably do.

He and Mr. Brown made an odd duo on the sidelines: Mr. Greek with his knapsack and foreign cap and Mr. Brown with his 8mm movie camera, filming his son at every game. They kept each other company.

I happened to glance to my right and saw Mike Endler walking toward me from the stands, which were pretty full. He circled behind the touch line and came up behind the netting. Coach frowned on anyone coming near me during a game, but in a match like this I welcomed company. After all, I didn't have to look at anybody to shoot the breeze as long as the ball was downfield.

"Hey George!" he yelled. I didn't turn, of course, but waved at him. Endler was a pretty good pole vaulter, besides shooting in the low eighties in golf. I played with Mike once, at his club, which actually had been our club the previous year. We'd been kicked out of the place just because Wolfie had driven a golf cart into the lake on the sixth fairway. He'd said it was an accident, but the week before he'd piloted a cart into the pond by the fourteenth green. He told me later he wanted to see if any of them would float.

Anyway, Endler came up behind the woodwork.

"Hey Mike. What's up?"

"Nice game so far. Hey listen, they just arrested Franz' dad. It's all over the news."

What?! Ted Franz' father? The guy who took us to the movies and a couple of ball games when we were small, and a swell camping trip to the Poconos in ninth grade? I actually turned and glanced at Mike for a moment.

"What? What do you mean?"

"He got arrested in New York. I guess at his office."

Mike knew I'd want to know right away; he'd also gone

on the Poconos trip and a couple of times to the picture show with us and Franz's dad.

"It's on the tv?"

"Yeah, WOR had a thing about it." WOR was big time New York television. Wow.

"What for?"

"Embezzlement. They say he stole a quarter million bucks from his company."

"Holy shit. Do you think he did that? Mister Franz?"

"How do I know?"

Could this be true? I was stunned. I conjured up a mental picture of Mister Franz being surprised in his office, handcuffed and led away. He was a jovial guy, usually with an infectious grin, and maybe now I knew why. I'd bet he wasn't grinning today. Did they let him put on his suit jacket first? Did they handcuff office people in the front or behind their backs, like violent criminals? Were they plainclothes cops or uniforms? What did his office look like anyway? I imagine it had plush wall to wall carpet and maybe a coffee table and big windows looking out on Wall Street, but maybe that wasn't right. Did they lead him away cuffed up, paraded past his secretary and all the other company people?

I returned to the game with a start when the Morris Plains fullback lofted a long ball down the right side and the winger picked it up. He dribbled toward the end line and sent a perfect cross toward the charging center forward, who headed it goalward. I had to leap out and punch it away. The Greek picked up the loose ball and sent it downfield; that was the extent of the action until the final whistle.

The next morning, when Ted Franz came to school, it was like he was in an invisible bubble. No one, including the faculty, seemed to know what to say him. I guess, though, what was there to say?

Leave it to the Wiener. He rounded up Brownie, Jones, me and a bunch of other guys at the end of first period and we intercepted Ted in the hall.

"Hey, Ted," the Wiener said, "listen. We all saw the news and it's no use pretending nothing happened."

Franz had an odd look.

"We all want you to know we think your dad is aces and we're behind him a hundred percent, even if he did it. If anybody gives you or your family any crap, let us know and we'll take care of it."

It was one of those embarrassing moments when somebody struggles to keep his emotions inside. I thought I saw Ted's eyes glisten.

"Thanks, Wiener, all you guys," he croaked, after a few seconds. "Really appreciate it." And that was that.

We never had practice the day following a game, so I was in the Sweet Shoppe at 3:10. Mr. Franz was the topic of conversation. Like Mike said, he'd made the WOR nightly newscast, briefly, but luckily for his family there was no film of him being arrested or led away. The news anchor guy said he lived in Windham, and made it sound like it was the Vatican, for Chrissake. Of course he called it an "upscale bedroom community." Didn't anyone think we had living rooms or kitchens in our goddamn town? I'll bet the Chamber of Commerce was having an ulcer. They were probably wondering how to deport Mr. Franz.

We all felt sorry for Ted and his family, whether the charges were true or not. Ted was a likeable kid who lived over on Rolling Hill Drive in one of the grander homes. No wonder.

We hoped his dad was innocent. He always seemed genuinely glad to take his son's friends to ball games and the Poconos. If the charges were true, then we supposed we'd been squired around with stolen funds.

I guess it was a step up from eating country club meals on the Wolf's phony charge numbers.

Chapter 21

Didja hear about Louis Miller?
He disappeared, babe
After drawing out all his hard earned cash
-   Mack the Knife, Bobby Darin, 1959

"I'm moving out."

Freddy Hirsch and I were eating a bag of hamburgers at the White Castle around nine-thirty on a balmy Tuesday evening. Freddy could easily put down a dozen of the little fellows. He'd decided what to do after his father stole his life savings.

"Yeah? Where?" Wow. I was relieved. At least he wasn't going to dismember his old man or ventilate him with the Luger. I was glad I didn't have to deal with that.

"I got an apartment in Mendham. Are you gonna help me move Saturday?"

"Yeah, sure." Besides relief, I felt badly for Freddy, but I guess he didn't have much choice. I hoped maybe someday they could patch things up, but I wasn't hopeful. His dad seemed Old World stubborn. He talked in grunts, with an occasional *Ja* or *Nein* thrown in.

Helping Freddy move really wasn't too difficult because he had hardly any possessions. The whole thing was kind of embarrassing because I felt like I was in the middle of a private family dispute. I guess it was okay with Mrs. Hirsch, though, because she cooked me a big German spaghetti lunch. I didn't feel like moving stuff after that; I just wanted to take a nap. At least Mr. Hirsch wasn't around.

Later, when we were rummaging around in a storage area looking for Freddy's duffel bag and some baseballs and crap, I came across a framed poster. I wiped off the dust with a curtain and held it at arm's length.

"Woah. Look at this." There was a picture of this blonde kid in some kind of uniform shirt looking off. Behind him was a faint image of Adolph Hitler with his stupid little moustache, glowering in the same direction. The legend said "Jugend dient dem Fuhrer" in big letters across the top. Underneath, it read "Alle Zehnjahrigen in die HJ/HN."

I peered at the kid, who was maybe ten, and his nifty shirt. He looked just like most kids who grew up in Windham, but without the shirt. It sure as hell wasn't a Boy Scout uniform.

"What's this? Whose is this? What's it say?"

Freddie came over and looked at it. "I think it's my mom's. Pretty cool, huh?"

It sure was. My mom didn't have anything like that, as far as I knew.

"HEY MRS. HIRSCH," I hollered.

"Ja?" When she came through the doorway, she stopped and gazed at the poster with a smile, like you'd look at a faded family picture that reminded you of the good old days.

"Ah," she said, looking rapturous.

"What's it say?"

"Jugend dient-"

"He means in English, ma," Freddy said.

"On top it sez 'Youth serves der Fuhrer. Der leader. Den down dere it sez 'All ten year olds into der Hitler Youth.' Dot's vat it sez. Vere did you get dat?"

I pointed to a pile in the corner. "It was over there under some stuff."

She took it from me, handling it as though it was a holy relic.

"Ma, you still got your shirt?" Freddy asked.

"I godt it all," she said, still smiling.

Just in case, I figured.

It kind of made me wonder what Freddy's father did during the war, and what other souvenirs might be strewn around the property. Like maybe a Mauser or potato grenade or jackboots. He probably wasn't size twelve, though.

The last words his mom ever spoke to me:

"Eat, liebchen."

Chapter 22

I have waited, waited so long
For your kisses and your love
Please come, come to me
From up, from up above
-Come Softly to Me, The Fleetwoods, 1959

Sunday morning was dead time because of church, except for my brother Wolfie, whom I guess you could classify as pretty religious because he used to take fistfuls of money out of the collection basket for candy during the week. Mom had us take little Raymond to the St. Francis' nine o'clock service pretty much since he could toddle. The purpose was not to introduce her youngest son to religion, but more so she could get some relief, I think. Taking Raymond to church wasn't too hard. He was fascinated by the votive candles and would watch them without blinking for about the whole Mass. He would just stare and lick his lips, besides licking the varnish off the pews.

I don't recall us ever going to church as a family, though, in my whole life. I think I would recall that if it had occurred. Funny, when I was small my mother tied my tie and cooked and all, and tried to bring me up right and everything, but I don't recall ever going to church with either of my parents. I would think I would remember that. Wouldn't you?

Anyway, one of the worst things about being Catholic was Catechism class, a requirement before First Holy Communion and Confirmation. Every kid got a booklet with questions and answers and old-timey drawings, not too unlike the drawings they gave me at the institute, except these were in color and mostly depicted shepherds in raggedy outfits with long staffs. The answers were even dumber than the questions and didn't really answer anything, like what does the word Catechism mean, what is Confirmation anyway, and who the hell is the Holy Ghost? The Holy Ghost was a mystery to me. Where did he fit in? I could sort of understand God talking to his Son Jesus from time to time, giving advice and maybe a pep talk now and then when the Romans and Jews began persecuting him. But I had no idea who or what the Holy Ghost said or did, or how he got along with the other two. The nearest I could figure is he was like The Shadow, the crime fighter guy who no one could see because he could cloud men's minds. Nobody ever prayed to the Holy Ghost, at least as far as I knew. I asked about it once but Sister Cecelia wasn't in the best of moods and just gave me a stern look.

I got through Catechism all right but it was mostly because I had a knack for being able to think about other stuff while half-listening to what Sister Cecelia was saying, which was handy if I got called on. The only time I got in trouble is when I asked what the V really stood for in BVM. I already knew the Blessed Virgin Mary was something special, because we learned that straight off, but the details were kind of sketchy. Of course, I was just a kid at that time but Sister Cecelia let me know there were certain things one didn't ask. It was awhile before I realized the Blessed Virgin Mary hadn't had sexual intercourse with her husband. I can only imagine how pissed

Joseph was to get shut out after probably expecting a big wedding night. He must have gotten quite a surprise when she told him about the little package incubating inside. I guess that's what you call Faith. It wouldn't work too well in Windham, I don't think. I can just see Brownie's future wife, or Jones' wife, telling him on their wedding night to stay on his side of the bed and that she was already pregnant. Yeah, right.

Actually, I couldn't imagine Brownie's future wife at all.

Anyway, I have a lot of respect for the nuns. For one thing, they have to wear those starchy white cardboardy things around their faces which must be uncomfortable, much less having to keep them spotless. Plus the black robes are probably pretty hot. Wearing that stuff all the time and praying all day can't be easy, and I believe they are very devoted people, although they can be cross at times. The theory is that nuns don't marry anyone on earth because they are married to God, and I couldn't help but wonder which of the Holy Trinity is the groom. Maybe that's what the Holy Ghost does, I don't know. I couldn't imagine the details, though, and I sure as hell wasn't going to ask.

A couple of years ago a new priest named Father O'Shea came to St. Francis, right off the boat from Ireland. I don't think he was very old, maybe mid-twenties, and his hair was the exact color of a ripe pumpkin. We seemed to get a new priest off the boat from Ireland every few years, and sometimes it was a little tough to understand them until they'd been here awhile, learning English and finding out there was stuff to eat besides fatty meat and boiled potatoes.

Unlike most of the other priests, Father O'Shea would greet the parishioners after Mass. He always said hello and asked how we were, and seemed to actually listen to our answers. Since Wolfie, Raymond and I were always alone, I wondered if he thought we were orphans, at least until Wolfie told him our mother was an alcoholic who couldn't get out of bed until noon on Sundays. My brother said this with a straight face. I think Father O'Shea actually believed it. He seemed to take an extra interest in us after that, at least until he met mom at bingo one night.

Actually, he might have believed it afterward, for all I know.

When Wolfie was maybe eleven, Father O'Shea proposed to my mom that he become an altar boy, and you could tell the idea lit her right up. Thank God no one had thought that one up for me. Father Corr and I got along fine, but from a distance, you know? Wolfie began going to altar boy practice, and my mom didn't even have to take him. Father O'Shea would come pick him up in the parish auto, a 1949 Rocket 88. I guess they were real buddies. I mean, a priest can't have kids, so I guess somebody like the Wolf was a good substitute.

When Wolfie told mom he didn't want to go to altar boy practice anymore, she shook her head no and said he needed the responsibility. He asked me to help get him out of becoming an altar boy, and I said I'd try. He seemed quite upset about it, but never verbalized his feelings. I did actually talk to mom, but she brushed me off too.

Wolfie, who had always been what you might characterize as mischievous, changed a bit after that. He'd go to altar boy practice once a week, and serve Mass on Sunday, and he got real quiet for a time. Maybe all the church stuff was making him more serious, but after awhile his anti-social behavior increased and we got kicked out of another country club in record time.

I guess religion didn't agree with him anymore.

Chapter 23

You got me pushin'
When I oughta be shovin'
Don't you just know it?
- Don't You Just Know It?, Huey "Piano" Smith and
the Clowns, 1958

Rich Venzoni's family owned the Italian deli off Main Street on Washington Road. We called him Greaser, which he hated, and were always asking him to bring in spaghetti or a pizza or thin sliced pepperoni. Actually, he did have this jet black hair and it looked pretty greasy, probably because he put olive oil in it, while most everybody else used Vitalis. The Greaser combed his hair in a D.A. and wore a black leather jacket even when it was warm. Hardly anyone outside of New York City wore a D.A., or a black leather jacket, unless they were in jail.

They say opposites attract, and sure enough right around Halloween Rich (The Greaser) Venzoni started dating Mary Anne Moffitt. This was shocking, because Mary Anne Moffitt was about a 9.5, with huge tits that weren't man-made. She actually went for The Greaser, it seemed. Brownie asked Rich if he slid off her when they were making out. If it bothered the Greaser, you couldn't tell. He just smiled his sly oily Italian smile and nodded his head slowly.

It was a topic of conversation at the Sweet Shoppe. We were crammed into the corner booth, which was the most coveted spot in the place, even though the seat had a big rip in it that Mr. Schmid had covered with tape. The juke box was even louder than normal. Mr. Schmid thought he had gone one up on Better Homes & Gardens, having hung one crummy paper jack-o'-lantern on the wall by the bulletin board. Very festive. What he really needed was a lighthouse to find the door. Mary Anne Moffitt's tits were often discussed, and it was always the same. Falsies were sharp and pointed, and you could always tell, but Mary Anne Moffitt's were round and full of promise and you could see the outline of her nipples. Jones said when it got cold, her nipples would stand out like erasers. Or maybe now like pimientos, since she started going with the Greaser. You knew they were real, unlike Doris Harris' or Mindy Wafford's, whose falsies looked like torpedoes. Doris was Julie's sister.

"Hey, what do you think of the Greaser? You heard about it?" asked Brownie.

"You mean about him and Mary Anne Moffitt?" I asked.

"Nah, everybody knows about that. I heard something you guys won't believe. Listen to this."

Brownie looked around the room, as if anyone could possibly hear what he was saying, since we could hardly hear what he was saying and we were all in the same booth. He leaned forward and gestured with his head. "You guys swear to keep this to yourself?"

"Yeah, sure," we chorused. This was just a ritual. If the story was any good, we'd have it all around the class by tomorrow morning.

"OK, look. Really, this is supposed to be true. The Greaser's popping her mother too." Brownie nodded sagely and sat back.

Jones went into convulsions.

"WHAT?" I said. "You're out of your mind, Brownie. What a load. Who told you that, the Greaser?" I started to laugh, too.

Robbie van Arsdale and Tommy Lynch, a funny guy I didn't know too well, said pretty much the same thing. But then we got quiet. Mrs. Moffitt had even bigger tits than her daughter, and of course in our minds she now became the mysterious and desirable older woman. The more I thought about it, the more I realized Mrs. Moffitt might actually be a better piece of ass than Mary Anne, although to my high school brain I hadn't tended to focus on Mrs. Moffitt sexually, despite my nightmarish relationship with Mrs. Carnahan three years back. Or maybe because of it. But once I did, thanks to Brownie, it was hard to get the thought out of my mind. Of course, there was really no possibility The Greaser was screwing Mrs. Moffitt by herself, much less both Mrs. Moffitt and her daughter. Even if there was, it would have to be separately because I was sure each of the Moffitt females wouldn't want the other to know she was screwing The Greaser. Come to think of it, I couldn't dream of any female on the planet admitting they were screwing the Greaser, even one of the shoats. Like I said, of course it was nonsense, but we all have imaginations. Mine can be pretty active, sometimes, especially in Social Studies class.

We had grown quiet for a few moments, in our testosterone reveries. Mrs. Moffitt's earthy image grew fuzzy with lust. The mind of a high school senior was 95%

hyperactive medulla, anyway, boiling away at about 451 degrees. I imagine Robbie van Arsdale could conjure up the best mental picture, being a Mormon and all, and not allowed to do much else but screw his brains out and marry as many women as he could handle.

The Chantels jarred me back to the Sweet Shoppe.

"MAY-AY-BE, IF I PRAY EVERY NIGHT, YOU'LL COME BACK TO -O ME-EE, O-O-O-O-O MAYBE (maybe maybe maybe)"

May-ay-be the Greaser really was screwing Mrs. Moffitt. It could be an omen.

I lit another Marlboro and looked at my distorted reflection in the Zippo. I'd jammed a finger in practice a month earlier but hadn't missed any games. I still couldn't snap my fingers and get the wheel to spark, though, even with the good hand. Forget about the guitar; I couldn't play at all. By now we'd missed a slew of band jobs and my discretionary dough was running low.

"Let's ask the Greaser," said Alan Allen.

"Yeah?" asked Brownie. "What good's that gonna do? He'll deny it if he's doing it and he'll say it's true if it's not, won't he?" There was wisdom in that observation. He paused thoughtfully.

"So maybe we oughta ask him."

Thinking of missed band jobs reminded me of the bulletin board. I was looking for a solid body guitar case and a couple of extra cords, so I wandered back toward the juke box. There was no musical merchandise, but there was that curious unsigned notice again:

℀ Notice ℀
The 2640 Club will meet on Thursday
at the usual time and place.

    Out of the corner of my eye, I thought I saw something scuttle across the wall and disappear behind the juke box.

    Something was still nagging me about that number.

       *   *   *   *

    None of us asked the Greaser about Mrs. Moffitt, actually, except David Klinghoff did a couple of days later, and the Greaser just winked and smiled at him. It made you wonder.

Chapter 24

Hurry Home, Hurry Home
-   *Return to Me, Dean Martin, 1958 -*

Brownie worked on occasion at Nick's Authentic New York Pizza in Madison. He did it for gas money, since fuel had gone up to a quarter a gallon. Nick made terrific pie, just like New York City Times Square pizza, with real mozzarella and the crust burned just right with dough bubbles that crunched when you bit into them.

Brownie was kind of inventive as a pizza apprentice, although Nick didn't know it. If Brownie didn't like the people who called in the order, or he judged they were rude on the phone, he would often add some extra ingredient he'd found crawling across the top of the pizza oven or behind the cheese cartons. A large pepperoni cost $1.65, with or without the extra component, but it was worth it, especially if I wasn't paying. This pizza was completely unlike the franchise thing from Morristown, which wasn't pizza at all, but something made from old tire compound.

Jones, the Greek and I met for dinner at Nick's on a misty Tuesday evening. The Greek was always up for pizza at Nick's or Chinese food at the New York Tea Garden or a Wallyburger at Two Bars, probably because he had to eat Greek things at home, including his mom's plaster of Paris cookies. He never patronized the Sweet Shoppe. He'd had pneumonia or something as a kid and couldn't take the soup that passed for air in that joint. Whenever Brownie was making pizza, we ate for free, of course, unless Nick was working also. Sometimes Brownie would use us as guinea pigs for his creations. That was all right with us, since the price was right, as long as he left out his secret crawling ingredients, and anchovies or fruit weren't involved. This night we had pepperoni, our favorite, with peppers, onions, garlic and pimientos. It combination was pretty good, actually. We all sat at the counter to keep Brownie company.

The Wiener wasn't with us. Earlier, he'd gotten detention for drop kicking a basketball into the gym scoreboard, denting it so badly the numbers wouldn't drop into the slots. It had made a really hilarious sound, though. The hostilities between Coach Weber and the Wiener were escalating.

"The Wiener's out of control," Jones said.

"That's not news," the Greek said.

"Listen," Brownie said, pulling down the oven door. He checked a couple of pies with his long spatula. "Something you guys don't know. His dad's moved out."

"What do you mean?" I asked.

"What could I mean?" Brownie replied. "His old man's living at the Y in Madison temporarily."

"Did he leave by himself or did his mom kick him out?" I asked.

"What's the difference to you? How the hell do I know?"

"How do you hear about it?" Jones asked.

"It's not for publication," Brownie said. "The Wiener told me Saturday night after a six pack of Knickerbocker. The guy's been gone for a couple weeks now."

"Boy that blows," Jones said.

We looked out the front window as a car pulled up. The fine mist seemed like fireflies floating around the lights, dancing through the exhaust. Brownie opened the oven again, lifted two pies with his spatula, inspected the crusts and slid them into waiting boxes.

"They don't look too done," Jones said. The cheese hadn't completely melted.

"I know," Brownie said. "But the guy that ordered them just pulled up and this way we'll have some privacy."

The guy came in, paid for his underdone pies and left in the rain.

"Do you think it's permanent? Are the Wiener's parents getting divorced?" I asked.

"How the hell would I know that stuff? The Wiener doesn't even know. Maybe his parents don't know either."

"Well, that could explain it," Greek said, biting into another slice. "Wiener's taking out his hostility towards his dad on Coach Weber."

"What're you, Sigmund Freud now?" Brownie asked, taking a dough ball and kneading it out. "Want more soda?"

We nodded. Brownie produced refills. I held the glass up the light to see what I had.

"It's called transference," the Greek said.

"It's think it's root beer," I said. Free root beer was better than not-free sarsaparilla, I figured.

"The Wiener's always been sort of out of control anyway," Jones said.

"Anything we can do?" I wondered.

"Well, we could have a counseling session with his parents, I suppose," Brownie said.   That was sarcastic. Actually, the Greek probably could pull it off. He was pretty smart.

"Any of you guys know anybody who's parents divorced?" Nobody did. Not in Windham, anyway. From time to time we'd had suspicions of carryings-on, but the veneer of civilization in Windham was pretty opaque, if thin.   Mrs. Moffitt was an example. Of course, teacher-student relations were another matter, as I'd known since ninth grade.

"Does this mean we have to treat the Wiener with some understanding or something?" Jones asked, looking pained.

"Hell, no," Brownie said. "It's just the Wiener."

"The guy's about as sensitive as a toilet seat anyway," Jones said.

We were all silent for a time, I guess imagining what that might be like if our own households split apart. Wolfie once told me that if mom and dad did split up, he figured they'd both give him lots of stuff vying for his attention. That was bullshit, though. It would be horrible, and what would anyone say to little Raymond? It made me almost shudder. I didn't want to think about the concept, really. No wonder the Wiener was the way he was.   Although he'd kind of been the way he was for as long as I'd known him, actually.

Chapter 25

Come along and be my party doll
And I'll make love to you, to you
And I'll make love to you
- Party Doll, Buddy Knox, 1957

When Mary Anne Moffitt decided to give a holiday party for the senior class, we couldn't wait to attend. For some of us, the feature attraction would be ogling the voluptuous Mrs. Moffitt, because we had been privy to one of the most salacious rumors ever heard in Windham. It was like *Peyton Place*, the racy novel that had been very popular a few years before. Actually, I saw the author's picture in the paper and she wasn't too good looking, even for a Greek. Maybe it's the homely ones who think that stuff up, I don't know. It kind of makes sense, though, because they're probably not going to experience those stories in real life.

Anyway, Jones and Brownie picked me up around eight on Saturday and we drove over to the Moffitts', right around the corner, actually. The house was large, with about five levels and comfortable, traditional furniture. Mr. Moffitt was already three sheets to the wind, which is how most people saw him no matter what time of day or night, apparently. Maybe ten years ago he might have been a handsome guy, and he and Mrs. Moffitt probably had made a smashing couple. Now, though, there was too much flesh on his face and his nose had these spidery blue alcohol veins in them. He was wearing a smoking jacket, for Chrissake. I thought they only wore those in the movies. He was holding a drink in one hand and a cigarette in the other, and had this dumb grin on his face. He stayed that way all night. He couldn't even scratch his ass. It made me feel sorry for Mary Anne, in a way, despite her good looks and effortless grace.

It's funny about the impressions you get from how a house looks, and how wrong they can be. The Moffitts' home was large and comfortable, and you would think you could be at ease there. I pictured the three of them sitting around the living room, reading by the table lamps, and once in a while discussing the authors or where Mary Anne was going to matriculate. Old man Moffitt would be smoking a pipe and listening in his stupid smoking jacket which somehow wouldn't look as stupid as it did in real life, sagely dispensing advice from time to time in a kindly way to his daughter while he puffed away. The whole scene in my mind was like a Walt Disney creation.

But I knew that wasn't the case at all, even though the house gave one that impression, because Mr. Moffitt was plastered all the time and smoked cigarettes, anyway. If the Greaser was really poking Mary Anne and her mother, then my mental picture wasn't true by a mile and the atmosphere beguiled me into a false impression. You never can tell about houses. They might have had an interior decorator who had her own ideas, anyway.

Robbie van Arsdale would have liked to have been there with us, of course, but then again he was a Mormon or whatever and couldn't go to the party. He could poke any or all of the girls who were at the party, as long as it wasn't actually *at* the party. If he walked across the Moffitt threshold, he would go to Hell. In truth, I was much more certain his parents would go to Hell for cruel and unusual punishment. I guess you can tell how I feel about crackpot religions. More people have been killed in the name of religion than all other causes combined, or so Mr. Kritzinger was fond of telling us in class.

None of these thoughts occupied my mind at Mary Anne's party, though. Mrs. Moffitt was wearing a cocktail dress, which was fairly low-cut and there was no doubt she had enormous tits. They preceded her like heavenly mountains, filled with a rubbery erotic promise. Those boobs were soft sensuous swells in a sea of alpine bliss. I could go on and on, mixing metaphors into a milkshake of desire. I guess you can tell I coveted her. The whole atmosphere around Mrs. Moffitt was sultry, like some Elizabeth Taylor character out of one of those steamy southern novels. They are always calling southern novels steamy, and I suppose it fits, and in this case there probably was no better word. Mrs. Moffitt seemed to pour through the party in a steamy vapor. When she came over to our group to say hello, I could hardly breathe. She laughed and threw her head back, probably at something Brownie said, and her teeth were very white and even and her tits stuck out even more when she did that and right then I hated the Greaser's guts.

We left the party convinced the rumor was completely unfounded, unless it really was true. We were certain that if Mrs. Moffitt was inclined to go for a May-December type deal, it would be with one of us and not the Greaser who was, after all, greasy. What bravado.

There were two funny things, though, that happened at the Moffitt's. Jones and I were in a hallway off the living room when Brownie came up, tapped me on the shoulder and beckoned us to follow. He led us to the door leading into the garage. He opened it and the three of us stepped down onto the cement floor. He closed the door behind.

"What –"

"Sshh." Brownie snapped on the garage fluorescents. There were three cars in the large area. "Look," he said in a low voice, pointing.

"Wow." Against the far wall, facing outward, was a gorgeous new silver Mercedes 300SL Gull Wing convertible with red leather seats. This was major dollars. Brownie led us over and pointed again. On the far side, next to the wall, the right fender was dented all to hell and the windshield spider webbed. He raised his eyebrows in a questioning manner. We retreated back to the party.

"We have to talk about this later," Brownie said, and headed off toward the living room. That was the one funny thing.

The other funny thing I hesitate to mention because I'm not really sure of my interpretation. A few minutes later, I had wandered into the kitchen, looking maybe for some eggnog in the Moffitts' refrigerator, and was startled when I looked up and saw Mrs. Moffitt leaning on the counter next to the open refrigerator door. She just smiled at me while she toyed with her drink. For some reason, I felt my face getting hotter and hotter, until I was pretty sure it was lit up like one of the red bulbs on the Moffitts' Christmas tree. This is a character flaw I seem to have. I don't know if I was more embarrassed by her seeing me raiding her refrigerator or because she smiled at me or what. Actually, my whole body was kind of on fire and I felt my motor reflexes jerking a little bit, kind of randomly. I know

I gasped for some cold air, right there with my head in the Amana. Then she said the damnedest thing, slowly and breathily:

"I don't make you nervous, do I, George?" She smiled this kind of secret smile at me, while I jerked around like a stupid fish on a line. I said something like:

"Aaah - well - aaah - I - eggnog - nice dress there."

Ohmigod. Not again. What is it about me?

"I know you live around the corner from us, George. Stop by sometime." She smiled again as I started what felt like a grand mal seizure. My body temperature would have melted lead. I never told anyone, not even Jones.

Stop by sometime. My God.

Not again.

Chapter 26

I begged him to go slow
But whether he heard I'll never know
Look out! Look out! Look out!
-    *The Leader of the Pack, the Shangri-Las, 1964*

"We gotta discuss this," Brownie said, licking the chocolate ice cream dripping from his cone. Windham rolled up the sidewalks at ten o'clock on Saturday, so we were in Summit at the Friendly Ice Cream shop. It was only about eleven, but the Moffitt party had pretty much petered out.

Actually, I didn't think Mrs. Moffitt had petered out at all. If anything, she'd gotten more fueled up as the night went on and looked even hotter.

"Mrs. Moffitt or the Mercedes?" Jones asked, noisily slurping his shake.

"The car. Well, first, anyway."

Brownie took a bite and started ticking items off on his fingers. "Okay. First, nobody's been arrested for running over that colored guy. Second, the other two cars in the garage were parked head in. That one was parked backwards. Why would that be except to hide the damage? Third, who puts a new Mercedes in their garage when it needs to be fixed? It's not even street legal with the busted windshield. It would've been towed from an accident right to the dealer."

He crunched the last of his cone. "Right?" Jones and I nodded.

"Is there any other reasonable explanation?" Brownie asked.

"Maybe it just happened so he hasn't brought it in yet," I said. "Maybe he hit a deer or something and he was shitfaced like he's supposed to be all the time so he didn't want the cops to come." Brownie shot me a look.

"Yeah, okay. It's probably not too likely," I said.

"If that's the case," Jones said, "then he'd bring it in to the shop Monday or Tuesday, right? Why don't we check in a couple of days?"

"How would we do that?" I asked. The others just looked at me like I was a moron.

*   *   *   *   *

On Thursday, the weather had turned, and the wind that whipped across the soccer field felt like little ice particles. At practice, everybody else got to run around, but as goalie I had to do jumping jacks in place to stay warm. At least I wore long pants.

Jones caught up with Brownie and me afterward in the parking lot, which was mostly empty. We sat in his '54 convertible. The top was up, thank God.

"The car's still there in the garage. It's still dented. Hasn't been moved."

"How'd you find out?" I asked.

"I parked by your house and cut across the back yard. The blinds were drawn on the garage windows but there was a gap I could see through."

He did this in daylight?

There was silence for a time. "Okay, so now what?" I asked. "Do we tell the cops or what?"

"Well, here's our options," Brownie said. "We could blackmail the guy, probably, and make some dough out of the whole deal. They've got plenty, we know that. We could forget about it, or we could turn him in. If we turn him in, it would have to be anonymous, especially because Mary Anne's in our class."

That seemed to about cover it.

"She's too good looking to screw over, though, much less her mom," Jones said.

"Their good looks don't do us any good. They only do the Greaser any good," Brownie said. "That asshole."

"I don't think I could forget about it or blackmail the guy. I think we have to turn him in." I still remembered Po fixing my bike for free, of course. I do have a sort of conscience, anyway.

"Wait a minute," Jones said. "How do we know it wasn't her? Mrs. Moffitt, I mean? Maybe that's her car."

We hadn't thought of that. Mrs. Moffitt liked her sauce, too, it seemed.

"It really doesn't matter," Brownie said. "It doesn't change anything." That was probably right, I realized.

"What about if we blackmail him and turn him in anyway?" Jones asked. "That way, you've got a clear conscience and we all get a little dough."

I shook my head. "You guys can do it, but I'm out."

"Worried about the risk?" Jones asked.

"Well, there's that, too, but mostly I think we gotta do the right thing here."

It was growing dark: the days were definitely shorter now.

"Turning him in is the right thing. Blackmailing him also is an intelligent thing," Jones said. "They're not mutually exclusive."

I just shook my head.

"Okay, we'll just turn him in," Brownie said. "Who's gonna make the phone call?"

Chapter 27

Many a tear has to fall
But it's all
In the game
-   *It's All in the Game, Tommy Edwards, 1958*

I hadn't really thought too much about my Princeton interview ahead of time. I had applied to four colleges, one of which was my 'safe' school, but we weren't to hear for another couple of months. Being of sound mind, I had no idea what I wanted to major in except sports, without the History of Sports part. Also, I wanted to make a lot of money playing rock 'n' roll, which was going to require forming a new group, getting another agent, rehearsing, etc. There would be a lot of work to do. When you're in a band the girls usually take care of themselves. I don't mean to sound egotistical, but you could put an electric guitar in Quasimodo's hands and the girls would flop over. That's why I wasn't really too concerned about the mediocre crop I had seen so far at Princeton.

When the doorbell rang, about seven thirty, I was already uncomfortable because my mother made me wear a tie. I had this clip-on job from when I was a kid with Tom Mix and a lariat on it, and I put it on for a joke, but mom didn't see the humor. It only came down to the middle of my chest, anyway. She was getting pretty uptight. I refused to wear my blazer, which was a little short in the sleeves, because mom had been too cheap to get me a new one. She said I was growing too fast. As far back as I could remember, she didn't buy me clothes because I was growing too fast. I was a regular goddamn weed, and if you listened to her, I would be about sixteen feet tall by now. Even the stuff she did buy me wound up eventually with Wolfie, and then with Raymond. I felt sorry for them even more than I felt sorry for me, but at least they didn't have to put up with that new-clothes itch. Most of the tags said IRREG, which I thought was a brand name for the longest time. At E.J. Korvette's how much could you spend, really? Eighteen bucks on their best sports jacket?

The Princeton representative was maybe 6'3", just about my height, but somehow he seemed taller. He stood very straight. The best thing I can say is that he looked like the New York Yankees of the Ivy League set. Words like polished, tall, suave, immaculate came to mind. At least I fit the tall part. Looking closely at his jacket, I could tell he got it from Brooks Brothers, and it probably came in an exact size, not just L, M or S. His tie had some sort of royal crest like maybe he was related to Queen Elizabeth, for Chrissake. I was tempted to ask him where his vacuum cleaner was, but I didn't think he or my mother would have appreciated the humor. She fawned over the guy, and practically offered him a restaurant menu, but Mr. Ivy League just wanted soda water.

It took me a second to figure that out. Soda water? Did he mean seltzer? I guess my mom knew what the guy wanted, because that's what she brought. He didn't even want an egg cream, which was kind of a waste of good seltzer. For awhile, I thought she was the one trying to go to Princeton, because all I did was sit there while the two of them chatted about Princeton-type stuff. My mom made sure the interviewer knew she was a concert pianist from Juilliard, the #1 performer in her class, and had toured professionally until I had the nerve to get born. So we were all in the same social stratum. Didn't the guy see, then, that I had to go to Princeton to even things out?

After about four years, the guy very suavely asked my mother to leave the room. I don't remember exactly how he did it, but it was really slick and subtle. Anyway, I saw her kind of blink and her head jerked a little bit. This was unplanned. The situation could get out of control. I could see her wheels turning. How could her whelp be trusted to complete a Princeton interview by himself? I might say anything. Actually, I wondered the same thing. Anyway, she had no choice and after a few seconds excused herself.

The guy, whose name was Mr. Luther, gave me this sappy, *intimate* type smile that meant now that my mother was gone we could talk about some real Princeton stuff. I guess he didn't have a first name, or else I was not privileged to know it unless I got in.

You know that point on a roller coaster ride near the beginning, when you've taken the slow, agonizing trip all the way up to the dizzying edge of the great precipice, and now you're just about to plunge to certain death? That's about where we were.

"Well, George, perhaps you can tell us how you might contribute to the educational process at Princeton."

What? Us? There was no one else in the room. Contribute? Did he mean band money? Educational process? What the hell was that? The only thing I understood in his whole question was 'Princeton'.

My mind was frozen, like the snowball from years before. All I could think of, crazily, was bashing that cop on the side of his face.

"Well - well, I - , what?" I asked.

And this was the good part of the interview. I'll tell you a couple of others, which won't take very long, but I did have a semi-lingual moment or two.

Mr. Luther looked at me a little sideways. "Maybe you can tell me why you want to go to Princeton. The Princeton *experience*."

Experience *this*, I thought.

"Oh," I said. I couldn't exactly say that my mother and the guidance counselor were pushing his school up my ass, could I?

"I studied all the college handbooks and read everything I could and talked to a few alumni who really enjoyed their Princeton *experience*. I especially think I would enjoy the setting and that big tower with the ivy on it. I think I want to major in Journalism and I know Princeton has the best department on the east coast."

What? Was I hearing myself right? What crap! I never even thought about Journalism until this very second, and I was praying they had a Journalism department. Since our crummy guidance department had about three handbooks, the statement about reading them all was probably true. Princeton, Dartmouth and maybe Wofford or something. I liked the Wofford one because it was quite colorful. If you went to Dartmouth, you could run a hotel, I heard. Or maybe that was Cornell. Who would go to college to run a stupid hotel? All you needed was a fat guy with an apron.

"Which alumni have you spoken with, George?"

"I don't remember all their names, but there are several members at our country club."

That was another good answer, my only other decent one, because it aligned me with the country club set. That was very important, I figured, unless I was wrong. For all I knew, really, the navy blue blazers I saw at Canoe Creek meant those guys were on the staff, rather than being Princeton alumni. Come to think of it, I kind of remembered one of them holding a door open for me. I wouldn't imagine this guy would know, though. But that was the last time I had my head above water before going down for the third time.

The rest of the interview was too painful to recount. I volunteered something about the Hasty Pudding Club, which I found out later was really at Yale, or somewhere. He asked me all this annoying personal stuff about goals and ideals and crap that nobody ever thinks about until they're old, or it's too late - the only goals I ever thought about were the ones I had let in during the state championships. The more I made things up the more my answers contradicted themselves, I thought. The only other card I had to play was my soccer career, but to this guy I might have been talking about fencing, or some other fag sport.

My mom practically fell into the room when I opened the door to let the guy out, about twelve years later. After he left, which was right away, I knew the interview process wasn't quite done yet. There was mom.

"What? What happened? What did he say? What did you say? Could you tell? Did he say you were going to be admitted? What?" She was a real machine gun, spitting questions out one after the other.

"What?" I said.

"AAAHH TELL ME" she said through gritted teeth.

"Well, ma, put it this way. I think I saved you a lot of tuition money. That's an expensive place. I can get just as good an education at any of the other schools I applied to."

She stared at me as if she had just learned I had been adopted.

"Also I saved you the cost of the blazers."

Chapter 28

Young blood, young blood, young blood
I can't get you out of my mind...
Young Blood, The Coasters, 1957

I've been putting this off, as you probably know. This is the other chapter that won't be in here if I do turn this in to Assistant Professor Murphy. It concerns my relationship with Mrs. Carnahan. If I'm truthful, I have to tell you that my feelings in this matter have been difficult to sort out. I think, frankly, I kind of became obsessed with her over the marking period. In fact, I know I became obsessed with her. You know how you can put feelings in a mental box, and take them out when you want to enjoy them? Especially when you're in someplace like Social Studies class and the clock seems to slog through molasses? You can do that for most things, anyway, like maybe a first date with somebody or getting your first car or a new guitar and all. Well, my Mrs. Carnahan box wouldn't close. Stuff just oozed out and soaked the rest of my brain.

I'm not entirely certain how this happened exactly, but after she asked me if I liked her things got a little hazy. After detention I know she wanted me to help carry some files and stuff to her car, which is where we wound up, right there in the Windham High School faculty parking lot, which actually was the same as the student parking lot. I remember thinking I could look out her car window and see my home room, which somehow seemed a million miles away at that moment. I can't explain it, but I believed I was pretty much able to get along with the opposite sex, and not fumble around, but as a ninth grader that was probably wishful thinking. I didn't behave in a very assured manner in Mrs. Carnahan's Plymouth Fury. For one thing, it hadn't gotten completely dark yet, and I was in fear that someone would see us. It didn't seem to bother Mrs. Carnahan that much, though, at least as far as I could tell. We didn't really do it, but we came close. Actually, the only reason we stopped, I think, is because she seemed to have a sort of climax. That's enough detail.

Anyway, after that she treated me as kind of a co-conspirator but for some unexplained reason I found the reality a lot less comfortable than the fantasy, if you know what I mean. I'm not sure I know what I mean. She suggested that I come over to her house, on Passaic Avenue in the borough, not too far from the Greek's home. That kind of scared me. What if Mrs. Greek or the Greek himself saw us? Worse, what if Mr. Carnahan came home? That would be a horror show, and I might get shot or arrested or something. Mrs. Carnahan assured me, though, that wouldn't happen. It's not that I believed her, exactly, but of course I had to continue on, like some goddamn lemming racing pell mell for the cliff. What else could I do? We hadn't done it, and there it was on a platter, so to speak, so by anyone's moral standard I had an obligation to see it through.

I guess.

She had suggested the following Monday, so over the weekend I didn't know whether to dread or look forward to that day. Now the stupid part is that I couldn't drive, so I had to kind of walk behind the school for a block or so until Mrs.

Carnahan drove up and I bolted into her Fury. She lived in a really small house on a tiny lot, and it wasn't too well kept. The rooms were full of cobwebs in the corners, and the space under the bed had dust tumbleweeds. The place needed painting, too. I don't know what Mr. Carnahan did for a living but I'd bet he wasn't on the Erie Lackawanna every morning.

I'll tell you what was weird. Well, a lot of things were weird but Mrs. Carnahan was not what you'd call a normal sex fiend. I guess if I thought about it, I'd have to classify myself as a normal sex fiend, unless I'm deluding myself again, but Mrs. Carnahan was definitely on the edge of the bell curve. For one thing, she pulled a bunch of colorful silk scarves out of the nightstand, and asked me to tie her right to the bed. I suppose I had no choice: what was I going to do, say no? So I tied her up and then what? I wondered. Fortunately, or maybe unfortunately, Mrs. Carnahan told me exactly what to do. I have to admit I didn't quite get it. Not that it was so bad, though, just weird.

She had other things, too, leather stuff and handcuffs and I don't need to give an inventory, for Chrissake. But that's not the weirdest part. The second weirdest part was that her house was across from Memorial Park, and sometimes I could hear the sounds of ball playing if the window was open. That was very unsettling. All those kids were doing normal after school things, playing ball and all, and here I was doing definitely abnormal things with Mrs. Carnahan. I had never realized it, but my own classmates were doing everyday things as well, at least compared to what I was doing, and it made me appreciate that relative normalcy. After a couple of times, I really didn't want to be there anymore but I had no idea how to end it.   After all, Mrs. Carnahan was my math teacher, for Chrissake. It was kind of a dilemma.

Okay, here's the weirdest part, and I'm only going to tell it once and not dwell on it. It was maybe the fourth time we were together in Mrs. Carnahan's house fooling around on her bed. When it happened, I felt the bed shake. It might have been Mrs. Carnahan, but I don't think so. I believe somewhere close the spider had shifted and the whole web quavered.

I heard a sneeze.

It came from the closet, through the louvers, and it wasn't anything you could mistake for anything else.   Mrs. Carnahan got this kind of shocked look; her eyes darted between me and the closet door.   I jumped up and without thinking too much whipped open the closet and there was this older man with no pants on, in an excited state if you get what I mean.   We stared at each other for a millisecond, or maybe about forty years, and I swear I didn't think about what I was going to do. I just did it. I kicked Mr. Carnahan as hard as I could in the balls. Even though I didn't have my shoes on, he dropped like a rock. While Mrs. Carnahan was making these horrified noises I quick grabbed my clothes and darted out of there.

After that, I made goddamn sure my Mrs. Carnahan mental box was closed and locked up tight. When I saw her the next day in math class, we didn't make eye contact. Suffice it to say we stumbled through the rest of the marking period and I got an A-, which is about what I deserved anyway.

Math. Christ.

Chapter 29

Little bitty pretty one
Come sit down on my knee
-Little Bitty Pretty One, Thurston Harris, 1957

On a dreary, cold Saturday evening, Wolfie slipped out the house after supper and rode his bicycle to St. Francis Church. There he met up with a classmate, Jimmy Harris, Julie's younger brother. Wolfie and Jimmy had attended altar boy practice that morning. They stood across the street from the rectory and fired rocks through a dozen windows before they were stopped. Apparently Wolfie was pretty near hysterical; I don't know about Jimmy Harris. After the startling phone call, my parents rushed out of the house and met Wolfie and the cops at Overlook Hospital in Summit. I guess he was in pretty bad shape. I found out later that no one got hurt by the rocks or showering glass, fortunately. It was serious enough.

My parents left me home with Raymond, and I have to say I was really shook up. I'd only heard snatches of what was said during and after the phone call from the cops before they took off for the Emergency Room. What was happening? It seemed like three years instead of three hours before my parents came home with my brother. I didn't get much of an explanation from anyone that night. Like I said, I was stunned. Wolfie's behavior was so un-Wolflike I didn't know what to think. My parents were huddled up with him until I went to bed; by then it was past midnight. I didn't sleep very well. I thought I hear my mother sobbing, faintly, and something else, something scrabbling on the wall behind my headboard. It gave me the creeps big time.

No one went to church the next morning. Wolfie came down for breakfast but didn't say much. I think mom might have stayed with him in his room. I figured he'd talk to me when he felt like it, and so I didn't ask anybody anything. You wouldn't have either; the atmosphere was leaden. It was a very strange, subdued morning.

After lunch, Father Corr came by. Mom suggested I take Raymond over to the Fairmount Avenue elementary school playground. I put my brother in this red jacket with a matching hat, the kind that flops over your ears. There were little cowboys with lariats here and there on the jacket and hat. Of course, they had been passed down from Wolfie after I'd outgrown them. Mom didn't dress him in that outfit very often but I liked it. Under normal circumstances, I would have enjoyed my outing with the little tyke. Off we went on my old bicycle to the playground. We passed old Mr. Hofmann on the way, rocking on his porch, and waved to the old geezer. He got so excited he dropped his book and waved back energetically. I hoped this wasn't going to be the biggest thing in his day. It was overcast and cool; the monkey bars were cold to the touch.

As I've said, most of the time Raymond drifted in his own world but he could be very funny if he wanted to. Once in a while he'd do something that let me know he really liked me. At least, that's what I like to think. Sometimes just a secret smile, or maybe his little hand on my knee. When he did that, I kind of hoped he'd stay a little kid forever, and that he would pat my knee from time to time. I knew that when I went off to college I'd miss many of his formative years. I wouldn't be there to watch him or help him grow up, and that was kind of sad. Stupid college.

Anyway, Raymond and I stayed at the park until about three and biked back home. It wasn't far. Old Mr. Hofmann's rocker was vacant; I guess it had gotten too cold for him. I was surprised to find Father Corr still at our house. I didn't know what to think. He'd never been to our home before. I know he'd visited Alan Allen's house once, but that was because his brother got polio.

Chapter 30

Put a chain around my neck
And lead me anywhere
-Teddy Bear, Elvis Presley, 1957

I don't know what I expected might happen after Wolfie's strange incident at St. Francis, but surely *something*. As far as I could tell, the cops never came back or anything. Wolfie didn't get punished, nor did he come to me in a day or so and tell me what the hell was going on. Father Corr visited again, and he seemed overly friendly to my parents, smiling and laughing for no good reason, and even asked me how school was going. I think he would have patted me on the head if I hadn't been six inches taller than he was. I believe he might have taken my parents to dinner a week later. It marked an abrupt end to our churchgoing, though, which was fine with me. I suppose Wolfie's candy consumption took a big hit, since he wasn't in church to boost change from the collection plate. All I can surmise is that mom should have paid more attention when my brother said he didn't want to be an altar boy anymore.

There was one thing, though. I guess you may have figured out by now that my dad and I weren't exactly too involved with each other's lives. I mean, that's not a bad thing, and from what I could tell that was the norm for every other kid in Windham. Except for that goddamn Little League, I mean.

The bastard that invented Little League should be strung up and made into a piñata with his own bats. Anyway, my father called me into the living room one night around maybe ten o'clock, when Wolfie and Raymond were already asleep. Somehow mom wasn't there, but I don't know why. He gestured me into a chair, which was unusual, since the living room furniture was normally off-limits. Not that our stuff was so hot, or big deal expensive, but I think because we didn't have that shitty plastic on the arms. If I recall right, it was about three weeks since the incident.

My dad sat on the sofa opposite. Vaguely, I remember thinking I'd never seen him on that couch before. In fact, the only time I could recall anyone even being in the living room was when my parents threw a cocktail party my junior year. It must have been a pretty wild affair, at least as far as parents go, because somebody spilled a drink on the wall to wall carpet.

"George, I need to talk to you about something."

Now this was rare. This was mom's ballpark; he'd never had to talk to me about anything, at least since he found all those automobile emblems. He had a serious expression. Briefly, I wondered which undiscovered felony was on the docket.

"It's about Wolfie, when we brought him home a couple of weeks ago." I was relieved; I wasn't in trouble and maybe now I'd find out what had happened.

"Okay, dad," I said, kind of man-to-man. "I'm listening."

"Sometimes, growing up isn't always easy. Sometimes, kids might have a hard time. I'm sure you know what I mean."

I nodded. I had no idea what he meant.

"Wolfie had a bad reaction to becoming an altar boy. I think he told your mom about it, and I guess we didn't really listen to him."

So what? I thought. What else is new? I could have a bad reaction about cleaning up my room, or getting a summer job, but nobody really listened to me either. I'd just like to see what happened if I busted out a bunch of church windows because I had to mow the lawn or wash the Buick.

"Anyway, your mother and I would appreciate it if you didn't ask him about it. He doesn't want to talk about it, we're sure. He told us he doesn't want to talk about it, so I'm asking you to respect his wishes."

There was a moment of silence. I nodded my head, slowly, as I weighed all this. Wolfie would ninety to nothing talk to me before he talked to our parents, so something was definitely hinky here.

"Okay, dad," I said.

"Good."

And that was that. To my surprise, Wolfie never did bring up the subject and I didn't ask him about it. I didn't ask him more because I respected Wolfie than because my dad had told me not to.

Father Corr stopped coming around, then. I do know Father O'Shea got transferred somewhere, so Father Corr had to take over altar boy training again. What the hell, it couldn't have been that hard. What else did he have to do all week, unless somebody died?

There was one funny thing. One night, in the bowling alley parking lot about a month later, I thought I saw a shock of flaming hair in the passenger seat of Coach Weber's jalopy as it was pulling out. It was dark though, and I was probably mistaken since I don't think Coach was a Catholic. Somebody said he was Lutheran.

Chapter 31

I know you send me
Honest, you do
-You Send Me, Sam Cooke, 1957

Along about this time a colored family, unnoticed by anyone, bought an old clapboard house near the township border. On the day they moved in, the news ripped through Windham like a sonic boom. The guy was an engineer working for Bell Labs, over in Morris Plains, where they invented the transistor. Maybe he was one of the guys who worked on it. He probably could read formulas and engineering texts, and no doubt was a respectable law-abiding citizen, probably. That wasn't the point. Property values were in danger, and that struck fear into the hearts of all the corporate executives. After all, why the hell did they bother to commute from so far out if the town was going to get infiltrated? The wives were even more frightened. Car doors were locked, back doors bolted. It simply could not be allowed. The problem was how to rectify this disruption in the natural order of Windham, hopefully in a Christian way if possible. After all, this wasn't the South.

Actually, it was worse. There were meetings behind closed doors as the adults attempted, unsuccessfully, to grapple with the situation. Sure, the new folks might be a nice enough couple, but what would happen when the guy's cousin Rufus showed up from Newark with his bottle of Ripple? What if they decided to send their kids to school, if they had any? Once they started to breed, they would have a dozen in about three years. How was this crisis going to be dealt with? The town seemed paralyzed.

The teenagers had no such problem. They weren't paralyzed. Within a week, all the windows in the colored family's house were smashed with rocks. From what we heard, the perpetrators were from the junior class. After the windows were fixed, they did it all over again a few days later. Believe it or not, it wasn't so much an act of prejudice as one of opportunity. The kids knew the cops would take their time answering the couple's frantic calls for assistance, which they did, and the gang could get away with a little mischief.

So pretty soon that was the end of that. The town hadn't needed the Klan, which was mostly active downstate, and who had graciously expressed their willingness to drive up from the pine barrens in their pickups and chopped roadsters to take care of Windham's problem in an even more direct way. The colored family moved out, probably back to Jockey Hollow or wherever they had come from. I kind of felt sorry for these people, but I could appreciate the town's point of view as well. In a way the couple had asked for it. I guess there was no satisfactory solution; at least the end result made most people breathe easier and inconvenienced only the colored family. After all, why would you want to live where nobody wants you? I couldn't understand that.

The momentary shudder in Windham's natural order had ended quickly. About two weeks later, though, the Wiener brought the subject up in Mr. Kritzinger's class. We were discussing current events. This was something only the Wiener would do.

"Mr. Kritzinger, I have a question about a current event."

"And what is that, Mr. Frankfurter?"

"I wanted to ask about the colored family that got driven out of Windham after their house got vandalized."

Now this put the class on high alert. Some things just weren't discussed. I could tell Mr. Kritzinger had been taken aback.

"I believe their house experienced some minor mischief, but I don't think you can draw that conclusion," he said.

"I didn't know who they were," the Wiener replied. "The paper never wrote about it. That's part of my question, how come the Courier didn't cover the story."

Everyone's head swiveled from the Wiener to Mr. Kritzinger. He knew it, too.

"Well, I suppose that was an editorial decision." Did he think we were that dumb?

"The Star-Ledger didn't cover it either. They cover all kinds of crime and stuff," the Wiener persisted.

"I doubt if minor vandalism in Windham would get printed in the Newark Star-Ledger," Mr. Kritzinger said. "Anything else?"

Vanity Fair's hand shot up. Yes, that was her real name.

"I know who they were."

There was a moment's hesitation; it seemed as though Mr. Kritzinger really didn't want to prolong the discussion. But it was too far along, now.

"All right, who?" he asked.

"The Cooks."

"How did you know that?" Mr. Kritzinger asked, unwisely.

"My dad moved them. They went back to Morristown."

Vanity's dad, aside from demonstrating a grotesque sense of humor in naming his daughter, owned Fair Deal Moving and Storage down on Commerce Street. "They're related to Sam Cooke the singer, without the 'e' on the end."

Sam Cooke Sam Cooke? The r & b singer whose top hits included "You Send Me", "I'll Come Running Back to You" and "Only Sixteen", among others?

What? What was this?

There was a kind of collective intake of breath.

"How do you know that?" the Wiener asked.

"He paid the bill."

Ohmigod. We – the golden youth of Windham – what had we done?

Chapter 32

I'm gonna tell Aunt Mary
'Bout Uncle John
-   *Long Tall Sally, Little Richard, 1956*

"You guys aren't going to believe this. Anybody ever heard of something called the Urban League?" Jones had convened a special meeting. The three of us – Jones, Brownie and I – were having burgers and beer at Wally's Two Bars in Livingston before going to see Gregory Peck in *Pork Chop Hill.*

"Never heard of it."

"Me neither."

"Well, get this," Jones said, after swallowing a bite. "It's some Negro organization, some national outfit I think. They've offered a reward for whoever ran down that colored guy Jackson. Anybody with information leading to the arrest and conviction, blah blah, blah, they'll pay two thousand bucks."

Two grand?!? My God. That was almost twenty band jobs. A fortune.

"What? Where'd you hear that?" I asked.

"It's in the Courier, like a paid ad."

"Cool," said Brownie.

Thanksgiving was days away. It had been a couple of weeks since Brownie had called the Windham cops from the

Sweet Shoppe pay phone and told them about the dented
Mercedes hiding out in the Moffitt's garage. As far as we
knew, though, nothing had happened.

"Holy shit," I said. "And we called anonymously. Now
what?"

Jones looked at Brownie. "They probably couldn't hear
a thing you were saying anyway, with that goddamn juke box
blaring."

Both Jones and I noticed Brownie was grinning.

"What," I said.

"I'm not as dumb as you look. I got the name of the
cop I told, and I said we wanted any reward that might get
posted. So I gave him a code name and told him to make a
note."

"No. You're not that smart," Jones said. "Are you?"

"Maybe he is. What's the code name?"

"Milner."

"Who's that?" I asked.

"It's my mother's maiden name. I wanted a link so no
one could dispute it later."

"Who was the cop?"

"Martin Rohleder." Martin had graduated a couple of
years ahead of us. His brother Jimmy was in our class. There
was a pause. Maybe we were all thinking about how to spend
that kind of dough. Jones looked at me.

"He is that smart I guess."

"They might be investigating and how would we
know?" Brownie asked.

"We wouldn't know," Jones said. "So what should we
do?"

"What if we give it a week and then follow up with another phone call?" I asked.

"I suppose so," Brownie said. "Want another beer?" Jones and I shook our heads.

"What do we do if the cops haven't done anything?" I asked.

"Maybe Moffitt had an explanation," Jones said. "But if he's some kind of VIP and pulled strings, we should take it to the state cops."

"Yeah?" I asked. That would be cool. The New Jersey State Police had these stupid Smokey the Bear hats, but they also had nifty uniforms and jackboots. A lot of them were pretty big guys, too. I wondered how they would react to interviewing Mary Anne Moffitt. It made me realize the state cops might not be such a hot idea.

"Look, it's probably not that Moffitt's got big connections, but he's a rich white Windham guy and there's a dead colored guy from the next town over. Think the Duffer's gonna give a shit?" Brownie said.

I hated to think Brownie could be right, but I supposed he might be.

"Well, then, we'll call the Star-Ledger. We can't let the money just slip through our fingers," Jones said. The paper had done investigative reporting on occasion. After all, they were in Newark.

The movie was pretty good, if grim. It was billed as sort of true. The only thing was, Gregory Peck always looked like he'd just stepped out of the shower and his uniform had just come back from the dry cleaners. Somehow, I didn't think the real Pork Chop Hill battle looked like that.

Chapter 33

Do you wanna dance
Under the moonlight...
-*Do you Want to Dance, Bobby Freeman, 1958*

The party season was in full swing. My bum hand had healed without incident, so our band worked at least once a week. Normally, music and soccer didn't interfere with each other, but one Friday we got back late from an away game and I had to perform in my uniform. It was kind of cool, actually, except I really needed a shower. Our standard rate for a three or four hour gig was $110. We had visions of upping our rates drastically, when we recorded for the big labels, but since we didn't crack the top 40 we were still in the $110 bracket, along with Hog Creek, the Hot Nuts, and the Ten Screaming N-----s out of Baltimore.

Billy Deane had wangled another deal with Columbia Records, and so we took all our band crap into New York City and recorded six sides in their studio, including "Vegetable Love (It Just Grows and Grows)". The recording session took all day, which I kind of expected. The studio guys never get the drums right. You'd think they'd have solved the problem, since they did it about every day for Chrissake. It was about six o'clock before we were all satisfied with the results.

As always, my hopes were sky-high, although, in the back of my mind, I knew that was really dumb. Most likely we would only add another few inches of vinyl to the vast mountain of unreleased would-be Top Ten hits.

We had exactly one groupie, Shirley the Machine. None of us seemed to know how or why, except we'd first noticed her late junior year. Actually, it would have been hard to miss her, since Shirley was probably the only girl that ever crossed the Windham city line without a bra. She'd actually followed our band down to the shore in the summer, staying in some cheesy Beach Haven motel. Shirley seemed to always find out where we were playing and show up, usually uninvited, sometimes with an escort. The guy would find out his sole function was to drive her to and from the party, because she paid him no mind once she got near our band. Shirley had no known last name, unless it was Machine, and if she went to school no one knew where. She was this sloe-eyed blonde who seemed always in a dream; languid and purposeless, it appeared, except to smile casually, as if favoring you with a secret shared only by the two of you, drifting through the party and trying to bed every band member except me.

"I like you, George," she told me once. "I like the way your guitar sings to me." Sing *this*, I thought. What bullshit. "But I'm not going to screw you, because I'm saving myself for when we get married."

At first, this was very frustrating, especially since Billy Deane, our bass player, and everybody else told me she was actually dynamite in the sack, despite her outward demeanor, but after awhile it got like a disability. I learned to live with it.

Chapter 34

I'm stuck in Folsom Prison
And time keeps draggin' on
-Folsom Prison Blues, Johnny Cash, 1955

Mister Franz made bail the morning after his arrest and returned home to Windham. At least he wouldn't have to spend the holidays in the slammer. I don't suppose life was too normal at the Franz residence, but Ted seemed to be getting along as well as he could, at least at Windham High. Most of his schoolmates expressed some form of support. After awhile, being teenagers with attention spans roughly equivalent to that of tree gnats, we kind of forgot about the whole thing.

About two months later, though, the Star Ledger ran another story on page two. The article said Ted's father (who lived in the "posh, upscale suburb of Windham") made a deal and was going to plead no contest in return for cooperating with the authorities. We guessed that meant showing them how he did it. The Wiener said he wished Mister Franz had consulted us first; maybe he could have passed on some useful information.

Brownie got the idea we should attend the sentencing hearing. He brought it up after practice as we waited for the hot water. You had to turn on all the showers and wait two or three minutes, which nobody appreciated standing around all sweaty and mostly naked. And this was a new school.

"Listen, you know we might be able to mitigate his sentence," he said. We had our towels around our waists.

"What? What does that mean, mitigate?" I asked.

"You know, get it reduced."

The Greek drifted over. "How?" he asked.

"Testify at the sentencing hearing."

Could anybody do that?

"Are we allowed to go to that?" I asked. Finally, the stalls were starting to steam up.

"What's the matter with you?" said Brownie. "This is America. It's a goddamn courtroom. Didn't you ever hear the expression 'open court'? Didn't you pay attention in civics?"

Maybe civics was an eighth grade course, because I had no memory of taking it. I wasn't totally dim, though.

"If he made a plea deal, then the sentence is already a done deal, I think," I said.

Brownie shrugged. "What the hell. Never up, never in."

What the hell.

So that's how it started. Formal sentencing was to be in the U.S. District Court, Southern District of New York. The judge was some guy named Murphy, unless it was Dunphy, but I may be thinking of Don Dunphy the Friday Night Fights announcer. Jones called the court and found out sentencing was set for 1 pm on a school day, which I thought would have ended the whole scheme.

I underestimated my friends. Somehow they convinced Mr. Kritzinger this would be a kind of civics field trip to see American justice in action, and that maybe we could help our

friend's dad by getting a few years shaved off his time in stir.
Mr. Kritzinger spoke to Principal Dunwood, who was horrified
at the thought and turned us down flat. The Wood Pecker told
Mr. Kritzinger in no uncertain terms that in no way were the
degenerates of the Class of 1959 going to turn a serious matter
into a circus, or cast a poor reflection on old Windham High.

Left with no choice, then, we played hooky on
sentencing day: Jones, Brownie, the Wiener, myself and Mike
Endler. Our parents had no idea what was afoot. We all rode
the Erie Lackawanna to Hoboken that morning and then
transferred over, winding up in Manhattan in time for a Horn &
Hardart early lunch. Jones, anticipating our repast at the
automat, had brought a bunch of washers to use in place of
nickels but they didn't work. In fact, he jammed a slot and we
almost got busted then and there.

We arrived at the courthouse about fifteen minutes
early. I should say that no one in the Franz family had any idea
we were going to the hearing. Ted and his mom were
flabbergasted to see us as we trouped in and sat in the spectator
seats. We gave Ted the thumbs up and waved. Mister Franz
was huddled up with his lawyer at the table where Perry Mason
usually sat, and hadn't yet seen us. I looked around. I have to
say the place was impressive, almost like a church, except the
pews didn't have kneeling pads or anything, and instead of the
cross there was that blindfolded justice lady, who looked like
she might have been related to that phone book person with the
lightning bolt.

After awhile, this bailiff guy came in and announced the
coming of the judge, and we all stood up like the guy was Jesus
Christ himself. It was just like in the movies. I was surprised at
the short amount of time the court was in session before the

judge got down to business. He asked the defendant to rise and that's where the Wiener went onstage.

"Your Honor?" he called out.   Everyone's head swiveled to Jack Frankfurter. For a second, it seemed as though no one really knew what to say, so the Wiener spoke up again. Now this is not an exact reconstruction, but it's damn close.

"Your Honor, all these people you see here before you in the stands are here on behalf of the accused. We all feel we have something to say in regard to Mister Franz' sentencing."

I looked over at Mr. Franz, who had a confused, horrified expression on his face. His lawyer just had a confused expression.   People at the prosecutor's table looked at the Wiener as though he were a talking insect. There was a kind of weighty silence.

Finally, the judge spoke up.

"Who are you? Where did you come from?"

This was a mistake.   All the Wiener needed was someone to engage in dialogue, and he was home free.

"My name is Jack Frankfurter.   I and my fellow companions that you see here before you are all classmates of Mister Franz' son Ted at Windham High. We came here at great expense in our classmate's time of trouble and we feel we have some relevant things to say here in Federal District Court, even though we understand everybody made a deal already.'

Mentally, my jaw was slack. Great expense?

'Plus, we're skipping school without permission and possibly jeopardizing our future college careers so that we could bring certain facts to your attention.'

Well, that was gilding the lily, but we were certainly far from Windham High during school hours.

'Plus, this won't take long and I'll speak for all of us," which was fine with me.

At that, the Wiener, who had cleverly sat at the end of the pew, or whatever they called it, moved to the aisle and up to the little swinging gate. Even he, though, stopped at that point and looked at the judge as if for permission to continue his journey. His Honor looked over at the prosecution table, but got no meaningful indication as to what they thought of the proceedings. There was silence for a time.

"Very well," the judge said.

Very well? Was I on Mars? Quick as a bunny, before the judge could change his mind, the Wiener slid inside and stood before the bench. Now what follows is a totally accurate reconstruction because, unbeknownst to us, he'd written it out on index cards which he gave me later. The only ad lib was the word "Okay".

"Okay. Thank you, your Honor. It is indeed an honor and a privilege to address this court, which being a federal court is way above municipal and state courts as well as the many magistrates administering justice throughout our land. We are all classmates of Mister Franz' son Ted, who is our friend and obviously raised by Mister and Mrs. Franz to be a upright and contributing member of our society, with about a B plus grade average, reflecting favorably on Mister Franz."

Here the Wiener made a deferential gesture towards the defendant.

"Now what you may not know is that during our formative years, going way back, Mister Franz spent a great deal of time and money taking us all to the picture show on numerous occasions and also to Yankee Stadium, home of the great New York Yankees and Mickey Mantle. One summer he even took us all on a camping trip to the Poconos where we learned things like whittling and horseback riding."

The Wiener was doing a great job, and throwing in the Yankees was, I thought, a brilliant touch. How could the judge go against the Mick?

"Now I cannot say all the reasons Mister Franz borrowed a quarter of a million dollars, if we are to believe the newspapers, which as we all know tend to exaggerate in order to sell more papers, which I venture to say would be yellow journalism. But I can say that he spent a considerable amount of those dollars on the youth of Windham, where we are all from, and which the New York Times has called one of the most desirable communities to live in the New York environs."

This, I thought, was kind of a stretch. If old Mr. Franz lifted a quarter of a million big ones, he probably spent two hundred fifty bucks on us, tops. I did a quick calculation: that would be one tenth of a percent, if I had my zeroes right.

"Now we all know the root of common law here in the United States of America is the English common law. I mention this because another figure in history, perhaps more famous than Mister Franz, also stole from the rich and gave to the poor."

Poor? He'd just finished telling the judge we lived in a rich suburb. Still, I could see where he was going.

"And that figure would be – Robin Hood. Yes, that fabled legendary folk hero of England was guilty of the same crime that Mister Franz has been accused of!"

Besides ending his sentence in a preposition, the Wiener was forgetting that Mister Franz had copped a plea.

"So is not Mister Franz, by extension of the English common law which forms the basis of that lady up there with the blindfold, also a folk hero? Yes, in our eyes. We, the youth of Windham, humbly ask that you consider our thoughts when you pronounce sentence on Mister Franz, who is seated right there, and keep in mind his wife and child who will be punished as well during the entire length of his incarceration, if any. And finally, if you want him to make restitution, he can't return all the money because of the considerable sums he spent on us, as I have previously described.'

'Thank you for your time and we are certain you will do the right thing, your Honor. God bless the United States of America."

There was a long silence as the Wiener turned, exited through the little swinging gate and sat back down. Everyone was looking at him with strange expressions, including me.

*   *   *   *

Four years. With time off for good behavior, he'd be out in two and a half.

Chapter 35

Come on baby let the good times roll
Roll all night long
- Let the Good Times Roll, Shirley and Lee, 1956

On New Year's Eve my parents got together with the Schwerins, who had a kid in Wolfie's class named Norman, and had a small New Year's celebration at our house. Norman seemed quiet and respectful, not the sort of kid my brother would pal around with, except that he had no choice that night because the Schwerins brought him along.

The next morning, I wobbled downstairs and saw mom sitting at the breakfast table. It was around 9 am.

"Hey, mom, Happy New Year."

She looked at me, nodding slowly. Mom looked a little thrown together after last night's big soiree. This was likely to be serious.

"I have never had to talk to you about anything, George, have I?" She paused. The question was rhetorical. "Except that time when the policeman brought you home for smacking him with a snowball. Remember that?"

I didn't answer. How could I not remember? She was forgetting about the car emblems, though.

"Or the time your father opened his old briefcase in the basement and found all those car emblems."

No, she wasn't.

That had been just a phase, like I said. Everybody was doing it. Well, a few guys, anyway. You jammed the screwdriver under the little Bel Air emblem, or Oldsmobile rocket, or whatever brand of auto you needed, and yanked. The emblem popped off and you stuck the pins through your garrison belt and wore the adornments. If my parents hadn't gotten so off the wall about the whole thing, the old man could've had his Cadillac. All he had to do was buy the Buick, and I'd have changed out the medallions in no time. Presto - instant Coupe de Ville.

At least I wasn't destructive, like Wolfie. He knocked the taillights off 1958 Imperials with a baseball bat. He must have creamed a dozen of the Chryslers. The stupid taillights stuck up on stalks, right above the fins, daring you to knock them off. It was sort of an early, spectacular version of tee ball.

Or when he got Huey Lenihan next door to get the baseball out of his father's trophy case when we lost our last ball in a pickup game. How were to know it had been autographed by the 1927 Yankees Murderers' Row?

"But you've been a good boy most of the time, George," my mom was saying. "That's why I know last night was something that won't be repeated."

What?

"What do you mean, mom?"

"Not all the girls in this world are like the ones you know from school. Girls who live here in Windham."

She said Windham like the nuns would say "Heaven." Could mom see that well into Marty Stringfellow's car windows? They were tinted, for Chrissake. God, she had eyes like a hawk. Marty had pulled into my driveway with two bimbos from Madison in tow. We'd taken them to the reservoir, which was fine if you overlooked the faint moustaches and Bazooka Double Bubble. I needed to cut this off fast. I decided the best thing was to act contrite and hope she'd buy it.

"You're right, mom. I feel badly about it. It won't happen again."

"That's good, George," she replied. "I have enough to deal with this morning with this business about your brother."

Instantly my mood changed. What was she talking about? Which brother? It must have been Wolfie. Raymond just drooled around the house and stared at the sun. Hah!

"Whaddya mean, Mom? What did he do?"

"I suppose you'll hear about it anyway. Last night the Schwerins and your father and I were thinking back over the years, and we were both congratulating ourselves on how fine our boys were turning out." She shook her head - wrong.

I got a stripped-down version of the story from mom, but Wolfie really gave me the details. It seems that while my delusional parents and the Schwerins were congratulating themselves on their wonderful kids, Wolfie and Norman were blowing up mailboxes over on Rolling Hill Drive. I guess it was in the genes; I felt a kind of older sibling pride. Some of it was probably because that meant Wolfie was all right again, or at least I hoped, now that he was back doing normal things. I mean, I know I'd been a bit critical of some of his actions, like ruining Kathy Obermeister and all, but that's just out of brotherly affection. You know what I mean. If anybody did anything to the Wolf or Raymond, I'd –

I don't know how I got off on that tangent. Anyway, none of the parents knew these kids had even left the house while they were entertaining each other. Norman had an arsenal of ashcans and cherry bombs, the really good kind that are hard to get anymore and cost a dime each. These were powerful and waterproof. Several times a year some kid would light one in a Windham High boys' room and flush it down the toilet, dart out the stall and close the door. BOOM. End of toilet. A huge geyser.

When the police caught Wolfie and Norman, they had blown up maybe a dozen mailboxes. It seemed maybe Norman wasn't so quiet and respectful after all. The thing was, though, they were so stupid they did them all right in a straight line so the cops had a trail of shredded metal and thunderous noise to follow. Really, I thought I'd set a better example than that.

I asked Wolfie about it later. He kind of looked at me sideways, with a sly grin.

"I'm a lycanthrope," is all he said.

What? I had to look it up.

Hey, the Wolfman was back!

Chapter 36
Ah be careful what you say
Or you'll give yourself away
Odds are you won't live to see tomorrow
-Secret Agent Man, Johnny Rivers, 1964

When the feds raided Windham on a snowy Thursday evening in January, I had already fallen asleep listening to Gene Shepherd on WOR and so I missed the whole thing. Actually, I would have missed the whole thing anyway because Robbie van Arsdale lived maybe two miles away and they didn't use sirens or anything, they just drove up to his house around 11 p.m. in khaki colored sedans with stenciling on the sides. It wasn't until the next morning when I was called out of class, along with Brownie, Jones and Dieter Becker, that we had any inkling we'd become involved in the Cold War.

Mrs. Kritzinger had rushed into 8:30 a.m. math class looking as though she'd been caught playing The Doctor Game with Mr. Freisler again, all disheveled and her mouth an O. She announced breathlessly that Brownie, Jones and I were to get down to the office *right now*. We looked at each other as we gathered our books and got up from our desks. The whole class was staring at us.

What had we done now? I wondered. Brownie just shrugged. All the way down the hall I mentally reviewed the felonies we'd committed back as far as the statute of limitations would allow, but couldn't think of much offhand. Misdemeanors, sure. It turned out Mrs. Kritzinger led us not to the office, but the library. Two military guys stood outside like they were guarding the place. They had these cool M-1 rifles. I realized with a shock they *were* guarding the place, probably. What the hell? We were ushered in, minus Mrs. Kritzinger. I never knew the soft click of a door behind your back could be an ominous sound.

This sure as hell wasn't going to be about an overdue book.

Dieter Muller and the Wiener were already seated on one side of a library table. There were four serious looking gentlemen on the other side, two in Air Force uniform. I mean, I guessed it was Air Force because I didn't think any other branch wore blue. Maybe it was Princeton. Was this some elaborate college acceptance ceremony? Not too likely. The other two were in suits, like Windham commuters. No one else was in the library, except Principal Dunwood, who sat at the end.

What the hey? My mind flashed to a couple of mailboxes we'd blown with cherry bombs a year ago. The mail was federal, I was pretty sure. That was the only federal offense I could think of, unless carrying fake I.D. across the state line to buy booze in Staten Island was interstate commerce, sort of. Suddenly I could think of all kinds of things we'd done that might fall under U.S. jurisdiction, including dropping a lit kerosene smudge pot onto an Erie Lackawanna freight engine as it chugged under a bridge in Madison. The ball had been marking a pothole on Kings Road and we'd grabbed it, not realizing the damn thing was filthy and the kerosene flame would coat the roof liner of Freddy Hirsch's car with soot as we drove to the bridge.   Plus it was really hot.   Anyway, we'd expected the thing to smash apart and the train erupt in a fireball, but all the stupid pot did was clonk on the engine and fly off, killing the flame.   I knew the railroads were federally regulated by the Interstate Commerce Commission, courtesy of Mr. Kritzinger's class.   Maybe they had a small ICC army.   Or was that the FCC?

Anyway, you can see how my brain was malfunctioning.

Boy, I was nervous as hell.   My heart felt like it was going to break a rib, booming inside my chest.   My throat was a desert.   I looked over at the others.   They looked much calmer than I.   I put my hands in my lap because they were shaking.   I hate when that happens.   I hoped my voice wouldn't quaver if I had to say anything.

I looked outside the big library window.   It was snowing, big fat flakes drifting down and piling up on the window sill.   It all looked so pretty and peaceful.   How could the sill look like that when we were about to face a firing squad, maybe?

Suit #1 spoke first:

"Boys, my name is Special Agent Langeman.   This is my partner, Special Agent White.   We're from the Federal Bureau of Investigation."

Eliot Ness!   The new TV series.   We all had watched it. Holy shit.   I felt a big jolt of electricity.   Special agents?   Did the FBI have regular agents too?   I couldn't bel-

"Can we see some identification?" asked the Wiener. No one spoke for a moment as all heads swiveled towards the owner of the voice.   My mouth was open along with Principal Dunwood's.   Was the Wiener super cool or just nuts?   I decided

I already knew the answer. I mentally winced, hoping the cuffs or rubber hose weren't going to come out, but both suits reached inside and came out with these neat leather fold over wallets and flipped them open. Unbelievably, the Wiener got half up from his chair, leaned over the table and held Special Agent Langeman's identification by a corner as he peered at the badge. He nodded, apparently satisfied. The suits put away the I.D. I hoped the Wiener wasn't going to ask to see their guns. Or Brownie. Or Jones, for that matter.

"Are those rifles loaded?" the Weiner asked, jerking his thumb toward the door. This was ignored.

"I believe you fellows are acquainted with a Mr. van Arsdale?" Special Agent Langeman said.

"You mean Robbie van Arsdale's dad?" Jones asked.

"No, I mean Robert van Arsdale, the boy in your class." If he knew Robbie was in our class, why would he ask? I thought. Maybe that's what the feds did, not take anything for granted. I didn't think they were just morons, but I was willing to keep an open mind.

We all nodded. What had Robbie done? Or maybe what had happened to him? Oh, shit, was he in jail?

Or worse?

For the first time in maybe ten years, I wanted my mom, kind of.

Special Agent Langeman eyeballed the four of us across the library table. "Do you remember sitting in the soda shop after school some weeks ago with Mr. van Arsdale?"

I cringed again because I knew what was coming:

"You mean Robbie's father?" Jones asked. Oh, God. He did it with a straight face, too.

Special Agent Langeman took a breath. I think that between the Wiener and Jones, the feds were starting to get an idea who they were up against, and Brownie hadn't even spoken up yet. I tried to look innocent and young. Maybe I could tell them I was only sixteen. Didn't they have to treat you like a juvenile if you were too young to drive?

"I'm only sixteen," I said, only it came out like a frog gargling.

"What?" asked Special Agent White.

"I'm an American," I croaked, only it came out like I'd swallowed a ball of feathers.

"What?" asked Special Agent Langeman.

"We're in the Sweet Shoppe all the time if we're not at practice," Jones said. "Robbie, too."

"Who are you guys?" Wiener asked, wagging his finger between the two men in blue.

"Do any of you recall Mister va-- Robert van Arsdale mentioning anything about national defense during any of those get-togethers?" Special Agent Langeman asked.

National defense? Was he talking about our soccer team? We had finished #1, after all.

"What are you talking about?" asked Brownie.

"You mean like *defense* defense?" asked Dieter.

Everyone looked puzzled for a moment, and then it hit me.

"The Titan missile silo!" I might as well have yelled there was a bomb in the room. The reaction was electric. The two guys in blue looked at me, eyes widening.

"Keep your voice down, please," said Special Agent Langeman.

"That's who you guys are, right?" I pointed at the two guys in blue. "Air Force. It's true. You're putting ICBMs in Convent Station! Wow! It must be true!"

Well, they never really admitted it, but evidently construction was only a couple of weeks away. They had a lot of questions for us, mainly concerned with who we might have told. Not to be outdone, we had questions for them, mainly how did they find out we knew anything? It turned out stupid Robbie had sent a letter to President Eisenhower and it only took about four seconds after it arrived at the White House before the goddamn Pentagon put out an alert.

We were told how serious a breach of security this was and were asked to sign some papers, which Jones and Brownie and the Wiener refused to do. Dieter said he'd think about it. Special Agent White tried to put the heat on us, mentioning something about a National Secrets Act, which I had never heard of, but then again maybe it was secret. Unbelievably, Brownie turned it around.

"We're all loyal Americans here. It insults us that you want us to sign something. But I'll tell you what, I'm sure we could be persuaded to forget all about it."

A bribe?!? Hush money?! Payola?!?

In the end, I suppose it was a standoff. Nobody signed anything and nobody got paid anything. I'd like to say I had a hand in any of it, but the two croaked comments were my only input. I'm sorry to admit I kind of caved. The Wiener asked if they were going to go ahead anyway, and how many missiles were going into the installation, and their combined megatonnage, and were they aimed at Moscow, or maybe Vladivostok, but he might as well have been pissing into the wind. He also asked how old he had to be to apply for an FBI Special Agent job, and they ignored that as well.

If the feds had come to Windham to try and contain the story, they sure as hell went about it the wrong way. Although none of us said anything, as far as I know, it was all over the school like a virus by lunchtime. It kind of made you wonder about our government.

Brownie, Jones and the Wiener were going to smack Robbie van Arsdale for awhile, even though they'd almost made a profit off the deal. Robbie showed us a copy of his letter.

```
Dear President Eisenhower:

     I am a senior at Windham High School
in Windham, New Jersey, not far from
Convent Station.    I understand the Air
Force is contemplating a Titan missile
installation in Convent, and I am writing
to urge you to change the location to some
remote area, possibly in the Midwest or
deep South.    It is my understanding that
these Titans do not need to be in close
proximity to the U.S.S.R. to be effective,
so it seems the choice of sites is perhaps
political.
     We citizens of Windham have enough to
worry about because we are within thirty
miles of New York City, which assuredly is
a Soviet missile target, probably with
multiple nuclear warheads, but if you put
ICBMs in Convent Station we will be
vaporized for sure.    There are many nice
families in Windham, Convent Station and
environs including small children who would
really like to have an uninterrupted
```

future, as would I and my friends and
family.   My   classmates   would   also
appreciate your attending to this matter.
        Thank you in advance.

Sincerely,

Robert van Arsdale III
"I like Ike"

P.S. - Please say hello to Mrs. Eisenhower
for me.

          *   *   *   *

After reading the letter, no one was mad at Robbie
anymore, since our classmate had tried to save our lives, sort of.
In a way, the whole thing was kind of cool if you didn't think
about what it all really meant.

Chapter 37

Poetry in motion
See her gently sway
- *Poetry in Motion, Johnny Tillotson, 1961*

When Mr. Glendenning announced an extra credit assignment, he gave us our choice of composing a poem or writing a critique of something already written. "Extra credit" were code words: if you didn't do the assignment your grades for the marking period were toast. Since I had the creative poetic ability of a woodchuck, I just wrote about the work I considered the greatest poem ever written, *The Love Song of J. Alfred Prufrock*, by T.S. Eliot. It was a little random, and bounced around all over the place, but there was really a great deal in the poem that could be pondered and a lot of graceful expressions, such as the one about the fog standing in drains and seeing it was late and curling about the house and falling asleep, like some kind of crazy cat. That T.S. Eliot could really write. I tried to explain what I thought it all meant, but words kind of failed me, and I was frustrated somewhat. It all seemed to work out OK, though, because Mr. Glendenning gave me an A-. I figured that was not so much a tribute to how good my essay was, but how shitty the others probably were.

When we had to turn in the assignments, Mr. Glendenning made the biggest mistake of his high school teaching career, I'm sure, even though I don't know anything about his career before coming to old WHS. His second biggest mistake had been letting the Wiener read his book report in class, and he was about to top that, which we would have thought an impossibility.

"Who wants to read their poetry essays?" he asked. Once again, the Wiener's hand shot up immediately. There was a silence. Then Mr. Glendenning nodded, slowly. Jones, Brownie and I exchanged glances. Another classic in the making?

"Mr. Frankfurter, I see your hand is up. Do you want to try reading in front of class again?" From the sort of amused way he said it, I believe he had no earthly idea what he was getting into.

"Sure, I'd like to read my poetry assignment," the Wiener said. He stood up, gathered his papers and came to the front of the room.

Here's what he said, more or less. I got the poems from him later, so that part is pretty accurate:

"Poetry Assignment
English 12A
Mr. Glendenning
Jack Frankfurter

'My assignment concerns an anthology of poems I would like to quote from." Here he stopped reading for a moment and looked up from his paper.

"An anthology is a bunch of stuff put together," he said to the class, helpfully. "In this case, it's a group of poems about similar subjects. OK?" He looked around the room for signs of understanding.

"Mr. Frankfurter," said Mr. Glendenning, "I believe we do understand what an anthology is. Please continue." The guy hadn't recognized the warning signs.

"OK. Let's see - oh, yeah. OK.

'I'll read a few and then discuss my analysis." The Wiener was warming up.

> "No use
> Knowing
> How to pick 'em
> If your half-shaved
> Whiskers stick 'em
> Burma-Shave"

There was a brief silence. The silence of a whole class, suddenly stupefied. Mr. Glendenning's jaw was slack, again, but he hadn't or wasn't able to speak. Naturally, the Wiener continued blithely on.

> "Violets are blue
> Roses are pink
> On graves
> Of those
> Who drive and drink
> Burma-Shave"

And more roadside wisdom:

> "Doesn't she
> Kiss you
> Like she useter?

Perhaps she's seen
A smoother rooster!!
Burma-Shave"

There was a squeaking noise coming from Mr.
Glendenning.

"Wh - what?" he said. It wasn't very loud, but I heard
it. Brownie had his arms around his head, down on his desk, and
I saw his shoulders shaking with silent laughter. Unbelievably,
the Wiener had done it again.

"The whale
Put Jonah
Down the hatch
But coughed him up
Because he scratched
Burma-Shave"

Honest to God, Jones had fallen out of his chair and was
on the floor, silently heaving. I saw tears coming out of his
eyes, he was laughing so hard. There were a few other muffled
sounds, so I knew the dam was going to break momentarily.
The Wiener must have sensed something, also, because he sped
up his delivery:

"Altho insured
Remember, kiddo
They don't pay you
They pay
Your widow
Bur-"

It all happened at once, then. It had been a delayed reaction, like to an accident. The class roared, louder and longer than I ever heard, and underneath it all we could hear Mr. Glendenning, who was just finding his voice:

"Aaargh! Frankfurter! Don't you ever - Don't you ever - Get your sorry -"

And the Wiener, incredibly, indignantly:

"WHAT? WHAT'S SO GODDAMN FUNNY? THIS IS AMERICANA, YOU KNOW?"

Chapter 38

American history and practical math
you study 'em hard and hopin' to pass
- School Day, Chuck Berry, 1957

There still had been no news about the hit and run death
of Po Jackson since we'd made our phone call to Windham's
finest. Brownie had made a follow-up call to the Windham
police and reached Martin Rohleder again. When he asked if
they'd interviewed Mr. Moffitt and examined the Mercedes, he
was told the department was "looking into the matter."

It sounded like a big stall to us, so Brownie called the
State Police barracks a few days later and repeated our
information. He told the troopers he'd given the same stuff to
the Windham police, but they hadn't seemed to have done
anything, and the staties were very interested in that. Brownie
used the same code name, Milner, for the reward. I still had
kind of ambivalent feelings about ratting out the Moffitts, but as
I had told Jones and Brownie I didn't think we had a choice.

One change on my schedule during the second semester
was study hall in place of driver's education. This particular
study hall was in the library, so we were grouped in tables of
six. I happened to be placed with Mary Anne. What luck!
There were many really knockout girls in Windham, as I have
described, all blonde Aryan cheerleader types, but Mary Anne

Moffitt was at the top of the food chain. Besides sniffing around the subject of the dented Mercedes, I thought maybe I could find out if the Greaser was really nailing her and her mother, although I figured Mrs. Moffitt wouldn't tell anyone, much less her daughter or her besotted husband.

Even though Mary Anne lived only about a half mile from me, we hadn't known each other that well before second semester study hall. We had taken the same school bus for years, but were really only acquaintances. Of course, I darted for the seat next to her the first day in the library.

Nobody really studied in study hall, except girls and maybe a few of the A.V. guys. We were allowed to talk, as long as we were fairly quiet. Bruce Himmler was at the same table. He wasn't interested in talking with Mary Anne Moffitt, or anyone else, and was only occasionally obnoxious by hissing at us to keep it down while he studied. I would return the favor with a Nazi salute. The only time I heard him talk, really, was when he opened his book bag and found two halves of a salami sandwich on white jammed in with his books. Someone hadn't wanted the lunch they had probably stolen. The mustard had dried into glue and stuck everything inside together. Bruce was all atwitter at the mess.

He never should have acted upset; two days later he found the crumbly remains of some Oreos and a melted Clark bar at the bottom of his fagbag. Pretty soon his briefcase was becoming a regular delicatessen. The worst was the remaining half of the Wiener's airborne egg salad sandwich, which he had stolen anyway from Michele Hoyt's locker. Another time, the Wiener lifted a chicken wing from her lunch and left it in one of Sherry Stahl's sweater pockets, hanging in the oinker's locker over Thanksgiving recess. You can imagine how ripe that was when we returned to school.

Anyway, I got off the subject again. (*Narrative urgency*, Mr. Williams. Stop drooling words!)

Over the first month, I talked quite a bit with Mary Anne Moffitt at our table in the reference section. At first, we chatted about school stuff, what teachers were any good, who did you like, what subjects interested you, and boring junk like that. Crap you would never talk about with other guys. Eventually, I steered the conversation around to automobiles.

"I thought I saw your mom the other day on Noe Avenue," I said. "What kind of car does she drive?"

"She has a Cadillac. A black Cadillac."

"Do you drive it?"

"Sometimes. It's too big."

"Yeah? What do you like to drive?"

"My dad bought a Mercedes when I got my license," she said.

She hadn't said My dad bought *me* a Mercedes. I didn't know if it was her car.

"I've never seen you driving it."

"It got banged up. My dad hit a deer."

"I'll bet that cost a fortune to fix. A Mercedes."

"I don't know. I know they're waiting for a part, so it's not fixed yet."

I immediately told Jones and Brownie about the conversation. It left us more suspicious than ever. There was nothing we could do but wait.

In study hall, Mary Anne gradually opened up about herself and her family a little bit. Mostly about her father. Fathers are very important in girls' eyes, as you probably know, and I think if they don't feel good about their fathers they aren't going to feel too good about themselves, or have wholesome relationships with boys. I don't mean just the sex part. That's just my observation, anyway. I think maybe that was why she was going out with the Greaser, because otherwise why would anybody go out with some hairy Italian? He had learned the secret of listening to Mary Anne, and clucking in sympathy at those things that bothered her. I think, though, that I got more intimate emotionally with Mary Anne, at least on the subject of her father.

"What does your father call your mother?" she asked me one day. Believe it or not, I had to think for a sec.

"I dunno. Mostly Mary, I guess, but sometimes honey. Mostly when he wants something, like maybe the paper or a sarsaparilla."

"Not baby doll or sexpot or anything?"

"What? Of course not." I probably shouldn't have said that. Her bottom lip got trembly.

And a minute later:

"Sarsaparilla? Not like a whiskey and soda?"

"Ahh, no. Maybe a cream soda, sometimes." I wanted to make something up, like a boilermaker, but I couldn't do that to my dad. Actually, I could do that to my dad, but I didn't think of it in time.

Mr. Moffitt was quite ambivalent in his daughter's eyes. She loved him, of course, but his drinking and sleazy behavior really disturbed Mary Anne. I tried to find out what exact sleazy behavior she was talking about, like maybe making a piñata out of old Po, but she never got too specific. A couple of times her eyes welled up in study hall and I quickly had to change the subject. I think it was mostly just his general manner and attitude. From my brief encounter with her old man the souse, I certainly could agree with her. Of course, that led me to wonder if Mrs. Moffitt was involved in any sleazy behavior as well, which would put things in an entirely different light, at least as far as Mrs. Moffitt was concerned.

Coveting Mrs. Moffitt was a break from coveting Miss Van Aldewehe, at least at any one moment. Maybe it was an older woman thing. Now before you bring up that sort of aberration with Mrs. Carnahan a few years ago, remember I was a lot younger then and relatively inexperienced. Plus I hadn't known she was nuts or that her creepo husband was a major pervert. And, as I said, that memory box is locked up tight forever. End of story.

It was funny, but the better I got to know Mary Anne Moffitt the more I liked her and the less I thought about sex as it pertained to her. I don't mean this in a faggy way. I knew Rich Venzoni was about as sensitive as a steam shovel, and so whatever consolation or emotional support he provided her was phony just to get in her pants, but I kind of regarded Mary Anne as a person, not just a girl. I looked forward to our study hall sessions. For some reason, I didn't tell Jones or anybody about our conversations. I don't think you would have, either.

The other thing was, of course, the fact that we'd finked out to the cops about the dented Mercedes. I felt guilty about that every time I talked to her, sort of. One third of two grand was $666.67, though, and I'd already figured out all the stuff I could buy with that kind of dough, like a new Stratocaster or Fender Twin Reverb amp. Part of me really wanted the money, but another part, maybe the bigger part, hoped the silver Gull Wing hadn't been involved. I felt kind of sorry for Mary Anne, even though she was a knockout and all the boys would kill to get in her pants and she probably would wind up winning Miss America or something. I wondered if maybe she knew or suspected anything about the dented 300 SL. That would have been a terrible dilemma: how do you turn in your dad? I decided she knew nothing.

There was one funny thing, though. Mary Anne was always perfectly groomed, with not a hair out of place, and she smelled like lilacs. Actually, I'm not sure what lilacs smell like, but they probably smell like Mary Anne Moffitt. She probably didn't even sweat during p.e., I'd bet. But when I sat next to her, I noticed her nails. They were painted and all, but she'd bitten them down to the quick.

Chapter 39

C. C. Rider
See What You Has Done?
- C.C. Rider, Chuck Willis, 1957

As spring blew its warm breath of promise into
Windham, activities moved outdoors. Our bodies quickened
with the natural rhythm of life, and even Coach Weber talked
about ending History of Sports for the balance of the year. His
experimental program had been a dismal failure, culminating in
the Wiener's shocking "F--- you!" in class.

It was all over a drawing. Jones, besides being a
maestro in oils and watercolors, was naturally inclined to
caricatures. These were of professional quality, inspired by his
clever sense of humor. The exaggerated figures unerringly
highlighted some major character flaw in the subject. History of
Sports, of course, was a great time to belt out a drawing because
there were no notes to take and no need to pay any attention to
whatever Coach Weber was saying or doing.

Sometime early in the school year, the Wiener and
Jones learned that Coach Weber owned a hunting bow. He
loved to hunt and the woods around Windham were occasional
deer country. On the first mild spring Saturday, Jones and the
Wiener followed Coach into the Great Swamp after first lifting
a bunch of expensive arrows and feathers from his car. They

waited until he fired off a handful, probably at some helpless woodchuck or squirrel. Now good arrows were not inexpensive, so a serious bowman would try and recover his missiles. Despite the danger, the Wiener managed to sneak up and snag a few, picking them off the ground or prying a couple out of tree trunks before Coach could get to the site. He stuck them in a rotting dead raccoon. This wound up costing Coach Weber a bit of money, and provided some hilarity amongst the gym class.

Jones' drawing showed just that. Boy, his caricatures were hilarious. Weber's gangly build was exaggerated so that he looked like a bunch of rubber bands in sneakers, and the vacant expression that usually graced his visage was now a moronic drool. The picture showed a whole bunch of arrows sticking in nearby trees while a deer was looking calmly at Coach, about 10 feet away. The quiver was empty. Of course, the Wiener was in the background, prying an arrow from a tree trunk.

It must have taken Jones all of five minutes to pen this drawing, which could have won a prize. He was that good. Of course, he had no regard for the value of his work so he just gave it to somebody near him, and it started around the class. When it got to the Wiener, he took one look and burst into laughter. Coach saw the transaction.

The pot that had been brewing all year between them was about to boil over.

"What's so funny, Mr. Frankfurter?"

"Aah, nothing, Coach. It's nothing."

Quick as a bunny Weber moved to the Wiener's desk and snatched up the drawing. His eyes bugged out.

"What the - " he said, astonished. That started Jones laughing, which in turn started several of us laughing, even though only a couple of us had seen the drawing. As I have said, Jones had that kind of laugh. Of course, the Wiener couldn't hold it in either.

"MR. FRANKFURTER GET DOWN TO THE PRINCIPAL'S OFFICE RIGHT NOW!" yelled Weber.

"What?" said Wiener. "What are you talking about? I didn't draw the goddamn thing."

"JUST GET YOUR BUTT OUT OF HERE AND DOWN TO THE OFFICE!" yelled Weber, gesturing toward the door. By this time, I am sure Miss Van Aldewehe next door was beside herself again.

"Hey, coach. I didn't draw the goddamn thing, I just told you. Somebody gave it to me."

"NOW. N-O-W NOW MISTER!"

This had become a seminal moment. Somehow, I know Coach Weber's entire teaching life would be forever altered by what would happen next.

The Wiener hadn't moved. The two stared at each other across the Wiener's desk for what seemed like minutes. Then came the two magic words I never heard in school before or since. Well, actually three words. The Wiener didn't even raise his voice, but said evenly, just loud enough for us all to hear:

"F--- you, Coach."

The class gasped as one. No one moved, not even Coach Weber, whose jaw hung even more ajar than usual. Finally, the Wiener got up from around the desk and walked casually to the front of the classroom. Without another word, he opened the door and left.

I don't exactly remember what happened after that, or what Coach Weber did or said after the Wiener left, because we were all in a slight state of shock. No one had even laughed. The Wiener had crossed the invisible line and now we would all wait to see just how the wheels of administrative justice would grind over Jack "The Wiener" Frankfurter. By two o'clock, the story was everywhere. The Wiener was either a hero or a madman, possibly both, but in any event what he had done was unthinkable. The student body held its collective breath.

And nothing happened. Nothing happened for two days until we figured out that the Wiener never did go to the office, but just hung out shooting baskets in the gym until his next class. Coach never turned him in to the office, either, so the whole thing just died right there. And after that, no student in Windham High would ever respect Coach Weber again, and doubtless that's why Dick Orr showered the chemistry lab class with glass and caustic chemicals.

Coach Weber would leave for another job at the end of the school year. I kind of felt sorry for him, then. In the fall, he had brought his wife and little boy to school for some social event, to meet us, which was something no intelligent teacher would ever do. I remember his little boy was friendly enough, and his wife, Araignée, had a sweet smile. I guess she was French, with a name like that, and a trace of an accent. Coach's biggest mistake was that he had tried to be nice to us, instead of an authority figure. He was doomed, like some Shakespearean character, with a fatal flaw. The world's screwed up, sometimes.

Or maybe it was us.

Chapter 40

And then along came Jones
Along Came Jones, The Coasters, 1959

Jones and I were on the track team in the spring. His specialty was the shot, and he could put the twelve pound ball into the next county.

Jones held the state record as he was enormously strong, a 5'10" tank, and his neck was as big around as my thighs, just about. That's why it was so funny he was an artist as well. I ran the hundred yard dash and was Windham's high jumper. I won my share of events, but was not very close to a state record. The shot put and the high jump always started late but at least I had the hundred to break the monotony. Jones had no other events and so most of the afternoon was really boring for him. We were hanging around the infield during our home meet against Westfield when I asked Coach Louden about running the half mile.

"Hey coach, how about I run the half mile?"

"What, you?" he asked.

"Sure," I said.

"Today? You ever run the half before?"

"Sure."

I had never run the half mile before, but I knew of course it was twice around the cinder track. After all, I couldn't get lost.

"Williams, you ever run a half mile before?" he asked again, narrowing his eyes. I interpreted his question in the aggregate.

"Of course, I have. I'm pretty good. Besides, there's at least an hour before the hundred so why not?"

Coach couldn't think of why not so he just shrugged and told me to go for it.

"Don't get in Pond's way," he said. Tommy Pond was our regular half miler, and he never won anything, so I hoped I wouldn't get in his way because that meant I'd probably be last. Three weeks after graduation, Tommy would come face-to-face with the spider, snagged in its tripwire. Who could yet know the eerie chain of events spun in the shadowy corners of our All-American town?

I reported in to the track official as Tommy came over. Pond was a friendly guy, but kept to himself, as far as I could tell. At least I didn't know what crowd he hung around with.

"Hey, George, gonna try the half, hey? Good luck." He grinned and held out his hand. We shook and I returned the greeting.

"Same to you, Tommy, but not too much. Coach says to stay out of your way. Just follow my shorts real close - I'm gonna jet along on farts. You'll come in second."

"OK, pardner," he grinned. As I said, Tommy was an all right guy, and I didn't know him too well, but he had gone out of his way years ago to be nice to me after the Johnny Broadhead thing. He had just come over in school, said a few words and patted me on the back. I always appreciated that; it was so thoughtful for a kid. Nobody else had said anything at all; even my parents avoided the subject.

A couple of my teammates wandered over to the half mile out of curiosity when they saw I was running. Actually, I was pretty keyed up at trying something new and everybody looked at me in disbelief when I knelt down on the track to start. I had forgotten you just start standing up, unlike the hundred, so I was embarrassed already and the race hadn't even begun.

That was nothing compared to what was to come. I made the sign of the cross, pretending I was genuflecting, and stood up, brushing cinders off my knee. I acted nonchalant, despite my red face, while Pond tried to hide his grin. The gun fired and we took off down the track. You had to stay in your lane for the first hundred yards or so, and by the time we could all run in the inside lane I was leading the race by several yards. I was amazed and from the yelling I could hear in the background so were my teammates. I thought I heard a voice from behind yelling "Go, George!" which could only have been Tommy Pond. We finished the first lap and my lead had lengthened to maybe fifteen yards.

I felt an incredible euphoria and, out of the corner of my eye, saw Coach looking at me as he trotted over for a better look. The crowd noise grew louder. We had about three quarters of a lap to go. I saw headlines in tomorrow's Courier.

Then I saw something else. Something odd. I saw spots in my vision, and suddenly there was no air at all. It was like I had run into the side of an invisible garage. My vision seemed to narrow and the dots were dancing around. I'm not sure what happened after that, except that I had the sensation I was running in slow motion and that everybody was passing me. Jones said that I finally staggered off the track onto the infield grass with about forty yards to go and tottered for awhile before collapsing on my face. He couldn't stop laughing as he told me. Some friend.

How embarrassing. It's embarrassing now, just telling about it, so you can imagine how embarrassing it was then. High school life is punctuated with embarrassing moments, and I certainly had my share. I hadn't known anything about pacing myself. You would think a high school student in reasonable shape from soccer could run a lousy half mile at full speed, but the truth is you can't. That's what I learned.

Unfortunately, of course, everybody in New Jersey heard about it before the weekend and I was the butt of a lot of ribbing. What the hell, at least I tried. That's what I told myself, anyway, but That Bastard Heileman said that was just a rationalization for knowing I had been an asshole. Thanks a lot, Heileman.

Jones broke the state shot put record again in the next meet against Convent Station and I managed to win the hundred. It was a lot easier without having passed out beforehand.

Chapter 41

So hush little baby
Don't you cry . . .
-All My Trials, The Shadows, 1961

Kathy Obermeister was pregnant.

Maybe. Jesus God.

I'd slept in Saturday, after our track meet with Convent Station and a Wallyburger and beers with Jones at Wally's Two Bars. You had to be at least twelve to drink beer in that gin mill. Wallyburgers were great; the secret was they never changed the grease on the grill. I'd gotten in around midnight and when I awoke the sunlight was streaming in my window. I turned to look at the clock and just about jumped out of bed. Wolfie was sitting in the chair next to my bookcase, looking at me.

"Christ, what're you doing? You scared the crap out of me."

Wolfie didn't say anything. He had a scared, far-off look.

"What's the matter with you? How long have you been sitting there?" I asked.

"I don't know. I've been waiting for you to wake up."

I propped myself up on an elbow. There was sleep in my eyes.

"Listen, George. I have a problem. I gotta talk to you about it. You have to help me."

"You're my brother, for Chrissake. What do you think? What's the matter?"

"Kathy Obermeister says she's pregnant."

What? My brain was full of cobwebs because I thought he said –

"What?!" About 110 volts spurted through my body. I was wide awake now. "You – she - what? How do you know? What did she say exactly? How does she know? What's she gonna do about it? . . . What the hell are you talking about?"

"She said she missed her period three weeks ago. I'm really scared."

Now I wasn't exactly an expert in the field, but I was pretty sure you couldn't tell much until you'd missed at least two.

"Listen, Wolfie, I'm no expert here, but I'm pretty sure you can't tell much of anything until she misses at least one more."

"Yeah?"

"Yeah. You didn't use a rubber or anything?"

I didn't ask this accusingly. Nobody used the damn things. All they did was leave a circle in the side of your wallet. I had asked Jones about it when we were sophomores.

"What're you, nuts?" he'd said. "Do you take a shower with a raincoat on? You think I'm gonna get some babe all hot and sweaty and ready to go and I'm going to call timeout and fumble around in the back seat and open the stupid package and try to roll the goddamn thing on? And you think she's going to wait and still be all hot to trot?"

"You're supposed to roll it on?" I asked. Boy, that was good to know. Jones had cracked up.

"Hey, I really knew that," I'd said, but I really hadn't. If Jones' philosophy was prevalent, I'd wondered how many Windham girls had gotten pregnant and nobody knew about it. Maybe they just went away for awhile or something. Or was that Madison?

Anyway, Wolfie shook his head. "I guess that was pretty dumb."

The whole thing seemed surreal. How could this be? He ought to be worrying about his nine iron shots, not making little Wolves.

Actually, his nine iron shots were right on the money.

"What am I going to do?"

My first thought was to call Jones and Brownie. They'd know, probably. I told the Wolf those guys would be discreet and he said okay.

They agreed to meet me right away, especially since I said I'd buy lunch at Fairview C C, where we were members at the moment. Fairview was a new club, without a doorman, championship tradition or nice old wood in the locker room. It had been carved out of The Great Swamp, so it was always soggy. They actually let women play on weekdays.

What the hell, we'd already been kicked out of all the exclusive clubs.

We sat out on the patio where we'd have some privacy. The weather was still pretty cool and so we were alone. We all ordered club sandwiches and milkshakes. I had one of Wolfie's bogus charge numbers so it wasn't costing anything. From where we sat, we could see foursomes as they approached the eighteenth green. It would have been a pretty sight, normally.

"I don't know this girl," Jones said. "Do you? What's she like?"

"She's nice," I said. "Sweet, innocent type."

"Not too sweet and innocent, though, is she?" asked Brownie. He had a point. "Let's look at the options. One, she's not pregnant, either because she's panicking too early or she's making it up. Let's say she's on the level. So if she turns out be foaling, she can have the kid or not. Mary Ellen Lundgren went away last summer, remember?"

I didn't remember. Wow. "She was pregnant?"

"Some guy from Morristown, freshman at Lehigh. You didn't know that? It was all around school."

"She gave it up for adoption?" I asked. Jones made a guess-so gesture.

Brownie resumed. "Okay. Adoption. That's an alternative. Obviously, she can't keep it – him – whatever. So that's not really an option. The other thing is to get rid of it."

"That's kind of harsh," I said. It wouldn't be like taking out the garbage, for Chrissake.

"I don't mean it that way," Brownie said. "You know what I mean. You got to face reality here. There aren't any good options."

"Do we know anybody?" Jones asked. "How about Herbie Schultz' dad?"

Out of the corner of my eye, I saw some golfer chip up and hit the pin from about a hundred and forty yards. It hardly registered.

Brownie shook his head. "Can't use a local doctor. First of all, he'd be required to inform her parents because she's a minor. I'm assuming she's not going to want them to know."

"He's right," Jones said. I wondered how they knew that.

"So who then?" I asked. "Some guy in Newark with a coat hanger and a Bunsen burner? We can't do that."

"They don't use Bunsen burners in Newark," Brownie said.

Jones leaned in, although the closest people were forty yards away, approaching the green. "Last year, I picked up something from this broad in Madison, like a rash. I went to some G.P. in Summit, a young guy. I told him I got it off a toilet seat. He said, what did you do, screw it?" Jones laughed at the memory. "Anyway, I could ask him."

Almost unconsciously, I moved my chair back from him a little bit. He noticed.

"Don't worry, I'm all fixed up. It's Barb that has to worry." He laughed harder.

"If she gets it done legitimately someplace, it's gonna cost," Brownie said.

"Where the hell can you do it legitimately?" Jones asked.

Brownie shrugged. "Mexico, maybe? Wolfie have any dough? Does she?"

"I don't know about her. Wolfie's got some money, yeah, in a savings account. But my mom's name is on it too. He can't take it out by himself." I thought a minute. "I guess I'd have to pay for it out of my band money."

"If that's what happens, we'll help out," Jones said. Brownie nodded. I kind of got a lump in my throat.

"Listen, speaking of money, we may be getting some," Brownie said.

"What do you mean?" Joes asked.

"Dick Orr said he was driving home yesterday and a tow truck was hauling the Moffitt's Mercedes out of their driveway."

"Yeah? Was it a cop tow truck? Was there a cop car there too?"

"Dunno. I asked him that. He didn't notice who was towing the car, he just noticed the car because it's so expensive."

"So it could just be getting fixed."

"Maybe but I don't think so," Brownie said. "Even if it wasn't exactly legal with the busted windshield, wouldn't you just drive the car to the dealer for repairs?" That sounded probably right.

The sandwiches came. Usually they tasted great, especially since they were free, but the lump was still there and this time mine tasted like sawdust.

Chapter 42

Come on, baby
Let the good times roll
Roll all night long
Let the Good Times Roll, Shirley and Lee, 1956

On a rare Tuesday track meet, we traveled to Florham Park and I lost my race. Although I was a little depressed, worrying about the Wolfie-Kathy Obermeister situation, the blame lay squarely with Freddy Hirsch. He had come to the Florham Park meet to watch me and Jones, and maybe try to bowl at Florham Park Lanes if they didn't recognize him. He had brought a large pepperoni pie from Nick's.

I suppose Freddy figured he was being thoughtful. We gorged on the pizza during the first half of the meet, while we waited for our events, sitting in Freddy's 1951 Chevy. He had been considerate enough to bring a few ice cold Nehi sodas along with the pizza. I only ate two slices because I was the only one of us who had to run.

Unfortunately, I miscalculated the speed of my digestive system. When I was getting into the starting blocks, I was still belching up pepperoni, propelled by the carbonation. The guy next to me from Florham Park made a disgusted face and waved his hand in front of his nose after one particularly deep, loud burp. I didn't even place. I told the Coach I had cramped up, which was not too far from the truth, except I was talking about my stomach instead of my calf.

A funny thing happened, though, right after the race as I sat on the infield grass. Because I had Freddy Hirsch's pizza sitting in my gut like a great big bowling dough ball, I started thinking about the pin setters he was always trying to knock off. A couple of the pin boys weren't kids, despite the name. They were adults. They had to be small, like jockeys, to fit back there. I always felt sorry for them. For one thing, the name pin boy was kind of demeaning for an adult, I thought. Who wanted to grow up to be a pin boy?

I wondered what those guys had wanted to be when they were in school, if they had even been to school somewhere. Maybe they were immigrants who didn't think in English, like the guys who made pizza, or our foreign grandmother's boarder, or Freddy Hirsch's father. But didn't they have dreams, even foreign ones? Didn't they have hope for the future? Maybe they didn't, and that was a sad thought.

And then I realized something. I knew why Beau Jackson, who had looked so dignified and serious as pallbearer at Po's funeral, had seemed familiar. He was a pin boy at Florham Park Lanes. Beau Jackson, that melancholy, proud young man who carried his father to his grave had been Freddie Hirsch's human target at the bowling alley. Beau was tall, and it was hard for him to squeeze out of the way.

That really hit me. The whole idea wasn't funny anymore, and I felt ashamed, even though I hadn't thrown any balls at those sad people. Right then I told myself I'd never bowl with Freddie again if he tried to hit the pin boys.

And what if they were orphans, some of them? The thought shocked me, thinking about Wolfie and Kathy

Obermeister and the little semi-person incubating in her hopper. It was a horrifying concept.

I hoped the pin setters at Florham Park Lanes were foreign, so they couldn't tell how sad their jobs were, and maybe wouldn't mind so much that Freddie Hirsch tried to cream them with a sixteen pound bowling ball. They probably were right off the boat, now that I thought about it, and setting pins was their first American employment. At least, I hoped it was their first job, and not their career pinnacle.

I guess you need immigrants around for things to function normally, if only to reset the pins and make the pizza. It took me awhile to figure that out because we had no bowling alleys or pizza joints in Windham. But then again we had our cops next door to the train station, so why would I have even thought about it?

Chapter 43

There goes my baby
You don't know how good it feels . . .
-There Goes My Baby, The Drifters, 1959

Kathy Obermeister wasn't pregnant.

Definitely. Thank God.

Kathy called Wolfie on Thursday evening, five days after I met with Jones and Brownie. My brother said it was hard to understand what the hell she was saying because she was crying and laughing and trying to talk all at the same time, but the gist of her conversation was that she had finally gotten her period.   I didn't know about Wolfie, but it felt as though somebody had lifted a car off my neck.   Actually, I did know about Wolfie because he said it felt as though somebody had lifted a car off his neck. He kept laughing and couldn't stop. All that tension poured out of him over the next half hour. Both of us, I guess.   Our parents were downstairs watching Soupy Sales and never heard anything.   They never heard anything anyway when Soupy was on. If Raymond was still awake and heard us carrying on, he never said anything either. Then again he never said much of anything at all.

When we'd calmed down, I asked my brother if he'd learned anything from the experience.

"Use a rubber," he said.

Sometimes I think I want to swat that kid.

In the morning, I found Jones and Brownie in home room. I gave them the good news and thanked them for their support. Brownie had gotten a name of a doctor in Essex County and Jones had talked to the M.D. who cured his "rash".

"All's well that ends well," Jones said.

"Hell, don't mention it," Brownie said. "Except me and Jonesie want to play golf and eat more sandwiches at your club. That was pretty good."

So we did, the following Sunday. Wolfie completed our foursome. I told my brother how helpful my friends had been and he was so grateful he showed them how to jimmy the golf carts so they ran backwards and the battery drained. As usual, he beat me by a half dozen strokes and only hit one ball into a foursome ahead of us on the sixteenth green. A good time was had by all.

It's nice to have friends in time of need, isn't it?

Chapter 44

Gonna shake things up tonight
-High School Confidential, Jerry Lee Lewis, 1958

The reason Dick Orr almost killed half the chemistry class was again due to the fact that Coach Weber was called into the office, this time when we were all out playing softball for gym period. We had played a couple of innings when a student appeared in the doorway to the field area and yelled to Weber that he was needed in the office for a minute. As soon as Coach trotted off, we quick as a bunny turned the bases around so that second base became home plate, home plate became second base, and the school building wall became the outfield. The whole second story, just about, consisted of huge glass panes making a large, inviting target.

Curiously, we had to justify the inevitable by actually playing the game facing the wrong way until somebody managed to poke one through a window or Coach returned from the office, where no one wanted him in the first place.

As fate would have it, it took just one batter. Dick Orr, a pretty good hitter, stepped up to the plate that moments ago had been second base. Since there was no place to go to play the outfield, we were lined up against the high school wall. Brownie served up a couple of meatballs, as slow and fat as he could. Orr fouled one off and then lofted a high, deep fly ball that flew unerringly toward the chemistry lab window. Naturally, all of us lined up against the wall ran forward and turned around to see what was going to happen. It seemed like we were always looking at something untoward to see what would happen. The softball hit the second story window with a resounding crash and bounced back out, but nobody tried to catch it since shards of broken glass were raining down along with the ball. With impeccable timing, Coach Weber had reappeared on the field just in time to take in the scene moments before the ball blasted Inorganic Chemistry 101 to kingdom come. Dick Orr had hit a home run.

The really unfortunate thing, which indirectly would ruin the summer for many Windham borough families, was that most of the chemicals and other stores were arranged on metal racks, one of which was in front of the target window. When the ball crashed through, it smacked a jar of sulfuric acid before bouncing back out. The acid tipped over and fell onto a lab counter below, where it splattered its lethal contents in every direction. Amazingly, it also hit a test tube containing a gram or two of sodium in kerosene that was sitting on the counter. The test tube flew into the lab sink, exposing the sodium to water, where it promptly exploded. Survivors of Inorganic Chemistry 101 told an incredible tale of flying glass, splattering sulfuric acid and exploding sodium.

Dick Orr's bases empty home run had become truly a one in a million shot, eclipsing even my sixth grade copkiller snowball, and it was probably only because the Inorganic Chemistry 101 students scattered so quickly that casualties were averted. Mary Penny, a junior with huge, dreamy eyes and a pretty smile, had been seated near the window when it disintegrated. She summed it all up with one of her smiles.

"Neat," she said. "That was so cool."

No one knew at the time the incident would spawn the seeds of destruction for the William P. Morris Memorial Municipal Swimming Pool.

They couldn't put everyone in detention, I suppose, but it was pretty well understood afterward that Coach Weber should not renew his apartment lease.

It rained for the next several days, and so gym class was held indoors while the Administration pondered this latest incident. After awhile they outlawed Backwards Softball. That's what adults do. They wait until a few clever kids figure out how create some mischief, and then outlaw it, not realizing that kids will just go on to invent something new.

We had convinced Coach Weber that rather than play dodge ball, that sadistic version of human target practice, we normally played Mayhem in the gym. Mayhem had been outlawed by every town in Morris County, because somebody always broke an arm or worse playing the game. Coach Weber was never enlightened, though, and of course we told him we played it all the time.

In case you are unfamiliar with Mayhem, it is basketball with no rules. You divided the gym class in half and threw the ball up in the air at midcourt to start. You didn't have to dribble, or pass, or do anything except try to score a basket by whatever means available. Tackling, punching, kicking, using a fire extinguisher: all was fair game. When somebody scored, which wasn't too often, the teams resumed their positions on either half of the court and the ball was thrown up in the air again. Very simple. It is quite a sight to witness a game of Mayhem, which one can no longer do legally, with about 25 kids on either side intent on - well, Mayhem.

Of course, somebody's arm got broken the first gym period we played Mayhem. It was one of the A.V. guys whose name I don't remember. Somehow the Gimp's arm got bent in a new direction, as well. This was yet another gold star for Coach Weber. I kind of hoped everything would turn out all right for him, but I knew in reality he was egg salad.

There was one odd thing, though. When Dick Orr creamed his towering fly ball, I ran forward and turned around to watch the softball fly towards the chemistry window like everyone else. For a second, I could have sworn I saw a face looking out at us from the floor below. It was hard to tell, because sunlight was reflecting off the glass.

I thought it looked a lot like Coach Weber. Or somebody.

Chapter 45

I'm gonna cut your hair off . . .
- The All-American Boy, Bill Parsons, 1959

Once you get your driver's license, parents send you on all sorts of errands that would normally be a pain in the ass. For me, this novelty phase lasted about a month, until the stupid license got suspended pretty much on a technicality.

"Need anything from the store, ma?" I'd ask. My American grandmother hadn't died yet, and so I didn't have a car of my own.

The first Saturday morning in April was bright and breezy. I was heading downtown to Dick and Art's for a haircut, which I really didn't need, but mom said to take her car so I didn't argue like I normally would. Plus she was having a cup of coffee in the breakfast room with Mrs. Tigner, so she knew I wouldn't make a fuss with company around anyway. I mean, for Chrissake, I was a high school senior and did I need grief about my head (!?) I could figure out how big it should be on my own. Little Marvin Tigner was spending a couple of hours with Raymond and did I want to take them along? Mrs. Tigner asked. He needed a haircut as well and pretty soon Raymond was coming too, since he could use a trim.

I get a kick out of small fry, and besides any kid whose parents named him Marvin needed all the help he could get, so I didn't mind. The three of us drove down to Main Street. The whole way, Marvin jumped up and down on the seat, laughing for some inexplicable kid reason, while Raymond fiddled with the radio. Danny and the Juniors were belting out *Rock and Roll is Here to Stay* as we tooled down Shunpike, and Raymond kept pushing the buttons in and out so that it came out "Ro- is here – it will – ver die." I know it sounds dumb but I was laughing too. After all, parents wouldn't let their own kids do that stuff, if you know what I mean. They would just get all annoyed and tell them to cut it out. Parents never let kids do stuff. It was the kind of memory you'd keep for awhile, anyway, and then probably forget when you got to be a parent.

I parked in back, even though there was a space along Main Street, because to tell the truth I wasn't too hot at parallel parking yet. There wasn't much of a line for a Saturday, and they took Marvin and Raymond at the same time. They put them on those boards that go across the seat arms when the patient is small. Raymond nodded off and just drooled while Dick cut away. He didn't even wake up when Dick moved his head around.

Marvin stayed very still while Art cut his hair, which was unusual for a tyke, I thought. He looked at himself in the mirror as old Art shaped him up, smiling most of the time. Art even mixed up some shaving cream in his mug and shaved Marvin with his finger. When he did that, Marvin's eyes got real big and he stayed stock-still.

It was morning, maybe 11:00, and the sunlight slanting in the window lit the scene with a kind of golden halo. Outside the door, the red and white stripes slithered up the barber pole on the wall. I know how corny that sounds, but it all made quite a visual impression on me.

"You guys hungry?" I asked as I paid Art. The kids' haircuts had been half price.

"Hungry, yeah," Marvin replied, still smiling. Raymond nodded. We walked outside Dick and Art's. The light breeze seemed to energize the air; the trees shrugged and whispered as we waited to cross over to the Main Street Luncheonette. Marvin and Raymond slipped their little hands in mine as we trotted across. I got a big kick out of that. Both kids wanted hamburgers with lots of pickles and chocolate shakes, so I ordered the same. Kids can eat a hamburger almost anytime and don't have to wait for noon, have you ever noticed?

It took about four years to get through lunch. I can wolf down a burger pretty fast, but I didn't need to. I actually chewed most of it as the kids played around and ate. Both of them slurped the extra half glass of milkshake out of the tin, although I wagged my finger at them as they laughed and drank. Marvin kept pushing buttons on the booth juke box, even though we didn't buy any songs. Whenever someone else did, though, Marvin lit up. I guess he thought he'd done it.

I thought about taking them to the playground, or something, maybe a movie, but probably Mrs. Tigner might get worried if her little boy didn't show up before dinnertime. We left the luncheonette and walked to the corner. Behind us, we heard a rumbling and clattering. Little Marvin got all excited and pointed to a westbound local rounding the bend toward the Windham station.

"Train, train, train," he said. I guess he didn't get down to the borough very often. We wandered over as it slowed. There were only three cars on a Saturday. The conductor swung off before the local came to halt. In a few seconds, two colored boys stepped down to the platform. One wore a sleeveless undershirt and the other a polo shirt; both had on jeans and sneakers. They were laughing and joking; one punched the other playfully on the arm. I didn't pay a great deal of attention until two uniformed cops were on the platform. They just seemed to appear. I heard them call to the boys, who stopped and waited as the officers approached. They weren't laughing and joking now.

The three of us stood and watched silently. We couldn't hear what was being said, but one of the colored boys reached in his pocket and pulled out a red wallet. A cop took the billfold and flipped through the contents. He handed it back and then both cops put their hands on the colored boys' forearms and all four headed off to the stairs that went under the tracks. In a few moments, they appeared on the other side. The boys sat down on the bench as the cops stood alongside.

I turned Raymond and Marvin around and guided them back to the corner. I wondered if either would ask me about the scene we'd just witnessed, but they didn't. As we crossed the street, I heard the eastbound local pull into the station. I didn't turn around.

Mrs. Tigner had started to fret, mom said later. Hey, I told her, it was Mrs. Tigner's idea in the first place and Marvin was a slow eater. She hadn't realized I would buy him lunch. Marvin might have been slow, but he didn't leave a crumb or a pickle slice. Before they left, Mrs. Tigner tried to pay me but I refused. I was sitting tall on my wallet, anyway, with all the band jobs we'd been doing. Besides, it was the best thing I probably could ever have spent my dough on.

I just wished we hadn't wandered over to the train station. I hoped the little guys wouldn't remember what they saw when they got older.

Chapter 46

So it must be raindrops
So many raindrops…
- Raindrops, Dee Clark, 1961

April was the month we read The Great Gatsby in senior English. Because my grandfather had been some sort of bond smuggler, I felt an affinity for Jay Gatsby, especially after mom inherited quite a bit of dough when our American grandmother died. At least I think she did, because she bought some new clothes and jewelry after the funeral and that seemed to balance the scales, emotionally.

Most of our class liked Gatsby right off, even though he was required reading. The guy really knew how to throw a party. Did you ever notice that if you have to read a book for English, it sucks, but if you read it later it's sometimes pretty good? Except for Beowulf, that is. That sucks no matter when you read it. There's another crummy book you have to read, by Chaucer, who should have stuck to serfdom or whatever the hell it was. The whole dumb book was a bunch of short stories with no redeeming value whatever, except for one stupid line in the whole stupid book:

Nicholas then let fly a fart,
As great as it had been a thunderclap.

That may not be the exact quote, but it's pretty close. I think it's from *The Miller's Tale*.

Our new English teacher, Mr. Glendenning, was always talking about *redeeming value* and the narrator being the *vehicle*. What the hell was that? The only important vehicle in the story was Gatsby's terrific yellow car. We all wished we owned that beauty, even after Daisy dented the fender on Tom's girlfriend, or the other way around. The narrator Nick - the *vehicle*, according to Mr. Glendenning - wasn't too smart, though. He turned down Jordan Baker, for no good reason except that he associated her with those other freaks that used to come over to Gatsby's parties.

We debated that in English. Brownie volunteered that Nick had laid Miss Baker, and so lost interest, but we weren't really sure because Fitzgerald wasn't too specific. Most of the girls in the class felt he hadn't scored, but that was just girls protecting their generic feminine reputation. You can't tell about those classical writers, anyway. Their characters sometimes think about different matters than you or I. Gatsby certainly did, especially that part about the self-improvement lists he made as a kid. His father was quite proud of that. The only lists I could recall were my Christmas lists and the song list for our band.

Of course, as Jones, Brownie and I knew, we had our own version of Gatsby right in Windham, with the Moffitt's silver Mercedes having been impounded. Only instead of two possible drivers, we had three. There had still been no word from Duff Carlin's boys or the State Police.

Mr. Glendenning would diagram stuff on the blackboard and analyze all these great works of literature. What a crock of shit. I'm pretty certain that a great writer thinks a little bit but mostly relies on inspiration. Oh sure, he may organize the stuff and rewrite awkward paragraphs, and everything, but he mainly writes from inspiration and instinct. He enjoys making things up. The lousy English teachers, who couldn't think of any of the great stuff these classic writers do, diagram and try to explain and overdissect the whole thing. I'm pretty sure the great writers would be amazed at what the English scholars and teachers did with their works. They'd probably flunk the class on their own book, because they wouldn't know what the hell the English teacher was talking about. At least, that's my opinion.

Also, most English teachers think a guy has to be dead to be any good. For instance, Ray Bradbury is much better than that goddamn Beowulf guy hands down, or Chaucer, or that windbag Henry James, who wrote *By Words Obsessed,* and most of the other authors we had to read. This Bradbury guy could write prose as poetry. But did they teach Ray Bradbury? Nah. Just because they were Martians didn't mean they weren't *human,* for Chrissake. Even *The Wind in the Willows* is nice, because it evokes images in your mind and a certain kind of mood.

Another example is Rachel Carson. If you ever read *The Sea Around Us,* you know what I mean. Miss Carson weaves your imagination into the fabric of her writing. That's the best way I can put it. You follow the ways of the sea, its invisible highways and beautiful life-forms, from birth through life journeys, silent struggles, death and disposal. It's all true stuff, quietly majestic. She doesn't need to make anything up; all the essentials of drama are already present. She chronicled God's handiwork, and you can't do better than that. Maybe those assholes in Robbie van Arsdale's church would do well to read a little Rachel Carson, rather than that guy who went around marrying every broad in Salt Lake City. Her book has started a revolution, environmentally, and speaking for our generation I hope it keeps up.

We were lucky to get Somerset Maugham. I liked Maugham's stuff. There was often some frail British wife who tried to be loyal to her colonial governor husband but wound up crying and screwing the lieutenant. Usually some event like her steamer trunk not showing up started her on her jag, plus it was always raining. If Maugham wasn't exaggerating, it always rained around the British Empire. Rangoon, Singapore, India, the British West Indies - it made little difference. What the hell, it was always raining in London, anyway, so maybe the British just liked to stay wet. That's probably why they seem so reserved, and drink all that tea. At least that's what I think. I didn't bring that up in Social Studies, but I could have. I could just hear Mr. Kritzinger, though.

"Mr. Williams, that's a half-baked theory if I ever heard one. You better pay more attention in class."

See what I mean?

*   *   *   *   *

I know this whole chapter was pretty much of a digression. I don't think I'm going to turn out to be much of a writer, because I keep wandering off. I can hear Assistant Professor Murphy now:

"A writer needs discipline, Mister Williams. Any idiot can let stuff splurt out like diarrhea. This is crap."

Hell, he can just skip it then.

Chapter 47

Somethin' heavy hit me
Like an atomic bomb
When I woke up
my head started to clear
- Stranded in the Jungle, The Cadets, 1956

April was also the month Windham borough filled the William P. Morris Municipal Swimming Pool, a tangible sign of impending summer. The Olympic-sized facility was drained every October, and covered with a tarpaulin. Last year, the town had emptied it a month early and resurfaced the pool. There were eight new black-lined racing lanes on the bottom, and raised platforms for the competitors. Swim teams formed in May, and competition continued until the fall, when school went back in session. The bulk of the time the pool was used for recreation and swimming lessons.

Young mothers congregated on the decks during the summer months, chatting and drinking iced tea around tables graced with gaily colored striped umbrellas while their toddlers learned to swim under Coach Otto and his staff. Hamburgers and hot dogs were prepared in the sparkling new kitchen facilities and served from the party pavilion. Graduating kids got shiny pins proclaiming their ability to navigate the treacherous waters of the municipal pool. The Boy Scouts sponsored lifesaving skills courses. Weekends featured barbecues and pool parties. In the township, people either swam in backyard pools or at the country club, but for citizens of Windham borough, the William P. Morris Municipal Pool was a central focus during July and August, kind of like an African oasis where all the wildlife congregates.

But it was not to be this year, thanks to Dick Orr's backwards home run.

Jones, Gerd Muller and I were languishing on a grassy slope by the shot put area during our home meet against Delbarton, chewing grass, when we spotted Dick Orr and Brownie headed across the track toward us. They had to wait for the half-milers, especially Tommy Pond, who was bringing up the rear as usual. I noticed the Bird had watched Tommy pretty closely; maybe he had a few bucks down with Willie G., our bookmaker in Madison, on whether Pond could beat somebody besides me for once.

As I sat there, something light scampered across my ankle; I swatted it away.

"Hey, mens," said Brownie, and we all exchanged greetings. He and Orr flopped down with us on the grass.

"Williams, how come you're not running the half-mile today?" Orr asked, and everybody laughed. You'd have thought they'd have gotten over it by now.

"What's up? You guys come to watch the high jump?" I asked, changing the subject.

"What're you, nuts?" Brownie asked. "Who gives a shit about your crummy high jump." It wasn't a question. "Listen, Orr's got an idea. Listen to this." He nodded towards Dick Orr.

"Well, I've been thinking," Orr said.

"Congratulations," Jones said.

"Remember when we turned the softball diamond around? The shot through the chem lab window?"

How could we forget? It had just happened a couple of weeks ago.

He continued. "Well, there was a gram or so of sodium in the test tube that exploded. Remember that? The sodium exploded when it hit the water in the sink." He paused. We all nodded.

"Mary Penny said it made a big bang. She could hear it even with all the other shit that was going on, like the crashing glass and everybody yelling and stuff."

"So?"

"Well, there's this whole jar of sodium on the shelf. It's got like maybe a couple of quarts of kerosene on top. The sodium is about the size of a human brain. You can't let it be exposed to water, like the softball thing showed."

"It's not the size of George's brain. His brain is the size of that speck that exploded," Jones said.

In fact, we all remembered how volatile sodium was. This was getting interesting. Maybe chemistry was a practical subject for high school students, after all, and not just the Nazis. The Germans had built rockets with solid fuel. The atomic bomb was physics, though. That was beyond our capabilities, plus we had no reliable source for U-235.

"What if we hack off a piece of the sodium in the kerosene and take it with us on the class trip? We could explode it in the ocean. Maybe yell about leftover German mines from the war. They'd have to clear the beach."

That would be fun, I supposed, but all of a sudden Jones lit up. He had a better idea.

"I got a better idea," he said, grinning. "Screw sawing off part of the stuff. They just filled the municipal pool. Let's dump the whole jar in the pool."

My jaw went slack. Everybody's eyes were on Jones, dumbfounded by this flash of pure genius. This had the potential to be one of the greatest events in Windham borough history, including George Washington's nocturnal visits. What an historic moment.

Orr became the designated sodium thief, and on Friday he brought a gym bag to Chemistry class. When the bell rang, Jones distracted Mr. Wisner, and in a flash Orr had the sodium jar in the bag.

Saturday night was clear, with a full moon. The four of us – Bird said he wasn't able to go - all jammed into Brownie's Rambler for the getaway car because of the two-tone paint job, since maybe he could try out his theory if things went badly. He parked the Nash over on Washington Street about two blocks from the facility, and we quietly carried the jar across Washington, up Passaic and over to the pool. The gate was locked, but that was just to keep little kids away from the water at night.

The wrought iron fence was only about three feet high. We hopped over it and approached the pool. The water was a silvery, flashing surface in the light breeze. Orr started to giggle softly until Brownie jabbed him in the ribs. We whispered, although there was probably no one within a half mile.

"OK," Brownie said. Orr was carrying the jar. "Unscrew the lid. Put the lid in your pocket because we don't want to leave any evidence."

He needn't have worried. "Who's gonna throw it in?"

"Jones, you throw it in. You're the shot putter," Brownie said.

"Your idea," said Jones. For the moment, nobody was volunteering.

"It's Orr's idea," I said.

"Hey, I already did my part with the softball," Orr countered.

That was true.

We milled around the pool deck, by the edge. Orr still held the open jar.

"Screw it," said Brownie. "Gimme the jar."

"Wait a sec," I said. "We gotta think about this a second. I guess it should go in the middle of the deep end. What do you think?"

"Guess so," said Brownie.

I remembered the kerosene smudge pot. "Make sure you don't spill any kerosene on yourself," I said. "You'll stink to high heaven. Be careful heaving it in."

"OK, you guys better back up in case this stuff really works," Brownie said. "As soon as I heave it, I'm heading for the fence."

We backed up toward the fence, at the edge of the pool deck. We were maybe twenty feet from the water. We looked at each other, and then we all stepped over the fence onto the grass, just as an extra precaution. Brownie slowly brought both arms back and then tossed the jar into the pool with a splash. Then he ran to the fence and hopped over as fast as he could.

The jar actually went in the water right side up, and from what we could tell in the moonlight bobbed up and down a couple of times before it sank. I thought I saw a rainbow sheen

of kerosene for a few seconds.   Nothing was happening.
Brownie spoke.

"What do you th - "

Patches of fire erupted in a ragged semi-circle on the
surface of the pool.   Smoke began to billow.   There was a
hissing noise.   A small fountain of sparks shot up maybe eight
feet in the air.

"Whoah," I said.   "That's so cool.   I nev - "

There was a blinding flash, like an atomic bomb, as if
lightning had struck two feet away, for an instant.   It was
brighter than daylight.   It was so bright I couldn't see anything.
I had only a split second to be terrified.

The next thing was this incredible noise, the loudest,
deepest boom I had ever heard, including the time a firework
misfired and landed five feet from me during the town's Fourth
of July celebration.   It was louder than thunder, it was louder
than anything, and then I felt this incredible concussion, this big
whoosh of air and the next thing an invisible locomotive
slammed into me and threw me through the air and I sensed
massive things hurtling past me at about the speed of light and
then I was on the grass on my back and couldn't hear a
goddamn thing.   Jones, Orr and Brownie were all scattered
nearby.

Dazed, we got to our feet.   I couldn't really hear too
well, and there was this ringing noise inside my head, and some
other hollow noise, but I thought I could hear Brownie through
it all.

"JESUS CHRIST LET'S GET THE HELL
OUT OF HERE!" he must have yelled, but it sounded like
"Jesus Christ let's get the hell out of here..."

Chapter 48

When I get the paper,
I read it through and through . . .
-    *Get a Job, The Silhouettes, 1957*

𝕿𝖍𝖊 𝖂𝖎𝖓𝖉𝖍𝖆𝖒
𝕮𝖔𝖚𝖗𝖎𝖊𝖗
April 14, 1959

Blast Levels
Municipal Pool
Concrete Hurled 200', Water
Vaporized
Cause Unknown, Special Task Force
Formed

Windham - The Windham Borough Police Department and Morris County Sheriff's Office today launched a combined investigation into a massive explosion at the William P. Morris Municipal Pool on Passaic Avenue Saturday night. The blast, which shattered windows a quarter mile away, was powerful enough to vaporize much of the 45,000 gallons of water and hurl sections of concrete up to 200' from the scene. The pool itself was a pile of broken rubble, with two remaining large concrete sections fractured and twisted. Pieces of the wooden three meter diving board were found on Washington Avenue.

The explosion, which occurred at 9:53 pm, caused an estimated $10,000 in damages. Umbrellas and pool tables were missing or broken, and all the windows to the party pavilion were blown out. Chief Duff Carlin announced the formation of the special task force to investigate the cause of the catastrophe.

"We know of no individual or group who would have done something like this," said Chief Carlin. "We are also investigating what type of explosive device could have caused this kind of massive damage. We are not ruling out natural causes, in any event. It is possible the gas lines feeding the stoves in the party pavilion may be involved. We are awaiting the structural drawings from the building department, although our early investigation shows these lines did not run directly beside the pool."

Due to the monetary assessment of the damages, Chief Carlin did not rule out asking the Federal Bureau of Investigation to

(continued on page 8)

Later in June, when classes were winding down and Mr. Wisner was taking inventory in the chemistry lab, he addressed the class while we were screwing around with Bunsen burners and hydrofluoric acid. Someone, Orr probably, had replaced the hole on the shelf with a jar some comedian had marked Zyklon B.

"Hey, what happened to the - where did the - "

Jones, Orr, Brownie and I exchanged furtive glances.

"Who had the sodium last?"

Chapter 49

I ran all the way home
Just to say I'm sorry
Just to say I'm sorry
I ran all the way
- Sorry (I Ran All the Way Home), The Impalas, 1959

We had just committed the Crime of the Century, right up there with the Brink's robbery, and figured we were facing twenty to life if the Duffer brought in the feds to help track us down. Moreover, we were already on J. Edgar's list for spying and attempted extortion, thanks to Robbie van Arsdale's dumb letter.

The Windham Police Department was out of its league with anything beyond a speeding ticket, but we knew the FBI had a sophisticated crime lab. They would figure out why the goddamn pool blew up, and then they'd find out the sodium was missing, and then they would subject us all to ultraviolet light or something that detected microscopic particles of the stuff. After all, crap like that happened in the True Crime magazines all the time, if you got beyond the broad with her revealing tight dress ripped provocatively on the cover, while she was tied to the chair and the hoods with the loud double-breasted suits and dago fedoras drooled over her. The magazines made it pretty clear you couldn't scrub off microscopic particles, because they always stuck to you like the gunpowder residue that told the G-men who did the shooting.

The irony was, Jones, Brownie, Bird and I got detention about a week later for something so trivial it was hard to believe we had to come in after school.

Active minds are the devil's workshop. Or is it evil minds? Maybe it's idle minds. Anyway, Miss Van Aldewehe was explaining some painting crap about perspective, and mentioned a focal point and some other stuff invented by Van Gogh or somebody, maybe the cave-dwellers who defaced the rock walls with their crummy stick drawings. I mean, if you assume cave-dwellers were subhuman, then the fact they drew anything at all was probably remarkable, but if they were considered humanoids or pretty much people then so what? It's not like they drew the Sistine Chapel, for Chrissake.

Anyway, inspired by the Impalas recording of *Sorry (I Ran All the Way Home)* Brownie, Jones, Bird and I all stood up at the same moment. Heads were swiveling, mouths open. Even Miss Aldewehe looked surprised. I snapped my fingers to set the time, since I was the only one with singing experience, and we began in a sort of half-assed three part harmony:

(slow intro)"SORRY, SORRY, OH SO SORRY...
(fast) I VAN ALDEWEHE HOME
DOO BAH DOO BAH DOO BAH
JUST TO SAY I'M SORRY
WHAT CAN I SAY
I VAN ALDEWEHE
DOO BAH DOO BAH DOO BAH
A YAY-AY-AY-HAY

That's as far as we got, although we had rehearsed the whole tune. The class was in an uproar, and we were laughing so hard ourselves we couldn't continue. Even Miss Van Aldewehe was giggling, her hand up over her mouth, looking as sexy as ever. Our art teacher evidently was current on her rock 'n' roll, which put her way up on the rest of the faculty.

Of course, in came Mr. Kritzinger, whose stupid classroom wasn't even next door, and the four of us got detention signed by Principal Wood Pecker Dunwood. We did it in Miss *Van Aldewehe's* class, but Mr. *Kritzinger* gave us detention. What kind of justice was that? Even worse, it was going to be a Saturday morning deal because it was already Friday and there would be no one to monitor us on Friday afternoon. Not even Mr. Kritzinger, who couldn't even take care of his own - or Miss Van Aldewehe's – detentions, much less his own teacup wife.

Naturally, Saturday was maybe the most gorgeous late Spring morning of the year, and we were going to be stuck in the library from nine o'clock until eleven. Briefly, we thought about skipping detention but of course we didn't, especially since we were likely to be on the FBI's Most Wanted list if the feds were called into the William P. Morris Municipal Swimming Pool case.

We pulled into school and were met by Mr. Kritzinger. At least we were going to screw up his Saturday morning, as well as ours. He directed us to the library, where Brownie and The Bird were already seated at the same table I occupied with Mary Anne Moffitt during study hall. It was almost like being in the Sweet Shoppe, without the vanilla cokes and egg creams and the smoke. The clean air was actually a bonus; this wasn't going to be too bad.

"Hey, mens," said Brownie. We exchanged greetings. Jones rattled a newspaper; somewhere he'd picked up the New York *Journal-American*.

"It says here *Your Hit Parade*'s going off the air."

"You mean we'll never have to see those assholes again?" I asked.

"Maybe there really is a God," Brownie said. "I still have nightmares about that fag Pat Boone trying to sing *Tutti-Frutti*."

That got a chuckle and nods of agreement. This guy Boone had shamelessly covered every decent R&B song he possible could, sucking money out the system that really belonged to the original artists, because the record people thought he had this squeaky image and colored singers wouldn't go over very well. They didn't know dick, because we loved Little Richard and Chuck Berry and Bo Diddley and Fats Domino, and really nobody gave a rat's ass about lily white religious fanatic Pat Boone.

Religious fanatics are really good at sucking money or favors out of other people, most of the time. They're so nuts, they can feel righteous doing it, which is one of the major benefits of being a religious fanatic. Somehow they think God wants you to give them all kinds of stuff, because they are his pal or something, and you aren't. Christ.

Strangely enough, that led to a discussion about our collective futures, which as I have related was a rarity. I guess it was because graduation was right around the corner.

"Hey, Bird," Brownie said, "you got a total free ride at Seton Hall?"

"Yep," he replied.

"You gotta take any classes?"

"Sure I do. I'm majoring in pre-law. Right now I think I want to go to law school after Seton Hall."

From what we heard, Bird's father was a pretty hotshot lawyer in New York who had made a lot of dough with some big railroad merger, or something. Maybe it was airlines. Funny how a guy who didn't need the dough got a full scholarship, just because he could shoot they eyes off a basketball. Some other kid who was only 50% from the free throw line wouldn't get to go at all, like Freddy Hirsch, whose father had stolen his savings account. Freddy's big roundhouse curve wasn't worth a dime. Probably the whole four year's tuition wouldn't make a dent in old man Mueller's bank account. But that was the American Way, and besides it wasn't the Bird's fault.

"Jonesy, you figured out if you want to be a dentist or a plumber yet?" I guessed Brownie was acting as the moderator again.

"Well, pretty much I think I'm going to be a dentist, unless I don't get in."

A thought struck me, which didn't happen too often. "How do you practice? Do they have dummies or what?"

"They rob graves," Brownie said. Jones shook his head.

"I don't think so. They round up homeless derelicts for dental school. They get like a buck and free soup."

Now it was my turn, it appeared. Brownie was still the Grand Inquisitor.

"Hey Williams, what about you? Gonna keep up with the music in college? What?"

"Oh, yeah, sure. I don't know about making a living at it, though. Pretty hit or miss. We haven't exactly cracked the

Top 40 yet." The Top 40 played every Saturday morning on the radio, and we were missing a big chunk of it by being in detention.

"Your parents know how much dough you make on your band jobs?" asked Jones. This was a sensitive subject.

"Not exactly," I said. "If they knew that, I'd probably have to chip some of it in for college." I usually had a pretty full wallet. "Not that I wouldn't anyway, if I needed to. But this way it's an option."

That seemed to make sense to everybody.

"What about if the music doesn't make it?" This from the Bird.

I didn't really like to think about that too much. Not too much. Secretly, I hoped I was a good enough goalkeeper to maybe play somewhere professionally, but it couldn't be in the U.S. since soccer was such a nowhere sport beyond college. I would have going for me the novelty of being an American player in some foreign league, if I could make it and stand stupid foreign food. But since I hardly ever got tested playing for Windham, I guess I didn't really know how good I was, and I didn't want these guys laughing at me if I told them what I was thinking.

They wouldn't be just like my parents, telling me I was impractical and I needed to prepare for a career, and to be realistic, but they would still just laugh their asses off. Not that my parents had said any of those things, actually. I just knew they would, if I talked to them about any of my thoughts, and I didn't need the grief from anybody. Besides, they were parents, so who would talk to them about anything like goals or dreams or the future?

Why were we having this desolate discussion anyway?

All of a sudden, my brain kind of went epileptic or something.

"Well, I don't know. I don't know. I can't see myself climbing on the 7:09 every morning, like some goddamn sardine in a can going into the crummy city, know what I mean?" I asked. Heads nodded. "Sitting on the stupid train next to some asshole you don't know belching up his breakfast and reading the goddamn New York Times? Who cares about the goddamn New York Times? What the hell could I do in an office? What does anybody do in an office? Why would anybody even want to go to an office? Just for the broads? Or wear a stupid suit, even when it's hot? And some dippy hat?" I was really warming up, now. I barely noticed something small crawl across the next table.

"It's like you're already dead, for Chrissake. And then you get home maybe at 7:00 and you're too tired to pay attention to your kids and all you can look forward to is playing a stupid round of golf on Saturday at the goddamn country club or Sunday if you can talk your way out of going to church with your wife and going to a Little League game and screaming at the coach because he didn't play your kid enough and embarrassing the hell out of the little guy and having a couple of martinis and listening to your heart because maybe it's not beating right anymore it's too loud in your ears so you better have another martini? Screw that. Son of a bitch. Screw that."

Wow, I was out of breath. What the hell was all that? I had to take a deep breath or two. It seemed to me like we were being handed a life sentence, just sort of by default, but that's about what we were expected to do. That's what just about all our fathers did, at least in the township. Screw that.

There was a silence for a time. Everybody looked at me, kind of surprised. I was kind of surprised myself. Where had that all come from?

"Woah. That's quite a speech there, Williams," said Brownie with a grin.

It got quiet for a minute or so as I calmed down. Maybe they were all thinking about what I'd said. My ass started itching.

The closest in our family to anybody working on Wall Street would have been my grandfather, the bond smuggler, and I don't think he walked around lower Manhattan or wore a suit either. He probably just smuggled stuff off airplanes and boats or forged signatures in the basement, and wore regular clothes, but I really didn't know.

I guess the only reason I thought I still could make the rock 'n' roll big time was because we'd just recorded six songs for Columbia, and had already signed two recording deals with major labels, albeit unsuccessful. We had a pretty decent following including the one groupie, and, after all, my mom had been a professional musician for awhile. Until I derailed that gravy train.

Then a new thought dawned on me, which was kind of ironic since I was sitting in school. What if it wasn't just the borough kids who had the dead-end jobs? What if I had it all wrong, and it was us, the golden youth of Windham Township, we who would march like Aryan lemmings off to college and cloak ourselves in the same trappings, weaving our own shrouds? Ride the Erie Lackawanna, that mobile steel coffin, suffocating our lives away in smoky club cars while we downed three martinis, swaying and clickety-clacking with mind-numbing repetition toward our enclave of privilege, vomited out in the twilight from the metal beast to waiting cars or waiting wives at the station, with enough alcohol inside so the edge was off and maybe we wouldn't remember to mind? Who were the dead-end people then? Maybe I had it all wrong.

Suddenly I saw the city as a living organism, an evil thing, taking a giant dump at the end of every day which was the Erie Lackawanna straight out of the city's ass, carrying all our fathers straight into the toilet. Maybe privilege was a trade-off, the big house, the two new cars, the whole thing. Maybe the reason I didn't like to think about it was because the price was too high, and I wasn't willing to pay it. It was fine now, because I got it all for free, but what about then? What could I do then? How could I explain this to anyone?

Oh, Christ. Somehow in that exact moment in the library I thought I saw it all, visualized the perfect snapshot of our lives, my life, the road that sloped downhill, led all the way by Mr. Moffitt, like some kind of half-assed Pie-Eyed Piper, in his ridiculous smoking jacket, endless cigarettes and stupid grin and martini, waving *come on follow me this way to the Big Top* with his hands full of cigarettes and martinis so he couldn't scratch his ass.

Really, the whole idea of a Windham-type future sucked.

Not me.

*   *   *   *   *

Mr. Kritzinger actually let us out at 10:30, saying something about what a beautiful day it was and hopefully we had learned a lesson and that Mrs. Van Aldewehe had gotten such a kick out of our song that maybe we didn't need to stay the full time. I got the impression Mr. Kritzinger was thinking about the fact that we would be graduating soon, and would have better jobs than his in about four years, so maybe he would be working for one of us. Also, he probably didn't want us to think of him as a total asshole for the rest of our lives, but really he was too late.

Chapter 50

Just for a moment I stood there in silence
Shocked by the foul evil deed I had done
-El Paso, Marty Robbins, 1959

It was a few days after the senior class trip, the one I told you about way back near the beginning, and long enough for our classmates to sober up and Jerry Garragues to dry out. Things had returned pretty much to normal, if that's the right word. The memory of Miss van Aldewehe's bathing suit was pleasantly imprinted on my brain pan, and Jones and I had survived Chief Duff Carlin's version of the Nuremberg trials. It was on to the next thing, except that on Tuesday Jerry experienced an excruciating pain in his elbow during class. He looked pale and shaky and so Mr. Glendenning asked Michele Hoyt to accompany him to the nurse's office.

When she hadn't returned in fifteen minutes, we looked at each other with quizzical expressions. The first inkling something was really wrong was when we heard the siren in the distance. It grew louder and moments later the Weiner pointed excitedly out the window.

"Look!" he said, as an ambulance flashed up the long drive and screeched to a halt by the entrance. Two guys in white spilled out and hustled inside toting a stretcher. We all crowded around the window and even Mr. Glendenning realized class was not going to continue. It seemed like forever before the attendants came out carrying a motionless figure.

When Michele returned a few minutes later, she told us Jerry had stumbled and become confused on his way to the nurse's office. She said his eyes lost focus and he didn't seem to know where he was. By the time Garragues slumped through the door, he was mumbling and incoherent, even more so than normal. They'd gotten him on the day bed and the nurse had dialed for the ambulance. Michele was ushered out and the door closed. Nobody told her to return to class, so she'd waited around and saw our unconscious classmate being trucked out by the guys in white. It's safe to say nobody learned much the rest of the school day.

Track practice was kind of unenthusiastic. After awhile, Jones wandered over to the high jump pit. It had rained at lunchtime and sawdust from the pit was sticking to me. The stupid stuff itched like crazy. That's probably why I missed two in a row at 5'10".

"You look like a chicken," Jones said with a grin, eyeing me as he hefted a shot. He handled the twelve pound cannonball like it was a BB.

I tried to brush the soggy shavings off, but they just slid around. "I feel like a pencil sharpener. What the heck is with Garragues?" It was maybe 4:30 and the dark clouds overhead added to the gloom of our classmate's strange ailment.

"Dunno. Maybe he had a stroke or something, from what Michele described."

"You don't have a stroke when you're eighteen, for Chrissake. Do you?"

"Well, it didn't exactly sound like a headache, did it?"

I knocked off the high jump. I didn't feel like practicing anyway. I was soggy and cold and distracted by the Garragues calamity. Jones gave me a ride home and after I got out of the car the seat looked like a box of Corn Flakes had spilled on it.

I told my family at dinner what had happened. Mom got up right in the middle of her meat loaf and called Jerry's house, although she said she'd only met Mrs. Garragues once or twice over the years. There was no answer. I suppose his folks were at the hospital.

"Maybe he's dead," Wolfie said, and I thought mom was going to swat him. She glared at my brother, who just looked at me and shrugged.

"Hey, I don't know the guy."

Actually, I didn't know Jerry that well either. We all knew he spent time on a stool by his fish tank, trying to stab goldfish with a number 2 pencil.

"It's not so easy with the refraction and all," he'd told us. "Plus, they learn quick for stupid fish."

As we drifted in to school the next morning the word was that Jerry was in I.C.U. at St. Barnabas Medical Center in Livingston. He'd suffered an embolism, they said, and the bubble had first lodged in a vein in his arm somewhere and then traveled to his brain. He was being decompressed in a hyperbaric chamber, they called it. I guess it's kind of like trying to get the fizz back into the seltzer bottle. Some of the girls appeared quite distraught and the shoats were crying. I thought Principal Dunwood would make some kind of announcement, but the p.a. remained silent throughout the day.

It rained again, so track practice was canceled, the one benefit of an otherwise gloomy day. Distant thunder rolled in the afternoon. At 3:30 Jones, Brownie and I were sucking on Marlboros and vanilla cokes in the Sweet Shoppe, which was a lot better than looking like soggy poultry in the high jump pit.

"Listen, this is really bad," Brownie said. "Garragues, I mean."

"Of course it's bad," I said.

"Not what I mean," Brownie said. "He got an embolism, right? In his brain, right? How do you get an embolism?"

Jones and I looked at each other. I wasn't too up on embolisms.

"Thinking too much?" I opined.

"Then you'll never have to worry about it. You get one from being underwater, sometimes," Brownie said.

Underwater? Brownie read it on my face, I guess.

"That's right, genius. Who do we know that was underwater for a whole minute or two last week?"

"Jerry was underwater," I said.

"Give the man a kewpie doll. And why was he underwater?"

"Because he fell in the trough on his way to England," I said.

Brownie shook his head. Jones raised his hand; Brownie nodded in his direction. "Because he was out of his mind on vodka," he said.

"Which makes us. . . what?" Brownie said.

"Whoa, wait a minute," Jones said. "I'm pretty sure you only get an embolism if you dive down deep. He never made it off the continental shelf."

"Who are you, Doctor Kildare?" Brownie asked. There was silence for a time. I began to realize we could be in serious trouble here, especially if Jerry didn't recover right away.

"Accessories, they call it," Brownie said. "Me, you two, Herbie Schultz, we're all accessories."

"Herbie Schultz?" Jones asked.

"He got the needle, remember? Out of his old man's doctor bag."

I have to say, it was a scary thought. Nobody spoke for a time as we digested this information and pondered its ramifications. Finally, Jones said what we were thinking.

"Suppose he freaking dies?"

Chapter 51

What do I see?
Poetry
Poetry in motion
- *Poetry in Motion, Johnny Tillotson, 1961*

A gray veil had descended over Windham. The rain didn't let up for three days. It was steady, monotonous; the showers were cold and showed the wind. Puddles became lakes, rivulets foamed into rivers. The ball fields had drowned. Alone in my room, I sat on the bed reading a little Somerset Maugham while I chewed on some Turkish taffy. I imagined myself one of Maugham's tragic figures, maybe a young lieutenant, posted in Rangoon or Singapore as I peered out my dormer into the gloom of late afternoon. Without a steamer trunk or pith helmet, though, I might have been in Jersey City. I was already depressed and worried about Jerry Garragues and so I sank even lower.

I looked across and up Rolling Hill Drive and gazed at the roof of Jamie Hofmann's house, which was about the farthest thing I could see in the mist. That made me feel even worse. Jamie was in Wolfie's class, and his grandfather had lived with the family. I guess he was a widower. The grandfather, I mean, not Jamie. Old Mr. Hofmann was about a gazillion years old. I kind of felt sorry for him because he would sit in a rocking chair on his son's porch and read books like Life Begins at 40 or ones with Bishop Fulton J. Sheen on the cover. He'd wait for people to walk by and try to visit with them. Since we had no sidewalks and most people just drove places he hardly ever got to talk with anyone, unless they were kids on the way to the playground over on Fairmount. He had befriended Raymond, and would tousle my brother's hair whenever he saw him. Once in awhile I'd take Raymond for a walk and the two of them got a real bang out of each other.

I didn't know too much about the guy, really, but one day the rocker was gone from the porch. My mom said old Mr. Hofmann had died. Somehow the rocker being gone from the porch struck me as really sad. I don't know why, exactly. I just thought they could have left the goddamn chair where it was, for Chrissake, at least for a few weeks or so. Kind of a memento, or something. If they'd left the chair I probably wouldn't have noticed old Mr. Hofmann was gone for months, I'll bet. But I noticed right away. Had they been waiting to grab the chair because they coveted it? Or what? That thought was bad enough, but maybe they just put it in the trash. I hoped not.

Then I remembered the last time Raymond and I had biked past his house, when Father Corr had visited my parents. I regretted only waving and not stopping for a minute so old Mr. Hofmann could talk to Raymond and tousle his hair.

Anyway, even though I knew next to nothing about Mr. Hofmann, I wrote a poem about the guy. Don't ask me why I did it, because I don't really know. I think I was inspired by Rachel Carson, or maybe T.S. Eliot, or maybe that other guy who didn't use capital letters. Here it is:

No More Questions All Misleading
By George Williams

He's kind of old and kind of dying,
Something in his chest is giving way.
But he's in no pain, just simply lying,
Savoring the twilight of his day.

His eyes are closed, he's slightly smiling,
A wisp of memory brushes by.
The lap of waves upon the piling,
The smell of fairgrounds in July.

The stars of youth were somehow brighter,
The crisp of night was never chill.
The weight of caring seemed much lighter
The world around is growing still.

A nurse comes in to fluff his pillow,
He lets her think that he's asleep.
He sees the sail unfurl and billow
On the shore she turns to weep.

His mind's an album, turning pages,
Photos fading, tinged with brown.
Many plays on many stages,
He sees the curtain coming down.

He makes no judgments, seeks no meaning,

There are no labels for his files.
No more questions, all misleading,
He has come too many miles.

No one knows he's in here dying
But if they did he knows they'd care.
He has no need to hear them crying,
It's just as well no one is there.

Not too long before he sees her,
Somehow he knows she must be dead.
He'll smile and hold her when he greets her,
Nothing needed to be said.

The day is over, night is falling,
No one hears him as he sighs.
Was it someone he heard calling?
A tear has fallen
and he dies.

*   *   *   *   *

    I thought about turning it in for our next Creative
Writing assignment, but I didn't. I could just hear Jones and
Brownie.
    "Fag," they'd say. "Hair ball."
    I wrote something about a soccer game instead, where
the goalie gets distracted looking at some broad in the stands
and lets in the winning goal.   The team loses the state
championship and the girl won't go out with the guy as a result.
    I got a B+.

Chapter 52

I'm dreaming my life away...
-All I Have to do is Dream, Everly Brothers, 1958

They weren't supposed allow visitors in I.C.U., but because so many classmates wanted to see Jerry Garragues and he wasn't an infection risk they made an exception. We couldn't go into the room, exactly, but they'd made him into kind of an exhibit. We could look through a window and see him in the bed, half-propped up and facing us.

It was eerie. The Greek, Jones, Brownie and I had driven to the hospital on a Saturday morning. Jerry wasn't sleeping, but he sure as hell wasn't too awake. His eyes kind of drifted here and there, and his mouth was slack, and you got the impression he wasn't exactly hitting on all cylinders. When he gazed at the window, he looked right through us.

"They've got him on display, for Chrissake, like a two headed cow. Maybe they could put a sign up over this window, up here." Brownie said, pointing. "Five cents, five minutes."

Jones waved at the window but got no reaction. "Maybe it's one way glass," he said. "Maybe he can't see out."

The Greek shook his head as he looked in. "Irreversible brain damage."

"Shhh!" I said. "Maybe he can hear us."

"You kidding?" Brownie said. "He couldn't hear an A-bomb."

I looked at the Greek. "How do you know it's irreversible?"

"That's the only kind there is," he said. A nurse walked by, carrying a tray with little paper cups of pills. She wasn't half bad, maybe early twenties, with that cute little hat. Brownie stared at her cute little ass.

"Say," he said, reading her name tag, "Miss Lange, what's wrong with our friend?"

"He's very ill," Miss Lange said, and started on her way.

"Just a sec, hey?" Miss Lange wasn't going to get away with a generic answer to this crowd. "What's his specific diagnosis?"

Miss Lange was not used to this. "You'd have to check with his doctors."

Brownie bored in. "We don't know his doctors, and we're not supposed to stay very long. Can you help us out here? He's our classmate."

Miss Lange considered for a moment whether to be a bitch or helpful. "He has an embolism, an air bubble that lodged in his brain. It's a very serious thing. They reduced it in the chamber."

The chamber of horrors?

"The hyperbaric chamber," she added.

"Well, then, is he okay?"

"The bubble may be gone but it could have done damage," Miss Lange said. "Really, I'm just speculating."

"How'd he get it?" Jones asked. We were all interested in hearing her answer.

"The air bubble? Well, I don't know if anyone knows. I certainly don't." That was good. Maybe they couldn't prove anything.

"Do you want some coffee in the cafeteria?" Brownie asked. She actually smiled.

"I can't. I'm on duty. But thank you."

Jones tried to help. "He has a two-tone car."

"How about a beer after you get off?"

"It's a Rambler. The seats -"

Miss Lange scooted away before Brownie could try again.

Looking at Jerry drool through a window got dull fairly quickly, so after maybe ten minutes we felt we'd paid our respects. We drove down Route 24 to the driving range, across from Wally's Two Bars, and spent an hour trying to hit the little cart that sucks up the golf balls out on the range. Jones tried to arc a few shots over the high netting into the miniature golf course next door, which was crowded on a Saturday. He only managed a couple of gutta percha bombs. We cracked up hearing a muffled hey! or a loud POK when the ball caromed off the pavement maybe twenty feet in the air, scattering whole family groups.

Later, at Wally's Two Bars – Jones called it Wally's Two Barfs - we sat at a round wooden table having burgers and beer for lunch. We were on the other side of the bar from the dart board and pool tables, so it was relatively private. As we chowed down, Wally came out of the kitchen and walked over to our table. He was wearing the same apron he always did, from probably the War of 1812. I recognized the stains; one or two reminded me of that ink blot test.

"Listen, you guys," he said, "the cops were in here last week checking I.D.'s. Take these."

He fanned out a bunch of phony drivers' licenses and tossed them on the table. We sorted through and each picked one. My new name was Elroy Hirsch. Crazylegs had retired from the Rams a few years back, so I figured it was okay. I noticed they all had the same birthdate: October 21.

"Hey, whose birthday is this? Is it yours?" I asked.

"Nah. It's Mickey Mantle's." I guess Wally was a Yankee fan.

"Aren't you worried the dates are all the same?" Jones asked. Wally shot him a look.

"They're cops, for Chrissake." Wally picked up the rest of his stash and retreated to the kitchen.

Brownie decided we should bounce our current problem off the Greek, who was pretty smart, for an outside opinion. Besides, since all Greeks who didn't own a restaurant were sponge divers, maybe he knew about embolisms. The Greek listened carefully.

"Well," he said after Brownie had finished, "it's not like you gave Jerry a loaded gun. All you did was provide a mechanism for the guy to get tanked. It was his responsibility not to eat a whole citrus grove."

"Like a brewery," I said. "Can't blame Pabst for every drunk behind the wheel." I started to feel better, like maybe I wasn't going to spend the rest of my teenage years in prison.

"On the other hand," the Greek continued, "if he doesn't recover, you could be civilly liable for his care, if not criminally liable. That could be hundreds of thousands of dollars. It's probably a few grand already."

Holy shit. I didn't think my dad made that kind of dough. Did he? My mood plummeted again. The Greek wasn't through, though.

"And if he dies, they could charge you all as adults."

Chapter 54

I looked at the sea and it seemed to say
I took your baby from you away.
-Endless Sleep, Jody Reynolds, 1958

They moved Jerry to a long-term rehabilitation facility out in Morristown. The Greek had been right; Jerry was apparently one slice removed from a lobotomy patient. They were going to try and teach the poor kid how to walk and eat by himself again, and maybe even talk, but he sure didn't look like Fulbright Scholarship material to us. We'd acted with bravado about the whole thing, but really – speaking for myself – I was scared shitless. Not just for any liability we might have, but because I knew if we hadn't acted like immature assholes and spiked the fruits Jerry would still be going to class and stabbing goldfish and living a reasonably normal existence. We'd committed a mortal sin, for Chrissake, as far as I could tell. I guess you could say I had pangs of guilt about the whole business. It made me wonder if that was how Teddy Wasserman's Jews felt about everything, kind of like he'd described.

I tried to think of the last time I'd been to Confession. How could I sandwich crippling a classmate in between smoking in the boys room and having impure thoughts about Mary Anne Moffitt? What if Father Corr recognized my voice?

Maybe I could go to Confession in Madison or somewhere, where they didn't know me. That town had a big colored population, so the priests were probably used to hearing lots of stuff about rape and murder. But then again, colored people were all Baptists, I realized, so that theory was wrong. I was starting to panic. Could I get up the nerve to try and save my soul? I wondered if Brownie or Jones or Herbie Schultz were thinking similar thoughts. Probably not, I decided. In Brownie's case, definitely not.

Jerry came from the borough, and his folks didn't have all that much dough, and we all knew his hospital bills must be the size of the national debt. Somebody had come up with the idea of a fundraiser cookout and pretty much the whole class showed up at Memorial Park for the event.

Normally I can gorge on grilled hamburgers and hot dogs and cole slaw and all, but I didn't have much of an appetite that hazy Saturday afternoon. It didn't help that Mrs. Carnahan's house was across the street; every so often I glanced at the upstairs window that let that foul light into her bedroom, where I had performed strange acts and kicked Mr. Carnahan in the balls. I thought I saw movement beyond the curtain. I shuddered, like after you walk through cobwebs and wonder if the spider's on you. I felt eyes looking back at me.

Actually, I was pretty hungry anyway, and I chowed down on two burgers and a hot dog, with a helping of baked beans. And a brownie with vanilla ice cream.

After the food, Mrs. Garragues stood under the bunting and thanked us all for coming. She seemed like a really nice person, and motherly, wringing her hands a lot. Not that I'm a Beau Brummell or anything, but her dress seemed kind of thin and if you looked closely it was frayed along the hem. I don't think anyone did her hair, either. I'll bet we raised a whole hundred bucks or so against probably twenty grand of hospital and doctor bills so far. At that rate, the Garragues' would only need about three years to catch up if they had a barbecue every day, rain or shine.

The whole thing made me feel worse than ever.

Chapter 55

And your future's looking dim
- It's all in the Game, Tommy Edwards, 1958

Finals were looming and some of us opened textbooks that had never seen the light of day. By now, most of the class had been accepted into college, but it was still important not to screw up at the end. Actually, we didn't think it was that important but that's what Mrs. Kritzinger told us. Aside from having cuckolded Mr. Kritzinger, Mrs. Kritzinger also taught home economics, or Marriage Prep 101, to the girls. I didn't know about her home ec skills, but she sure was a lousy guidance counselor. Thanks to her, I'd had to endure that stupid interview with Mr. Luther, the Princeton guy with the broomstick up his ass. A lot of the girls were destined for Smith or Vassar, or maybe Radcliffe - I forget which one was the lesbian place.

I was supposed to give the first speech at graduation, a fact that I'm sure mom had already told everyone at the Shop-Rite. She kept bugging me to write it. The dinner table was her preferred forum. She used the subtle approach.

"Did you write your speech yet?" My old man rolled his eyes. Wolfie just shook his head slowly. She'd been asking for two weeks.

I swallowed a mouthful of peas and carrots. They were pretty good, actually, for stupid vegetables. "No, ma, but I told you. I've got plenty of time."

"Graduation's right around the corner."

"I'm thinking about it."

Right. What I was thinking was that I had nothing to say, really, and I didn't want to say any of it. I guess I was supposed to talk about how wonderful everything had been at old Windham High, and how well our teachers had prepared us to march forth into the world, and how our futures were so bright we probably needed sunglasses to look past next week. Maybe I was supposed to comment on world or national events, but really I didn't know too much about what was going on outside Windham anyway.

I mean, I'd read this new doll named Barbie was selling all over the place, but who cared about that? Don Drysdale had hit his second opening day home run for the Dodgers and Alaska had become the 49th state, but there didn't seem to be much else to say about those things. They'd shut down the casinos and whorehouses in Cuba, but I figured that wouldn't be too hot a topic for a graduation speech, even though it might be important to us.

And all that career crap. My God.

"Well, you'd better get going on it," Mom said. "Want some suggestions?"

"That's okay. I'll start on it soon."

Mom was itching for me to write down some stuff, so she could helpfully edit it. Of course that meant toss whatever I'd written and write the damn thing herself, but she couldn't really do that until I'd typed some drivel.

"You've all got wonderful careers in front of you."

Yeah, right. Wolfie suppressed a giggle. Career *this*.

Anyone with any sense had no idea what he wanted to do, except the Bird and maybe a few people like Herbie Schultz, who wanted to be a doctor like his father, or Tommy Lynch, who was going to be a stand-up comedian. Lots of Windham kids were pretty smart, and realized they didn't want to do anything, except maybe inherit their parents' dough and just go around doing fun stuff or whatever they wanted.

This is another example of great, clear thinking. You couldn't really say that out loud, though. Actually, we did say that out loud, chewing the fat at the Sweet Shoppe when the discussion about Mary Anne Moffitt's tits lost steam, usually after about five minutes.

We also talked about how sometimes parents wanted their offspring to go to their own alma mater, like Dieter Becker getting shunted off to Yale, because of course they viewed their kids as extensions of themselves doing things they either failed at or didn't do very well or were denied the opportunity to do. The whole purpose of this was to redeem the parent, so he could sort of live his failures over again in a surrogate way and maybe the results would be better. We all agreed that our parents were delusional. Unfortunately, though, this meant the father – or in my case, mother - had to be completely intolerant of his kid's mistakes. Just like Little League. If the kid wasn't too rebellious and had nothing better in mind he would probably follow in his father or mother's footsteps.

I wasn't going to make the Juilliard concert tour with my electric guitar, but maybe I could still crack the Top 40 or learn bond smuggling like my grandfather. I sure as hell wasn't going to be one of those gray flannel suit guys on the Erie Lackawanna every morning, as per my flash of insight back in the library and I of course had my secret ambition to be a professional goalkeeper.

I knew there were several seniors who only wanted to be trades people, or work with their hands in some way, or do artistic things. Jim Lynch carved these terrific animals in Shop, for instance, but his parents wouldn't dream of letting him make a career out of it, even if he could. Windham parents, especially those in the township, would be horrified if their child didn't go off to college and pursue some professional career, so they could maybe wind up secret alcoholics like Mr. Moffitt because after all this was Windham, not Madison or Morristown.

Jones faced this dilemma, trying to decide whether to be a dentist or plumber, although I must admit his parents had nothing to do with it. His folks were very nice, and his mother always asked me interesting questions about my life. I say interesting, but that was only because she was so nice about it. On the surface, her questions *sounded* interesting and relevant but really they were more a pain in the ass that made you feel like you had to take a deep breath and scratch something. She asked me stuff like what did I want to be, and what did I want to study, and other crap that just would give you a headache if you thought about it very much. I was an actual *person* to Mrs. Jones, which only sounded like a good thing until you thought about it. Most parental interaction with their kids was carefully limited to the dinner table. It was really better, as I have already pointed out.

Apparently a couple of books about teenagers were popular this year, written by some obviously childless Ph.D.s. Consequently, some parents started trying to be *in touch* with their issue, like finding out what they were doing, or palling around with them, and so things went to hell. Those parents had phony guilt, like integration. Mostly the kids wanted to keep their distance as much as the parents, only they weren't confused with phony guilt. All the colored people wanted was nicer neighborhoods and stuff, with schools that went at kind of a remedial pace, and for guys like Pat Boone to stop covering R&B tunes, but not necessarily you or me as their neighbor. But white people with phony guilt don't understand that, although you'd think it was simple enough. Duh.

The school year drifted on toward its conclusion, the end of a major chapter in our young lives. We were looking forward to a relaxing, carefree summer before college, except for those of us who had to get a job because their parents had this skewed idea about a work ethic, as I mentioned earlier, or they couldn't afford college. Jamie had gotten our band a contract playing down the shore for July, and he'd even found a house we could use on the weekends. Summer was shaping up nicely.

Mr. Meyer, substituting in Social Studies class, asked everyone what their ambition was. Tommy Grayson, a kid I didn't know too well from over on Linden Lane, summed it up best. He echoed my thoughts from earlier in the year.

"I want to stay in high school forever," he said. I think everybody knew what he meant. Great thinking really means a kind of crystal clarity, like Tommy Grayson wanting to stay in high school forever or even Brownie and his two-tone Nash. I've noticed since that really great people or successful people have simple, clear ideas, not complex ones, although sometimes they may be the result of complex logic, but not too often. The end result is just focused vision. Even Einstein's $E = MC^2$ is a simple clear idea, although it's not too clear to me, exactly. These people figure out what's important, and just discard the other irrelevant stuff, even though everybody else might think it's the other stuff that's important. Usually you think, "Why didn't I think of that?" But you usually don't. If you did, you would be very successful or great.

Yeah, I know, Assistant Professor Murphy. Another irrelevant chapter. *Keep it moving, Mister Williams. Nobody wants to hear your bogus high school philosophy.*

Chapter 56

In the still of the night
I held you, held you tight
Cause I love, love you so
- I'll Remember (In the Still of the Night), The Five
Satins, 1956

Our Senior Prom followed the disastrous Senior Class Trip, and we were probably lucky it didn't get cancelled. I had asked Laurie Messler. Laurie was a junior, and my mom wasn't too pleased, because she said as long as there were any senior girls who hadn't been asked I shouldn't take an underclassman. I told her hey, you're the one who shoved me ahead a grade; at least Laurie wasn't older than me. There wasn't much she could say to that.

Mothers can be nuts. That's all I needed, to take some oinker like Julie Harris or Sherry Stahl. Mom wanted me to ask Marjorie Wentworth, because she was friends with Mrs. Wentworth. Actually, I could have taken Marjorie because I secretly thought she was pretty attractive, although no one else seemed to, and she didn't get asked out on too many dates. Marjorie was very quiet and, to my knowledge, didn't hang out with any particular group. She just had this soft, pretty smile. She had the last laugh, though, because in the summer after graduation she popped up on television out of New York, doing all kinds of ads and making a fortune looking incredibly glamorous. She never had to talk in any of the ads, just show off some stupid appliance or toothpaste or smile this terrific dazzling white smile. Maybe they painted her teeth, or something, because I didn't remember them being that white. Then everybody realized she really was good-looking, and I felt stupid because I always *thought* she was good-looking, but I didn't ask her out because I hadn't the courage of my convictions.

I wondered if every guy secretly thought she was attractive, like I did, but didn't ask her out because nobody else had. Maybe not, though. Maybe somebody just showed her how to use makeup and painted her teeth when she got to New York. Anyway, it just goes to show you to listen to yourself sometimes. Maybe not all the time, but sometimes. I'm sure you've kicked yourself many times for not listening to yourself.

Because my driver's license had been suspended just for going 120 mph on Rt. 80, which was deserted and six lanes wide for Chrissake, I had to double date to the prom. You had to be seventeen to get your license, and I was about the last person to get it in my class. The ink was hardly dry when they took it away. There were complicated reasons why I was the youngest person in my class, as I explained earlier, and I won't go into them again. They mostly have to do with my mother and her ambitions for me. It would not have occurred to her that sports would be much tougher, being younger than the rest of the class, at a critical time in my physical development.

How would a concert pianist have any ideas like that? I was barely a teenager when I started playing goalie. She had wanted me playing Bach, which she could do when she was about five.

Anyway, Jones and I double dated to the prom. Jones laughed at his own jokes, and his laugh was very infectious. He took Barbara Wilkes, who was very sweet and nice, and to whom he got engaged a couple of months later, which was kind of a waste of a prom. To her credit, Barbara ignored Dan's jokes, which often were directed at her.

All the boys rented tuxedos, of course, and doubtless that's why Divine Providence picked that night to piss on Dan Jones. Prom night was clear and soft, and Jones decided to put the top down on his 1954 Ford, which would prove a big mistake. He had picked me up first, since I lived closest, so it was just the two of us. I crunched across our gravel driveway and got in. Jones looked at me.

"Hey, let's put the top down."

"What about their hair and stuff?"

He shrugged. "We can put it back up if they want. It's too nice out for us. Look at all the stars, daddy-o."

You always have to put the top up for girls, it seems. Most of them, anyway. The ones that wanted the top down and just put on a kerchief were invariably much more fun.

Jones unlatched the windshield clasps and pressed the lever. Now in 1954 the Ford top was hydraulic, so that there was this loud whining noise and the top started backward. That was normal. What was abnormal was a baseball on the rear shelf behind the back seat. As the top retreated backward the ball got jammed in the folding frame. The whine grew much louder as the frame jerked and quivered.

"Hey," I said. "The top's not - "

Suddenly something let go with a loud bang and green hydraulic fluid from the ruptured cylinder shot out through the crack. It was as though the car had taken a petroleum piss right on Dan Jones' noggin, splattering all over the back of his head and neck and on his white ruffled tuxedo shirt and tuxedo collar, not to mention the fact that the top was now stuck with no hydraulics. Best of all, his head looked like vinegar and oil dressing, because the fluid didn't mix with his Vitalis.

"SHIT GODDAMN IT!"

I didn't say anything at all because I was laughing so hard. After all, I hadn't been hit with any oil. So Jones had to get out of the car and we went back inside my house and my mom cleaned him up as best she could, which was all right on Jones himself but his tuxedo was a mess, including even the bow tie. We were a little late picking up the girls, who thought the accident was as funny as I did, even though they hadn't seen it.

There was this problem that kept looming in my mind all during the prom. I had never dated Laurie Messler and she was quite nice, really, and pretty good company. She was really good at keeping everybody in the conversation, and listening, which is a talent most people don't have. Most people are just waiting for you to get through with what you are saying, because they are already thinking what they are going to say, and can hardly wait to say it. Look closely at someone you are talking to and you will see what I mean, sometimes. Their eyes dart around impatiently, waiting to interrupt. You can tell them just about anything at all and it won't make any difference.

Anyway, girls like Laurie Messler really faked me out in situations like a prom, because I couldn't treat them like objects or things you wanted to get something off of. I know that's bad grammar, ending a sentence in a preposition, but it's just an expression. That's why I had a problem. All during the prom I kept thinking about what I was going to do and how far to try and go with her. Of course when we started to dance I would get a clue, but actually Laurie was so light and responsive it was hard to tell. She really was a good dancer. She didn't cram into me, but she didn't keep any open space, either. The whole thing was looming larger and larger in my mind, and pretty soon it was starting to ruin the evening, so I realized I had to just take my chances and go for it. Jones had taught me that our junior year, when we dated the Kuntsler twins, Jeannie and Joanie.

"Never up, never in," he had said. "You don't want to be in a position where you wonder what would have happened. If it turns out you like her, you'll always wonder what you could have gotten off her the first date. It can drive you crazy after awhile, because you'll start to think maybe she gave it to somebody else who put the move on her, but you won't know because you didn't. If you don't like her, you blew your chances for a freebie. Besides, you don't want her to think maybe you're a faggot, do you? They expect you to go for it."

That was hard to believe, sometimes, but I guess as long as you stopped the second time they asked you to, they wouldn't get pissed off. Sometimes, though, they didn't sound very convincing and you had to wait for the third time, unless it was weaker still. It was a matter of judgment. Jones told me not to be nervous about it, but on occasion I would still get apprehensive about when to make the first move. He was much smoother than I was.

We suspected the Kuntsler twins switched on us once but we couldn't really tell. We only dated them about four times and dropped them because they wouldn't put out. It was a fine line. If you really liked a girl, she was way ahead holding you off because it drove you crazy and you had to reluctantly respect her. On the other hand, if you didn't really like her too much, it was easy to get mad when she didn't put out because after all why were you dating her?

About 1 a.m., after our last dance courtesy of Johnny and Joe's *Over the Mountain Across the Sea*, we all piled into Jones' Ford and wound up at Mel's Diner on Route 10. We had been able to get the top up by hand, although the frame was all cockeyed and took quite a bit of force, and it was a good thing because it was getting chilly. I was starving. Several other couples wound up at Mel's and the drunks, truck drivers and other one a.m. patrons got a real kick out of seeing us all in our prom duds. They nudged each other and smiled, probably because we brought back memories for those old guys. Either that or they thought we looked like real assholes, and the girls looked very attractive, which they did.

Actually, Jones kind of looked strange because the green hydraulic oil didn't really dry totally on his tuxedo and shirt. Barb had a hard time dancing with him, because her arm and hand would normally have gone up on the back of his neck, but she wasn't about to ruin her dress for the sake of correct dance etiquette.

The blue plate special was meatloaf, mashed potatoes and peas and that suited me fine. Normally, I made a dam out of the mashed potatoes and the gravy was a miniature lake or reservoir held in by Potato Mountain. Of course, we had a real reservoir nearby and Jones' car would probably wind up there after we finished eating. The peas and small meatloaf particles were the houses and vehicles in the make-believe town at the base of Potato Mountain. I would make a small breach in the top of the wall with my fork and the gravy would start down the mountain toward the town. The townspeople would see disaster coming and try to get away in their pea vehicles as I widened the breach but invariably the onrushing gravy would overtake them, drowning the occupants if they didn't crash first. I didn't do that, in this instance, because I was with Laurie Messler, trying to act like a reasonably mature person graduating high school, so it really faked me out when she asked me a question.

"Did you ever pretend the gravy is a lake and the peas are buildings in a town at the base of the mountain?" she asked.

I really liked her, then. "Yeah, sure. I do it all the time."

Suddenly I wished I had dated her all year long and that this stupid business with making out was already happening, so I wouldn't be nervous about it beforehand. I knew the clock was ticking and I would have to face this trauma soon. Part of me actually wanted not to have to make a move on her at all, but it had nothing to do with any fruity tendencies. It was so I could relax, but also because then I could put the whole night in my mental pocket with only good memories and no anxiety and save the making out for a night with some lesser event, like maybe a movie, in case things went badly.

You were supposed to remember your Senior Prom your whole life, I was pretty sure, and I wanted it all to be nice. But of course I couldn't do that because that would be queer and chickening out would be worse than having the night turn sour if Laurie took offense. It is a complicated business.

We wound up at the reservoir around 2 a.m. The night was still clear, and of course we couldn't put the top down anymore, but we could see the stars out the windows, shimmering quietly in the softly stirring night air. It looked like Someone had decked out the sky for prom night. I thought I saw Sputnik, tooling around the heavens reminding us of the

Communist menace, but nobody else could see it. Maybe it really was something evil, darting around in God's great vault on some nether errand, beeping like a lonely duck, but we didn't think so. We thought it was pretty cool.

Without going into a lot of details, Laurie Messler was perfect, like most of the evening, because she kissed like a soft promise and stopped me just when I secretly wanted her to. I mean when I wanted her to just for that particular night, which was our first date, and not for the whole history of us, which I was beginning to hope might stretch through the summer before college. Of course I tried one more time and she stopped me again.

That evening I'll always remember Jones' radio playing *In the Still of the Night* by the Five Satins, holding Laurie Messler and looking at the moon painting a quicksilver path on the lake, silently flashing cold silver fire when the trees began to shrug in the stirring air. *In the Still of the Night* is about the greatest make-out song ever written. Way off in the distance, in the low western mountains, an early summer storm was wobbling toward us on electric legs, rumbling faintly underneath the Five Satins.

Before we left, the air turned cooler still and the metallic smell of ozone drifted in the Ford's windows, clean and crisp, before the storm scrubbed everything fresh. My prom was really nice, and Laurie turned out to be a gossamer dream, and Jones turned out an oily chauffeur, but what the hey. He had to pay forty bucks to the tuxedo place for the stains.

*   *   *   *

And then it all went to hell in a hurry.

Chapter 57

Oh tell me the words that I'm longing to know
My prayer and the answer you give . . .
-My Prayer, The Platters, 1956

When mom got off the phone, I knew something was really wrong. Her face was the color of notebook paper. Dad looked over from the TV.

"What?"

"That was Mrs. Tigner. Marvin's in Morristown Memorial. He's on a ventilator. He's running a hundred and six degrees."

"From what?"

"Something bit him in their garage. His arm got all red, then he got a fever and had trouble breathing. He lost consciousness."

"Yeah? I think I met the guy once. He's a stockbroker, isn't he?" my dad asked. He wasn't too up on things, sometimes.

"Not her husband. Her husband's name is Gene, and you've played golf with him." Mom's voice had an edge. "Little Marvin. He's Raymond's age."

"Oh. Gee. That's a tough break."

"Tough break? Tough break?" I thought she was going to hit him with something. "That's what you say!?" Dad shrank back into his show, a Dragnet rerun.

I was completely stunned. It was a Thursday night – just an ordinary Thursday night – when we got the news. Mom immediately got in her car and drove to Morristown Memorial where little Marvin Tigner, his body having betrayed him, lay fulminating in Intensive Care. What first had been thought to be an annoying bug bite was infinitely more sinister. Just like that, he'd crossed over from being a normal, healthy kid who got haircuts and ate hamburgers with mustard and lots of pickles to getting fed through tubes and breathing with a ventilator. My mom stayed with Mrs. Tigner until very late; she slept in Friday morning and so I never saw her before school, which was really unusual.

Evidently Marvin developed a raging secondary infection late Friday, and slipped into a coma by Saturday. He was on oxygen and listed as critical. It sure didn't look too good. All I could think of was that little tyke sitting wide-eyed in the Emil J. Paidar while Art shaved him with his finger, and then slipping his hand in mine when we crossed Main Street for lunch. Sunday I decided to go to church, light a candle and say a few words for little Marvin. Wolfie said he wanted to come along, and so out of habit Raymond went with us. It was a Three Stooges reunion in old St. Francis.

It was strange, being in that building and actually trying to talk to the landLord. I couldn't really remember having done that before. I felt kind of guilty even asking Him to fix Marvin. I could just hear Him turning to His Son or maybe the Holy Ghost and saying, "Oh, NOW the asshole wants something. He ignores me for just about his whole life but now that he wants something . . ."

I prayed anyway, hoping that since my message wasn't a selfish one maybe it would do some good. I guess that's what they mean by 'fervent prayer'. I recalled Father Corr's sermons about praying for favors. They weren't too popular, I think. I've noticed that when good stuff happen, religious people thank Him. But when things go in the crapper, who blames Him? It makes no sense at all to me when you look at what really goes on in the world. It makes me think you'd have to invent another one just to stay sane, and call it Heaven, I guess.

But then I had a strange memory, those WW II newsreels showing all those bodies and carnage. They weren't just all soldiers, either, especially around those death camps, if they were really real, despite Mr. Kritzinger's scoffing. So then I started wondering if maybe He really was a laissez faire kind of Guy, for whatever reason I couldn't imagine. After all, we were supposed to have been made in His image, so wouldn't He feel fatherly towards us? What kind of Father lets his kid get bitten by some deadly creature and fall into a coma, especially when all He would have to do is wave a wand or maybe say a few old timey Bible-type words? Something was definitely off somewhere. I tried to reason it through.

We'd learned in Current Events that a great famine was gripping China, with possibly millions dead already. A couple of years ago, the Medog earthquake, a huge shaker along the Chinese-Tibetan border, killed thousands; those that were left were drowned when a bunch of dikes broke. Back in 1931, we'd read, maybe two and a half million Chinese perished in catastrophic flooding. It sure seemed like He had it in for the Chinese, maybe in retribution for the Korean War, I don't know.

Or maybe He had made Orientals as a kind of prototype for real humans, and they were sort of expendable.

I prayed as hard as I could, but I couldn't help the thought in the back of my brain that it wouldn't do any good, in light of all the destruction we'd learned about. After all, Marvin was just one kid and we were talking about millions of Chinese, not to mention any other races or countries, like the Japs in Hiroshima and Nagasaki. The only thing I could think of, though, was that supposedly Jesus had a different standard for actual Americans. History sort of seemed to bear that out. I was pretty sure Marvin Tigner was a real American. In fact, I was positive. After that, I felt better about the whole thing, like maybe I'd done some good.

Maybe. I supposed the next few days would tell.

Chapter 58

A white sport coat
And a pink carnation
I'm all dressed up for the dance
- A White Sport Coat (and a pink carnation), Marty
Robbins, 1957

Rich Venzoni, the Greaser, was still dating Mary Anne Moffitt, of course, and it was a foregone conclusion she would be his prom date. No one else asked her to go, although most of the boys in the class would have wanted to.

Right before I asked Laurie Messler to the prom, even though my mother wanted me to ask the secretly attractive Marjorie Wentworth, Mrs. Moffitt quietly left her comfortable, warmly furnished split level and checked into the Historic Morris Inn in Madison. She paid for a night in one of their expensive suites, and had a bottle of champagne brought up. She had taken the electric carving knife from her modern, well-thought-out kitchen.

The spider was spinning now.

About 2 a.m., she placed one phone call to her home, but hung up when her husband picked up the phone. That was reported in the Windham Courier. Then she turned on the bathroom sink, plugged in the electric carving knife, and sliced both wrists. The right wrist was severed so badly, with tendons and connective tissue gone, the police determined she sliced that wrist last because she couldn't have gripped the knife to do her left wrist afterward, even with the electricity on. That hadn't been reported in the Courier, but we got the story from Jimmy Rohleder, who of course had learned the grim details from his brother Marty on the Windham police force.

The news was shocking on several levels. Mary Anne Moffitt had become my friend, and I was helpless to comfort her. I didn't even see her afterward; the school year was almost over and Mary Anne did not return. I thought about calling her several times, but for whatever reason never did. I think I was afraid her father might answer the phone; after thinking about it enough, though, I was more afraid that wasn't the real reason. Rich Venzoni went into a state of shock and even That Bastard Heileman had enough sense to leave him alone.

Mrs. Moffitt had remained true to Windham, even to the end. She had crossed the township line to kill herself, and preserve the town from scandal in some symbolic way. She slit her wrists in Madison.

For the next several days, we discussed the tragedy at school in hushed tones. We had come to the horrible, unfunny conclusion that the rumors about Rich Venzoni doing Mrs. Moffitt may well have been true. After that, no one really spoke much to the Greaser and of course we didn't see him at the prom. He sort of quietly faded from visibility.

Brownie, Jones and I realized among ourselves there was another, more sinister factor in play. It seemed more likely now the Moffitt silver Mercedes, the Gull Wing with red leather seats, had been the vehicle that ran down and killed Po Jackson.

But who had been driving?

Then The Bird stunned us by wallpapering his family room with the back of his head.

Another strand, maybe the trip-wire, as the web took shape.

Our senior year was ending grimly. Graduation was days away. I still needed to compose my speech. I spent the next two days writing gibberish. The night before graduation, I practiced on Raymond while he downed his Oreos and milk. Somewhere he'd gotten hold of the can of furniture polish again, but I stopped him before he could mix it with the milk.

Raymond thought the speech was funny. I gave it to mom, figuring it was too late for her to write a new one, but she said she actually liked it.

She handed it back. "It's very good, George. I'm so excited about your future."

Some future. As it was turning out, not all of us had one.

Chapter 59

We'll remember always
Graduation Day
- Graduation Day, The Four Freshmen, 1956

Graduation Day weather was actually about perfect: a light breeze pushed a few white puff balls around blue sky, with the temperature in the low seventies. The show started right on time at eleven a.m. Mom was all lit up when I was introduced; I heard my family clap and cheer. As I walked onstage, I felt ridiculous in the cap and gown outfit with the dumb tassel hanging down, like you could pull it for the butler or to get off the trolley car. With all my stage experience in the band, I didn't feel too nervous, though. After all, I didn't have to sing. I hadn't really memorized my speech, so I took the notes, written in large letters, to the podium.

"Thank you. Principal Dunwood, distinguished faculty, proud parents and fellow students. It is with great pleasure that I – that I--"

That I what? I'd lost my train of thought, having spotted Miss van Aldewehe in the front row. She looked terrific, with her gorgeous legs and sweet smile. What the hell great pleasure was I talking about? I hadn't written that part down. I couldn't remember, exactly, unless it was her. Was it her? Suddenly I had the same helpless feeling as when I had the disastrous Princeton interview.

I looked down at my notes. I couldn't see them too well; something about the lighting, maybe. I blinked hard, blinking away cobwebs. The notes seemed – nonsensical. As I stood at the podium, they seemed even dumber than when I had written them, and they'd seemed really dumb then. I put the pages aside and looked out at everybody for a few moments, gathering my thoughts, sort of. Then I felt a surprising calmness, a sputter of inspiration. I would rise to the occasion.

"Most of my classmates, like myself, grew up in Windham, and it's a pretty good place to grow up, because we have big houses with lots of stuff and new cars and dough to spend-- "

A few rows back, I could see Brownie and Jones look at each other. Something small scrabbled across the stage in front of me and disappeared, into the audience I guess.

"— lots of stuff and dough to spend. Out in the township, anyway. Maybe not so much in the borough. There's this kid, Marvin Tigner, who's a friend of my small brother Raymond, and he's in the hospital very seriously ill with a spider bite. He's just a little boy and he got bitten by a dangerous brown recluse spider. I had never heard of a brown recluse spider. It happened right here in Windham. I don't know what to make of that.'

I could hear a rustling in the audience. A few people were looking around, or at each other.

'Not too long ago, before little Marvin got bitten by the brown recluse spider, the three of us were downtown getting haircuts when the cops rousted these two young Negro boys who made the criminal mistake of getting off the train in

Windham. They were laughing and joking on the platform. But Duff Carlin's men in blue were right on the scene, protecting you and me and Miss van Aldewehe, all the good folks of Windham, as they intercepted these two dangerous criminals and sent them packing, back towards Newark or wherever. The young Negro boys weren't laughing and joking anymore. Now little Marvin and my young brother Raymond and I all saw this happen, and I saw the looks on their faces, and it made me ashamed of my town."

There was a kind of collective gasp. Jones had half-gotten up out of his seat and was gesturing Brownie to do the same. I guess he was going to drag me away from the microphone. Brownie just grinned, though, and motioned Jones to sit back down. I'm sure he didn't want to ruin the show. Jones shrugged and sat.

All the adults were open-mouthed now, kind of frozen in place. I did see that Wolfie was wide-eyed, covering his mouth so he wouldn't laugh out loud, but I know he was laughing because his shoulders were shaking, and my mom was all horrified. She was still lit up, but now it was all white.

"Not as ashamed, maybe, as when that family the Cooks got driven out of town, when the junior class busted all their windows knowing the cops would take a half hour to respond.'

'And I haven't even started on that goddamn Erie Lackawanna club car, the one that gets our dads home for dinner half-sloshed, or that asshole Pat Boone, that fakey religious plagiarist fag who steals all the songs from Little Richard and everybody who's any good and robs them of their money."

Out of the corner of my eye, I saw Principal Dunwood lurch up from his chair on the corner of the stage. He beckoned for Coach Weber, but Coach didn't do anything. Instead, Mr. Glendenning got up. I spoke faster as they approached.

"And what about teachers who have sex with students while—"

Principal Dunwood grabbed for the microphone but I yanked it away.

"—some of you take turns running over hard-working Po the colored guy so the stupid Courier can give it a line or two AND LEAVING HIM ON THE SIDE OF THE ROAD LIKE HE WAS—"

Suddenly I was wrestled to the ground. I still had the microphone, though.

"—ARMADILLO---"

I poked somebody in the eye, accidentally.

"—AND THAT GODDAMN LITTLE LEAGUE—"

I guess I passed out, or maybe hit my head. From what I heard, mom had beaten me to it.

    *   *   *   *   *

I guess I screwed up Graduation pretty well, although I wasn't there to see the rest of it. They resumed the ceremonies after awhile but the adults were pretty much in shock. It got awkward when the seniors were coming up to get their diplomas, and they got to the W's, but Principal Dunwood just skipped my name entirely. I don't suppose he could have done much else, really. Afterward they served Kool-Aid and cookies from the Shop-Rite, for Chrissake, as everybody but me milled about in their mobile draperies. Not the good cookies fresh from the bakery, or even Mrs. Greek's homemade plaster patties she'd made her son bring to school on some foreign holiday called Theofany, but the crummy little prepackaged ones that probably had chemical preservatives.

Kool-Aid. I guess it was our crowning toast.

I was surprised by the reactions over the next week or so. The story, of course, had spread like wildfire. The Courier didn't cover it; Windham might lose its ranking as the third most desirable place to live in the New York environs. Unexpectedly, I turned out to be a real hero to the student body, and apparently even kids from neighboring towns had heard about my unscripted rant. The whole event was fast becoming legend. Somebody said Murray the K even mentioned it on WINS in New York, although I never heard it. Fellow graduates congratulated me. Jones and Brownie treated me to a pepperoni pizza, and even Wally chipped in a couple of pitchers of beer down at Two Bars. Everybody wanted to know who I was referring to in the sex part, especially since I'd mentioned the ravishing Miss van Aldewehe, but I just said I didn't remember. I could tell none of the students believed me, though.

The adults quickly made excuses, like maybe I'd had heat stroke or something, because after all what I had said couldn't possibly be true, and wasn't I a nice boy? I guess they kind of decided to feel sorry for me, and that it was just an aberration.

"You're my new hero," Wolfie told me later. "That was the greatest. All my friends think you're a living legend now."

A living asshole was more like it. I think mom and dad just didn't know how to react, or what to do, so they didn't do much of anything either. Either that or mom was in shock, clinically. I think I probably shortened her life span by about a decade, though.

Life went on. I'd punched Windham as hard as I could, but it was like punching a big bean bag. The dent just sagged back out again.

Chapter 60

I begged him to go slow
But whether he heard I'll never know
- The Leader of the Pack, The Shangri-Las, 1964

Now the spider was busy.

Three weeks after graduation, we were stunned again, attending our second funeral in a month when Tommy Pond made sausage pizza out of himself and his new Harley Davidson up on Route 80. The bike was actually four years old, a 1955 Hydra-Glide, but Tommy had just gotten it as a graduation present. It had been a clear, dry afternoon and Tommy had smashed into an abutment at an estimated 90 miles per hour. There were no skid marks. There wasn't much to bury; they probably could have fit the motorcycle in the coffin with Tommy.

Some of the kids gave a kind of eulogy, which was very nice, but of course they wouldn't let me anywhere near a microphone. Gerd Mueller's funeral had been a closed affair as well; what was left of his head wouldn't have looked very restful in an open casket. Between these two guys and my dead American grandmother, I was getting to be an old hand at funerals, all of a sudden. I don't think they are something you ever get used to, though, unless you get to be about sixty-five years old and your friends all start to go. But maybe by then death becomes more a part of life, rather than a jarring intrusion, I don't know.

The story was weird. Coach Weber, of all people, was about the first person on the scene and flagged down a passing police cruiser. This was really odd, because Route 80 was not that close to Windham and, as I said, didn't really run to anyplace one would want to go. Coach drove an old Packard, which I suppose was all he could afford on a Windham teacher's salary. It was the model where the Indian hood ornament lit up at night, I think a 1954, and so obviously he wasn't going to drag race anyone except maybe a turtle that wandered onto the highway.

I wondered, idly, what Coach Weber had been doing there. Route 80 was a heavily patrolled interstate since becoming a popular drag racing location, and there were initially rumors that maybe Tommy Pond had been racing another bike. Nothing ever came of it, though, and if there had been another motorcycle the rider would never be found.

Our band was working weekends at the shore, and so I didn't have a regular day summer job. It usually took me until about Tuesday to recover, anyway. I had spent the Fourth of July in Ocean City, or maybe it was Seaside Heights, playing a three night gig and so I missed the Windham fireworks.

It was a Wednesday around the end of July when I ran into Brownie at Tommy Wade's Esso station on Route 24, which of course was Main Street as it ran through our town. I was driving my deceased grandmother's 1955 Studebaker Hawk, a real piece of shit if there ever was one, but also a free piece of shit. Thanks, grandma. Like my mother's T-Bird, this was also powder blue, but all similarity ended there. Top speed was maybe 65 miles per hour, which was 65 miles per hour faster than I had been able to drive while my license was suspended. Raymond's American Flyer could give it a run for the money.

Brownie's two tone Rambler was up on the lift getting new tires. It was almost noon, and I had been out running errands, mostly getting stuff for college. It was a hot and muggy day, like a steam iron, and I felt sorry for the borough residents who were not going to be swimming in the William P. Morris Municipal Pool, which was everybody, thanks to us.

I offered Brownie a lift to the Sweet Shoppe while they put on his tires. We shot the breeze over a couple of burgers, fries and shakes. The American Dream meal. I wonder how many other countries' cultures we have corrupted with crap like burgers, fries and shakes, but then again we gave them Chuck Berry, rock 'n' roll's greatest lyricist, and the automatic dishwasher.

Brownie was on his way to England in another week to play soccer, having signed a big buck contract with Manchester United, and therefore had postponed attending Duke University. I was really excited about Brownie's good fortune and asked him a zillion questions about it. His dad had come to every game and filmed his son with his 8mm Bell & Howell home movie camera, rain or shine. Mr. Brown had become a fixture at all our games and after awhile we hadn't even noticed him cranking away, making his homegrown Brownie newsreels. Brownie said his dad had sent copies of all the spliced highlights to teams in England's first division.

What a smart idea, and it had all paid off. A couple of clubs had sent people to scout him, and we knew nothing about it. Not even Brownie had known at the time anybody was coming to watch him, which he said was probably much better because he would have been too nervous and not played well. I could never imagine Brownie too nervous about anything, though. The whole idea wouldn't have worked in my case, because the highlights would have lasted about two minutes for my entire high school career, since our team had been so dominant.

I was going to buy lunch, being flush from our busy band season, but in light of his sudden wealth I let Brownie pick up the tab.

"Got any more big speeches planned?" Brownie asked. Very funny.

"Very funny. Yeah, I was asked to be the keynote speaker at the Republican National Convention."

"Hey, remember that kid you mentioned? That kid with the spider bite?"

"Sure, Marvin Tigner."

"Whatever happened?"

"He's home. He's okay, just a little scar where he got bit. Mrs. Tigner told my mom he's lucky to be alive."

"That's good. I wondered about that."

The food came.

"Too bad about the reward money, you know?" Brownie said, ladling mustard on his burger.

"Well, doesn't sound as if you need any."

"Yeah. Do you believe the cops?"

The report had come out a week earlier; we'd gotten the gist of it from Martin Rohleder. The Moffitt's Mercedes had gone to the state crime lab and after scientific examination could not positively be established as the vehicle that hit Po. Deer blood lit up luminal anyway, and old man Moffitt said he tried to clean it with bleach, which also reacted with the stuff. It was pure bullshit.

I shrugged. "Sure. But we know it's the car anyway."

"Of course it's the goddamn car. I bet nobody squeezed old man Moffitt as to why he had it hidden in the garage and didn't fix it. That made no sense."

"Guess we'll never know which one of them drove it."

"I guess we won't," Brownie said, biting his pickle. "I don't guess a lot of people care that much."

I supposed Brownie was right. I knew another one who cared, though. He didn't own his own suit.

We ate for awhile.

"Hey, I ran into Coach Weber at the hardware store. Guess what?" Brownie said.

"What?"

"He's gonna be teaching in Pennsylvania next year. Somewhere in the coal country."

Pennsylvania mining communities were not exactly a step up. "I guess he's gonna move next month?" I asked. It would be a long commute.

"Next week, actually. He said he's just about packed up now." Brownie pushed away his plate, leaving half his fries.

"I never saw you leave food before, except in the cafeteria," I observed.

"With what they're paying me, I gotta show up in shape," he said.

"Yeah, that's why you're still sucking on your milkshake."

He shrugged. "Well, I mean within reason." He shifted gears. "You know, I asked him about Tommy Pond. I asked Coach Weber."

This raised my antennae. "What do you mean? You mean, how come he was there?"

"Yeah. He was surprised at the question and I don't think he had an answer. You were right, I think something's funny."

Suddenly I knew what we had to do.

"Let's go out there."

"Out where?"

"You know, Route 80. Where it happened. Let's take a look."

"What's the matter with you?" Brownie asked. "That's morbid, Williams."

"Yeah? Well, I don't mean it that way. I just think we gotta take a look. I mean, we weren't Tommy's best friends or anything, but he was a classmate and we liked him, didn't we?"

"Sure."

I remembered his pat on the back, years ago. I owed him that much.

"Besides, you're not working and neither am I," I continued. "We'll leave your car at the Esso station and be back by 2:30 or so. What else you got to do?"

Brownie shrugged. "Hey, it's your gas." At twenty five cents a gallon, fuel was becoming a consideration for some people.

I let him pay the check and we climbed into the Hawk. Boy, was that car misnamed. If they were going to name it after a bird, they should've dropped the H, or maybe called it the Turkey.

The day was hazy with heat and moisture. The Studebaker was noisy anyway, and with the windows down we didn't bother with the radio. It took us twenty minutes to get to

Route 80. The newspaper had said Tommy hit the abutment just over the crest of a hill, a quarter mile before the county line. I knew roughly where that was, and as we approached the area I drifted over into the slow lane, the Hawk's natural home.

"I guess that's it," said Brownie. The rise mentioned in the Courier was just ahead. As we cleared the top, I saw the overpass a quarter mile away. There was no traffic in the rear view mirror. I slowed to maybe fifteen miles an hour and pulled onto the shoulder. I eased the Hawk up to within about fifty feet of the abutment and stopped. I turned off the engine, which kept knocking and coughing and having tubercular Studebaker spasms. Maybe it was trying to lay a little Hawk egg. I had learned to put it back in gear to stop it.

Brownie looked over at me. It was one thing to visualize the scene mentally, but quite another to actually be there. It felt pretty creepy, even in the dazzling, diffuse sunlight. It was like looking through gauze, or maybe cobwebs. Ahead, the abutment shimmered quietly in the heat, waiting, Tommy Pond's giant concrete tombstone.

"Let's take a look," Brownie finally said, opening his car door. "It can't be any hotter out there."

We were perspiring heavily, and not just from the heat. I felt a shiver down my spine anyway. We walked slowly up to the bridge, looking around and taking in the scene. I silently imagined Tommy flying over the rise just behind us, maybe airborne a little bit at 90 mph, and then drifting off to the right as he lost control and splatting like a bug on a windshield. Maybe the bike had wavered a bit as he desperately fought for control.

I hoped he hadn't had too much time to realize what was going to happen. We reluctantly walked up to the concrete.

I don't know what we expected to find, but there were a few scarred gouges which might or might not have come from Tommy's Harley. They seemed about the right height. I don't know if I thought the concrete itself might be discolored, but the chipped surface was the only sign of the accident, a mute epitaph on the highway headstone.

Like I had with Mueller and his shotgun, I thought of the coroner coming out to the scene and doing his ghastly business, measuring and examining and taking pictures, none of which would be suitable for framing or the yearbook - just shards of twisted chrome and eggplant. Who would take a job like that?

Neither of us had spoken since we had gotten out of the car. We wandered around for another minute or so, heavy with our thoughts. Not a single car had driven past. What a spooky highway.

"I dunno, George," Brownie said. I don't remember him ever calling me by my first name before. "I guess it's a good thing we came, but I don't really know why."

"Yeah, I guess," I said. Maybe we just had to pay our respects in our own way. It was too late to pat Tommy on the back, which no longer existed in any event. I took one last look around before turning back to the Hawk.

I happened to look up toward the crossing roadway, maybe fifteen feet above, and froze. I stood stock still. Brownie saw me stiffen, and gave me a quizzical look.

"Jesus H. Christ," I said, softly. Slowly, I raised my hand and pointed. Brownie followed my finger. He saw it, too, as the spider danced across its infernal architecture.

"Son of a bitch," he said.

Sometimes they put a sign on bridges or abutments, telling you the name of the road you were crossing under. Not always, but sometimes. This one had a sign. It read:

HALF MILE ROAD

Chapter 61

My secret love's no secret anymore
- Secret Love, Doris Day, 1954

I dropped Brownie off at Tommy Wade's Esso station and looked up Coach's phone number around 3:30. Mrs. Weber answered.

"Hi, Mrs. Weber. It's George Williams. I was in Coach's class. I met you at the Get Acquainted Day thing at school, back in September, but you probably don't remember."

"Oh, hello, George. Well, there were so many students it's hard to remember them all."

"Sure, that's OK. Is Coach in?"

"No, he's getting boxes. We're moving, you know."

Now I felt even worse than I had a moment ago. "I heard. Would you please tell him Brownie and I would like to see him tonight, if possible? Could you give him that message?"

"Certainly. Why don't you boys call back in about an hour?"

We set it up for seven o'clock. I drove to Brownie's house, because he didn't live too far from Coach Weber. While Windham had no apartment houses, as such, there were a few places to let that had either been detached garages or were above some of the stores on Main Street. The Webers lived at

43 ½ Passaic Avenue, which proved to be a converted garage. Mrs. Weber let us in with a pleasant smile.

"Hello, boys. Why yes, George, I do remember you now." I guess she'd been to Graduation. Everyone remembered me now. "How nice to see you again. And you must be Walter Brown."

Brownie's real name almost didn't register with me. She must have looked it up in the yearbook. She led us back to the small living room, where Coach was busy putting stuff in boxes, dressed in his usual black and red sweat suit. I don't think I would have recognized him in any other outfit.

The place was kind of in disarray, but that was understandable. The thing was, though, it was really depressing. Not just the mess from moving, but the idea that anybody would live like that in somebody's goddamn garage apartment. The walls were these cheeseball thin wallboard sheets, instead of plaster, the kind you can't even hang a picture on without crumbling. There was no molding either, and I noticed a trapdoor in the ceiling which must have led to a storage area in the attic. The edges around the trapdoor were discolored from moisture, stained a disgusting brown.

Mrs. Weber was at least as nice as the landlady, I was sure, who lived probably in the main house which was about three times as large and no doubt had real plaster walls with molding and no leaking trapdoor to the attic. Capitalism can be pretty depressing. There was this threadbare old rug on the floor that didn't really fit the room too well; it went up the baseboards one way but was too short the other. The small window had these milky-white curtains, and they were rustling in the light breeze. For some reason, the sound made me shudder. I guess with all the upheaval, Mrs. Weber hadn't really cleaned the joint recently because there seemed to be dust and cobwebs everywhere. She asked us if we wanted something to drink, and she brought us a couple of cokes. You could tell they were trying to save dough, because nobody would buy soda in stupid cans instead of the 6 ½ ounce bottles unless they were watching their pennies. I was getting more depressed by the minute.

Mrs. Weber excused herself and said she was going to take little Coach for a walk in the stroller. Brownie, Coach and I chatted about his new job for awhile, until we were alone. It was pretty weird talking to Coach Weber as a regular person, and not just a teacher anymore.

Coach grinned at me. "Well, Mister Williams, I haven't seen you since your Graduation speech."

"Yeah, I know, I know. Listen, I saw the Wood Pecker wave for you to help him when they tried to get me off the stage. Thanks for not getting up."

"Hey, I wanted to hear the rest of it as much as your classmates."

"Coach, we - uh - we wanted to say so long and all, but also we needed to talk to you about something else," I said.

"What's that, boys?" I could tell he knew what we were talking about, because he was being sort of elaborately casual.

Brownie took up the cudgels. "Coach, we gotta talk about Tommy Pond. We went out to the accident site this afternoon. You know what we saw."

There was a long silence. I guess he was making up his mind.

"Look, Coach. We saw the sign. We saw the road sign. Tommy smashed up against Half Mile Road. Tommy was our half miler. That was no coincidence, was it? He never did too good in the half mile, did he, Coach? Maybe we wouldn't have known something, but how come you were the first guy on the scene? What's going on, Coach?"

Tommy had run up against his last half mile, and lost again.

Coach looked at us, one to the other, slowly. He let out a sigh. Brownie and I were sitting in the only two chairs in the small living room, and Coach was perched on a box where he had been packing up another one. I saw about a half dozen baseballs, a desk set, a couple of books and an old hourglass in the open carton. Somehow that was even more depressing. Then he got up from his box and went over to a drawer in one of those antiquated prescription file cabinets, like they used to have in the doctor's office.

As he opened the drawer, it hit me why the curtain noise was so disquieting. The swishing sound reminded me of Mrs. Carnahan's stockings; it was exactly the same. I glanced over to the window. What the hell were those curtains made of? I shuddered again.

Coach Weber reached under a pile of papers in the drawer and came out with a sheet of schoolbook lined paper. He came back over and sat down.

"You're not boys, anymore, men. We've had our moments, but right now I'm going to be speaking to you as adults. Do you understand me?"

We nodded. "What I'm going to tell you should never leave this room. Now I know I have no control over that, and I can't force you to keep silent, but I'm going to ask that you do. Nothing but heartache can come from this if you speak out."

What the hell was going on?

Coach shifted on his box. "What I'm going to tell you is known only to me and Chief Duff Carlin. I thought for a long time about not saying anything to anyone, but the police had a right to know. I could not withhold information from the authorities, but I implored Chief Carlin to keep this quiet, and he has. Now it will be on your shoulders, as well."

He raised a questioning eyebrow. Brownie and I looked at each other and nodded assent.

To what?

The spider was stirring.

"Some time after the softball game, when you guys turned the bases around - " he smiled, in spite of himself, "sometime after that, your gym class was playing a little soccer and I realized I had forgotten my whistle. I trotted back into the locker room and came upon Tommy and Gerd Mueller."

He stopped for a moment. I guess he was looking for a flash of comprehension, but we didn't give him any.

"I came upon Tommy and Gerd alone in the locker room. In the shower."

In the goddamn shower?

Jesus H. Christ. Son of - I felt like I had been hit with a ball bat. I looked over at Brownie. He looked like I felt.

There was a silence for the longest time.

"Coach, - coach, do we - do we understand what you're saying?" I asked.

Coach Weber just looked at us. "Under the rules, I was obliged to immediately report this incident. That was my obligation. But I chose not to report it. Later, I spoke to the two of them, separately. I offered to arrange counseling, not in Windham, and without their parents being informed. I was way out on a limb, but that's what I did.'

'Over the next couple of weeks, I tried to watch the situation closely and help the boys come to the right decision. Obviously, I didn't do the right thing. Mueller as you know seemed a pretty low-key guy. He had become very agitated, and then unresponsive. He stopped seeing Tommy Pond altogether, and wouldn't even speak to him. I thought I was going to have to do something further, but I didn't have enough time to figure out what. You know what happened next."

We knew what happened next. Bird Mueller blew his scholarship and his brains out. He had played it pretty cool with us, as though nothing was wrong, but I guess everything was wrong. Christ.

Weber continued. "Tommy Pond went into shock, quietly. I got him to start seeing somebody over in Morristown, but then he called me that particular day. He said he wanted to see me. He handed me this note and took off before I could read it. I don't know why, but later on I didn't show it to Chief Carlin. I guess I was afraid the note would wind up in the papers or his mother would see it."

We took the sheet of notebook paper. It was short and to the point.

Dear Coach,

Thanks for trying. It's not your fault. If you hadn't forgotten your whistle that day, somebody else would probably have come in and that would have been a lot worse.

I am like at the bottom of a deep well. I can barely see the light above, and there's no way I can reach it. The words have already been said. You tried to help, but its all just too deep. I'm very tired. Remember that road we talked about? Route 80? I guess it's my last half mile.

I'm sorry, Coach.

Tommy Pond

I handed the note back to Coach Weber. There was something oddly familiar about the handwriting. Brownie and I looked at each other; there was nothing we could say.

"Tommy told me about Route 80," Coach Weber said. "He got a real kick out of you and Jones taking your mother's new car to a hundred and twenty. He was something of a mechanic; he said nobody in his right mind would do that to a new Thunderbird. That cracked him up. He said that road was like his life, going too fast from nowhere to nowhere. He had seen that sign for Half Mile Road. I knew what he meant as soon as I read the note. By the time I had read it and jumped in my car, he was ahead of me and I couldn't catch up. I got there just a couple of minutes later."

*   *   *   *   *

It took me a few days to figure out the stuff about Tommy Pond's note, and why the handwriting had seemed faintly familiar. It didn't dawn on me until the next time I wandered into the Sweet Shoppe, and I connected it up with the three by five index cards on the bulletin board.

The 2640 Club. Now I knew why the number had seemed familiar, as well. The Half Mile Club. Coach had tried to help those two lost boys, without realizing Tommy had been involved since at least the beginning of the school year, and was, apparently, the leader of the whole sorry mess. Maybe he wasn't so much a victim as a predator. The whole idea of posting notes on the Sweet Shoppe bulletin board seemed to me either a message of defiance or maybe a muted cry for help.

I sure as hell hoped it wasn't a recruiting poster; kids from the junior high occasionally hung out at the place. I wondered how many members were in the Half Mile Club, and if the mortality rate of the organization had been 100%. I fervently hoped so.

I didn't even want to think about that pat on the back, those years ago, but I knew I would anyway, maybe for the rest of my life. Goddamn it.

Oh, damn it all to Hell.

Chapter 62

Stagger Lee shot Billy,
He shot that poor boy so bad . . .
-Stagger Lee, Lloyd Price, 1959

On the morning of the fourth of July, Lee Garragues, Charlie's dad, drove out to the rehab facility in Morristown for his daily visit. They said his son smiled when he saw his father, a vacant smile, drooling, and offered no resistance when Mr. Garragues gently laid him down, put a pillow to the side of his head and fired a .44 magnum into Jerry's malfunctioning brain. He sat beside his son for a few minutes, while all hell broke loose outside the room, and wept. Just as the cop cars screeched to a halt outside the window he held the .44 to his heart and pulled the trigger.

Brady's Funeral Home was the site of the first reunion for the Class of 1959.

Chapter 63
Rock 'n' roll will always be
It'll go down in history
-Rock 'N' Roll is Here to Stay, Danny and the Juniors,
1958

In the fall, we scattered like leaves before the autumn wind. Brownie probably traveled the farthest from home, at least initially, flying off to Manchester. Just about everyone went off to various colleges and universities, as I did. By October I had another band started and was keeping goal for the freshman soccer team. I really thought I was better than the varsity keeper, but freshmen weren't allowed on the varsity.

Before taking off for college, I reflected again on my years at Windham High. I wasn't sure what I had learned, or how well the school had prepared me for what was to come, but I thought the place had done a pretty good job. Many things stood out, as I have described, and some had a meaning beyond the moment. While not all the memories were golden, I valued my friendships and considered myself fortunate. I had felt the filament of the web, burning, like the man o'war, and shuddered; I had seen it trap others close to me, even bite little Marvin Tigner, and once I thought I saw that black shape scampering quickly across the trip-wire, in the dimness, and the blood-red hourglass. But that was out of the corner of my eye; when I looked directly, it wasn't there.

I didn't have many regrets during that carefree time - or so it already seems, even now – the biggest, of course, was the tragedy we'd indirectly caused to the Garragues family. That will haunt all of us forever, I know, even Brownie.

Probably.

And the other: coach Weber tried to treat us decently, kindly, and with perhaps more understanding than we knew; in return we had gleefully torpedoed his professional teaching career. There is one unfulfilled wish, maybe more so than planking Mary Anne Moffitt, or even Miss Amy Van Aldewehe. Well, almost as much, anyway.

I wish we had let Coach Weber be what he was, had let him stay in Windham, for he was perhaps the best of us.

Or was he?

Somehow I see him standing in the surf, looking down, motionless, for perhaps a minute while the lifeguards flail and dive maybe twenty yards away. And I see snatches of black and red through the pain as Heileman's fists make eggplant out of my face.

I have the impression there were clues I had not grasped, levels I had not seen or understood, but maybe I haven't the tools to comprehend them all. Somehow Coach Weber seems near the center of things. There are other explanations, possibly, but as I said in the beginning, I just can't be sure I fit it all together; I cannot tell if indeed the pieces form a whole. I hope one day I can.

And there's one other disquieting thing: I don't know why, exactly, but before I went off to college I went back to old WHS one final time. It was open for summer session, and there were basketball leagues in the gym. I rummaged around Coach Weber's old office, looking for I don't know what, but only found a few scraps of note paper in the bottom of his desk drawer that hadn't been thrown out. Here's one:

% Thurs. Dec 9 % -
History of Sports - bring Roman gladiator material - early games as forerunners to modern Olympiad

I thought I saw the web now, barely visible, stretching across Windham, lightly, shuddering in the summer breeze. Quietly co-existing, letting in the sun and the air, neither evil nor benign, I prayed, but as a filigree, simply there.

- End -

*   *   *   *   *

The Windham Courier

September 10, 1959

FBI Winds Up Investigation, Results Inconclusive

Windham- The Federal Bureau of Investigation officially closed its investigation into the William P. Morris Municipal Pool explosion, issuing a three page report indicating cause of the blast remains unknown.

"Without any motive or suspects, we feel the blast was likely caused by something like a natural gas pocket explosion, perhaps from lightning. Although the weather that night was clear, a phenomenon known as ball lightning or clear air lightning may have occurred," said Special Agent David Budworth. "Naturally, we would reopen the investigation if new evidence should warrant this action."

The pool complex was heavily damaged, but is expected to open in time for next summer's activities.

From the December 11, 1959 McKeesport-Clairton Daily News:

Hunting Accident Victim Found

A body found near the town of Clairton, Pennsylvania has been identified as nineteen year old Jack Frankfurter of Windham, New Jersey. Mr. Frankfurter had been a freshman at Penn State University and failed to return to school following the Thanksgiving break. His parents had reported him missing. Clairton police said the young man had been shot with an arrow in an apparent hunting accident, and the badly decomposed body was undiscovered for two weeks. "The hunter may never have known he shot someone," a police (continued on page 4)

From the March 8, 1967 N.Y. Times:

American Keeper Shuts Out British World Cup Champions

London (AP) - A packed throng at London's Wembley Stadium watched in disbelief as underdog Real Valencia, on the brilliant goalkeeping of American George Williams, shut out the World Cup British championship team 3-0 Saturday. Captain Marty Peters, besieged by reporters following the match, could offer no explanation as to why the Brits, who attacked in waves throughout the game, were unable to score on the Spanish team despite an amazing forty-three shots on goal. As the match neared full time, British fans jeered and whistled as their countrymen failed to put the ball past the former Princeton standout, (continued on page S3)

Epilogue
(written in 1999)

Time goes by so slowly
And time can do so much
- Unchained Melody, Al Hibbler, 1955

For some reason, when I think back on those days, one of my strongest images is those monarch butterflies dancing in Kathy Obermeister's garden. Kind of funny, really, but in a way that image represented the Windham of 1959 to me. Wolfie didn't really pull their wings off, I guess, as Kathy lay violated, sobbing on her pillow. Over the next decade or two, maybe it was the whole goddamn society.

Perhaps the terrible events at the end of the year were as a channel marker for the serene, meandering river of the 1950's, the fading backwater of the decade, as we entered more turbulent waters. For almost forty years, though, I can still ponder many of the same questions as I did then. Maybe the only thing I have gained is a kind of uneasy perspective, a less parochial view, an appreciation for things now lost - or maybe a resignation that there is no real finality, and that perhaps Windham needs to be held like Robbie van Arsdale's religion: acceptance without understanding.

Certainly I'm no smarter. In my mind, I can turn Windham as a diamond, reflecting light and color from its many facets, with a few inevitable flaws and spots of carbon. I'm at peace with the whole thing, on balance, although sometimes it's Mrs. Broadhead's wild, accusing eyes staring out at me from that sign, or Jerry Garragues' blank orbs, unfocused, wandering around the hospital room.

And sometimes still I see the headlights, the dark, faceted glass on that silver Mercedes, the Gull Wing with red leather seats, sitting silently, reflecting only the dim light that filters through the blinds and the dust in the Moffitt's three car garage.

But even now, what the hell do I know?

I think I know now that the spider spins mindlessly, without malevolence; as much a part of it all as the wind or the sea or the grass on the baseball diamond behind Windham High.

Or maybe I just wish it.

Maybe I just wish it, for sometimes the colors reflecting back are black and red, fleeting, for an instant only, not long enough to focus on, and then they're gone.

I remember the last dance at our Senior Prom. It was Johnny and Joe's classic from my sophomore year, *Over the Mountain, Across the Sea.* In a way, it was kind of fitting. We had come over the mountain, most of us, the Class of '59, with warm memories of what now, I realize, was certainly a most halcyon time in our lives, despite our casualties. We left Windham High School filled with hope, promise, and a concept of the world that would be found too seldom outside the tiny borders of our insular community. I came to believe, finally, not without struggle, that we had the good fortune to grow up in a pristine place, a pleasant gulag, in a world not as yet complicated by wrenching internal issues, disillusionment, fragmented families and a bad war. Our collective Windham sin, if we were to be judged, was being comfortable with our own kind and self-assured in our camaraderie.

The Cold War was just a game, another transient fad, a monstrous hula hoop after all. We were a golden moment, frozen in a tranquil time, ending a teenage decade. We were the rock 'n' roll generation, ushering in new music, new trends, fast cars and affluence, riding the peak of prosperity. Wrenching changes were in the mail, but we had by and large preceded them; we would largely be spectators to tumult, upheaval, and a chemical revolution.

Vietnam would catch some of us, but it would hit later classes much harder. We were sandwiched between the beatniks and the hippies, the Uncle Toms and the fiery Civil Rights preachers, the patriot soldiers and the protesters. Our brief generation would be forever undefined by any historical seminal moment, any particular war, any great cause; rather, we were measured by our music, our cars, our benign self-preoccupation.

A few of our peers would miss the opportunity, searching for causes that were yet to exist. We would, with everyone else, be stunned by tragedy in Dallas, Kent State, Los Angeles, and Birmingham, but would draw a pacific strength from our common wellspring, Windham High, and having done so move quietly, resolutely, unprotestingly on with our lives.

In the end, we had been instilled with a sense of responsibility alongside a cynical disdain for our 'duck-and-cover' limited future and the Cold War. The world beyond our borders was a black-and-white television show, with desultory ratings. We were, despite our attempts to resist, given a respect for institutions and authority and American values. Our World War II parents had passed these on, sometimes unknowingly, and we were the better for it. Our ship sailed into the sunset, as the wind freshened and the whitecaps appeared, having passed through a decade of calm waters. We may have been the last.

Maybe, in the end, we had it right: the music would endure while much else would fade away.

It was, as the saying had gone, great to be young and a Yankee fan.